NELL DIDN'T DO IT

But someone found the young heiress in hiding.

Someone's attitude got her killed.

Was it Nell's student Lyle?

"Whoa," Lyle said, puffing as he staggered up the path. "It's the little ninjas."

Technically, Lyle was an adult. But he was a college student studying some kind of physics, and his mind was not always in sync with the rest of his body.

Or the developer who wants to own all of Boulder, including Dad's farm?

"I don't care what he told you," said Jimmie Condo, his brownish-gray mutton chops blooming from the sides of his head. "He's bluffing. I won't offer him a penny more and that's final. Don't worry, he'll give in.

Or was it someone else?

THERE IS MORE NELL LETTERLY

AND MORE SUE STAR!

Murder in the Dojo **(#1 in the Nell Letterly Series):** The book that started it all. Available **now** from your favorite bookstore in trade paper or e-book format.

Murder for a Cash Crop **(#3) Coming in 2015:** When growing pot in beautiful Colorado begins to involve real money, things can turn deadly.

READ SUE'S SHORT STORY COLLECTIONS ABOUT OTHER STRONG WOMEN

Organized Death: Even the most organized women stumble when a crime occurs.
Trophy Hunting: Trophies come in all forms.

Available **now** in e-book format on all e-reader platforms

Read selections at: www.dmkregpublishing.com

Available as e-books from both Amazon and Barnes & Noble.

MURDER WITH ALTITUDE

SUE STAR

D. M. Kreg Publishing

DMKregPublishing.com

Cover Design: Renee Barratt, The Cover Counts

For Al, whose light shows me the way.

ACKNOWLEDGMENTS

Thanks to the many fine martial artists with whom I've trained, and especially, thanks to Mr. Reid. Thanks also to the writers who helped this project along the way: The Boulder Lunch Bunch, who first encouraged me to write about Nell; the Inklings, my awesome critique group; the Oregon Writers Network, whose support keeps my career on track; and my first readers who rearranged their schedules to accommodate mine. Thanks to my family for always humoring me and believing in me. Thanks also to Donald Kreg, editor and publisher extraordinaire. This book wouldn't have happened without any of you.

MURDER WITH ALTITUDE

SUE STAR

ONE

The body hung upside down, dangling against the rock face of one of the Flatiron outcroppings. At first I thought it was a climber, a hapless amateur tangled in ropes. Someone needed help.

Or maybe my eyes had fooled me. Flashes of May sunshine speckled the trail where my students and I ran and blinded me like a strobe light.

I dropped out of my running gait, thunked to a stop on the trail, and squinted at the spot of neon pink up ahead. Someone's jacket. That someone clung to the side of the gigantic slab of sandstone rising from the canopy of pine boughs. He or she wasn't moving.

I sucked in deep gulps of woodsy air. Over a mile high, there wasn't much oxygen to suck. Feeling dizzy, I waited for my students to catch up. A small group of us from Callahan's Karate had come out here on a training run today in one of Boulder's mountain parks, and I'd gotten too far ahead.

Because all along the way I'd had a dreadful feeling about that spot of pink that we'd kept glimpsing.

I waited a few more breaths, just in case my suspicion was wrong, but the rock climber in pink up there still didn't move.

She was dead.

My heart thumped, and I tore into my fanny pack, rattling through junk for my cell phone. Flipped it open.

No bars.

I defaulted into protective mother mode and whirled around in a one-eighty. Buster, my over-achieving thirteen-year-old student, nearly plowed into me.

"What's wrong, Ms. Letterly?" he said, running in place beside me.

"We have to turn around now."

"How come? Is there a bear?"

"Let's *go*." Farther away, from behind thick Ponderosa foliage, sounded the deep breathing and scuffing footsteps of struggling runners, my other students. They'd fallen farther and farther behind. Training for the Bolder Boulder was supposed to be an innocent rite of spring. Not a retrieval of bodies.

"Aw, do we have to go back already?" Buster's eyes widened with apparent dismay, and he bit his lip. "I mean...ma'am?"

"We have to find a place on the trail where there's cell phone reception." Reception faded in and out, this close to the pinkish sandstone geology that formed Boulder, Colorado's signature backdrop.

Buster's face twisted with questions that reflected his inner conflict. I could tell that he really wanted to ask me what the heck was going on, but his martial arts training taught him not to question any decision of his instructor.

Sure, I was his instructor, but I was also a mom. I'd learned to select my battles and turn a blind eye on a lot of the disciplinary slips that would warrant push-up punishment in another *dojo*. Not in my studio — Callahan's Karate. After only two months on the job, it still sounded good. *My* studio.

"You can do a round of drills while I make my call," I said.

"Yes, ma'am!" Buster's face shone at the mention of drills, but then his face always shone. He's the kind of kid who never comes to a full stop. He bobbed first to the right and then to the left, trying to look around me. "Hey! Wait! Is something wrong with that climber up there?"

I clamped my hand onto the shoulder of his sweat-dampened tee shirt. "We're turning around. *Now*."

He bobbed some more, craning his skinny neck farther. "Oh. My. God. I think she needs help."

"She's beyond our help."

"You mean... She's...dead?" His face twisted some more, and I thought he was going to cry.

"That's why we have to call for help. But I can't call without a signal. Move it!"

I didn't usually act Marine-like. At least not all the time. Only when I had to herd my cats. I would let them stray only so far. Most of my students were just budding adults, for goodness sake.

And then there was Lyle.

"Yes ma'am." Buster stumbled, whirling around and darting away, back down the trail the way we'd come.

I followed, tripping over each rock that I had glided across only moments ago. Now, my focus was shot. That let in the pain. My feet felt like they were on fire, pinched and scraped and twisted from the uneven terrain, uplifted with boulders. My legs were lead weights. My lungs wanted to explode, starved of oxygen.

Got to call 911.

I should've stayed home in the garden today, planting tomatoes.

Instead, I had to make a living. *Someone* had to be the grownup in my family and make the mortgage payments on our ritzy, north Boulder suburban home. Not my jerk soon-to-be ex-husband. Max had run off, leaving me in charge. But, hey. Two months into my new job, I was getting good at being in charge. Life was good.

Life could always be better.

"Buster!" I shouted as he disappeared, skidding around the switchback in the trail below. I was in pretty good shape for a middle-aged mom, but I couldn't keep up with him.

The trail butted up against the giant pieces of red-pink sandstone, shaped like their namesake, antique flatirons. Three main slabs of stone rose like skyscrapers from the tumble of the Rocky Mountains' Front Range, and then there were countless smaller chunks, like the one with the climber on it, soaring above our heads. Smaller, but they were still the size of multi-storied buildings. Usually, you saw climbers rappelling with ropes along the side of any of these Flatirons. Not bodies.

From where we'd started today's run, lower down at the trailhead, I'd seen the bright pink spot of color up there. I assumed then that it indicated one of the many rock climbers who are drawn to my hometown, a rock climber's heaven. After a half mile or so up the trail, the pink spot disappeared from view altogether, along with the Flatiron, because terrain got in the way. I worried, wondering if she was stuck. That's when I picked up my pace, drawing slightly ahead of my students.

Then the pink reemerged as I closed in, only a couple hundred feet away from the climber. No ropes held her. And I could see that she would never move again. I was pretty sure she was a woman, but in this college town, you could never be sure.

14

She looked like a broken doll with her red hair splayed between limp arms in her upside-down position.

Or a trapeze artist, the way her legs hooked into a crevice a hundred feet or so up from the base of the massive slab. Maybe five hundred feet down from the top.

Had she fallen that far?

By the time I rounded the bend, Buster was waving his arms at two of my other students, trying to lead them off the trail into a relatively flat and smooth area. What I liked about the kid was his take-charge nature. He was my highest ranked student, a high red belt soon to test for brown. He launched into jumping jacks, but the other two — fifteen-year-olds — didn't follow his lead. Jason, a blue belt, doubled over, groaning. Rachel, a green belt, flung herself into the tick-infested mahonia ground cover and moaned "Gawwwd."

"Where's everyone else?" I said, sliding on loose rocks beside the group. We'd started with a group of eight, meeting up at the trailhead about a mile back, and now there were three. I hoped we weren't disappearing like Ten Little Indians.

Rachel sipped from her fancy camel-back water carrier. "They quit ages ago."

Jason stood up. "They said to tell you not to wait for them. They're going back."

They should've told me personally at the last rest break, but I would deal with those issues later. I tapped my cell phone again. One bar. Moving out of my students' earshot, I punched in 911.

The dispatcher seemed more interested in my name — Nell Letterly — than my report. She instructed me to remain calm. I could do calm. No problem. But not in the forest with a dead body and adolescents whose safety I was responsible for. Including the ones who'd bailed.

Maybe I shouldn't have put Buster in charge of the training runs.

Or I should've vetoed his choice of this running route.

Nell, Nell... I could hear my sensei, Master Hwang's chiding voice in my head, always correcting my doubts, my number one weakness.

I breathed in deep, willing myself to relax. Training for black belt was more than just physical, more than endurance training, more than conditioning and strengthening. It was also about leadership and teamwork. *In. Out.* Okay. Time to push aside the doubts that always lurked at the back of my head, waiting to trip me up. Time to control my personal dragon.

"We'll take turns leading a few more rounds of exercises and stretches," I told my students with authority flowing along with my *chi*, my body's invisible energy. The dispatcher had said to stay here until the first responders arrived. It wouldn't be long.

Right.

"But can't we just rest for a while instead?" Rachel asked.

"We don't want our muscles to get tight," I said.

Jason smirked. "Make her do push-ups."

"Oh, go away." Rachel stuck out her tongue at him.

"You can't talk to us like that, Rache," Jason said. "We outrank you."

"Shut up."

I was about to intervene when Lyle staggered up the path.

"Whoa," he said, puffing. "It's the little ninjas."

Technically, Lyle was an adult. But he was a college student, studying some kind of physics, and his mind was not always in sync with the rest of his body. Besides that, he was *my* student. So I treated him like all the rest of the adolescents.

"I thought you gave up hours ago," Rachel said.

"You can't get rid of me that easy," Lyle said.

"No one's getting rid of you," I said. "We've been waiting for you."

"What took you so long?" said Jason. "Didn't your warp drive work?"

"No, stupid." Rachel rolled her chocolate brown eyes. "You don't know anything."

Lyle chuckled. "If I could build a warp drive, you think I'd be out here? I wouldn't have to go to school, and I wouldn't have to take karate, either, just to make girls go out with me."

Rachel squealed when Lyle advanced on us.

"Not you," he said. "Why would I want to go out with a baby?" He winked and glowed, like any adolescent with a crush, although maybe it was just perspiration. He smoothed a greasy clump of dyed-black hair, managing to muss everything into gluey spikes.

Rachel's face read "ewww."

"Seriously?" Jason asked.

"If you really want to know," Lyle said, "I was exploring multiple paths of the continuum."

"Huh?"

Lyle snorted. "You might try exercising your brains, as well as your bodies."

"Children," I said, adding a mom-like scolding tone to my sensei voice. "Black belts treat everyone with respect." Our goal was not just to earn the rank of black belt but also to adopt the black belt way of life.

Lyle ignored me. "Hey, Buster, couldn't you find any other adults to come along and baby-sit?"

Buster threw me a pleading look, pleading me to intervene on his behalf. I could tell that he was bursting to respond, but fearful that his retort wouldn't be appropriate, especially for his rank. He was probably right, but I wouldn't help him. I watched their drama play out. Martial artists had to learn how to handle themselves.

"Gimme ten push-ups," Buster said when I wouldn't save him.

Lyle slumped onto a rock instead. He might've been the only adult student here, but he was also the lowest ranked belt of this group, orange. According to our school's ranking system, orange was the third level for beginners. It must irk Lyle to know less about the martial arts than his juniors. He had the most to learn about proper martial arts attitude.

"You want to be buff, right?" Jason said. "'Cause you still got the hots for Fanny."

"Shut up, dude," Lyle said.

"She's the only reason you came along today, isn't it? You thought Fanny would come with us, too, 'cause she's going to run the Bolder Boulder, and she likes to train in those sexy little outfits."

A flush crept up Lyle's neck and engulfed his face. I didn't think it was entirely from his lack of conditioning. I positioned myself between Jason and Lyle, so that if they came to blows, they'd have to get past me first.

"How do you know that?" Rachel said. "I haven't seen Fanny in like for*ever*."

"Fanny?" I glared back and forth at Jason and Lyle and

wished that Search and Rescue would hurry up. "Who's that?"

"She came to karate back when Mr. Valencia was still there," Buster said.

"Only because *she* had the hots for *him*," Jason said.

"Shut up, dude," Lyle said.

I lifted my eyebrows. I was still cleaning up the various messes that Valencia, my ill-fated predecessor, had left behind in the studio before his untimely end. One of his problems had been womanizing. "Really? So, how old is this Fanny?"

"Don't worry," Rachel said, "she goes to college. But Jase is like so wrong. Fanny thinks she's way too cool for us high school brats. She's such a b — " Rachel clamped her hand over her mouth. "Oops, can't say that word."

"You're just jealous," Lyle said.

"Am not," Rachel said. "I work my butt off. Why else would I be out here with you nerds?"

"Okay," I said, "let's focus on what we're doing here today. We're conditioning not only for the Bolder Boulder but for the next belt test. And each of you is due to test." It would be the first test for me to conduct for my students. I'd scheduled it for two and a half weeks from now, which would put the test a few days before the ten-k race that Boulder hosts every year over Memorial Day weekend. Those events would kick off the new summer program for the karate studio, pun intended.

"Wait, that's who it is!" Buster shouted.

"*Who* is?" Rachel asked.

"That dead girl, hanging up there from the Flatiron." As soon as the words slipped out, Buster's eyes rounded. His face paled, and he looked about ready to faint.

I enveloped him in a hug. "I phoned the authorities, and

they're on the way."

"*What* dead girl?" Lyle said.

Rachel squealed. "Someone's dead?"

Jason's jaw dropped open.

"Fanny?" Lyle shouted, as if he could make the dead woman hear. He lurched off his rock and charged forward, pushing past me, brushing my fingers off of Buster's shoulder. Then he plunged into the shrubs, bypassing the trail, and clawed his way straight up the side of the hill.

I wasn't keen on the idea of trampling baby growth in the underbrush, scattering quails, or waking up hibernating snakes. Buster, Rachel, and Jason scrambled away after Lyle, following him with renewed interest. I looked around but didn't see any "stay on the trail" signs, so I shrugged and charged after them.

The main path we'd left a half mile or so lower down on the mountain was a seven-mile freeway clogged with tourists. It ran more or less north and south, parallel to the base of the Front Range. Off-shoot trails, like the one we'd chosen, headed west, up toward the Flatirons.

We didn't tree bash long, thank goodness. Soon, the dash up the side of the hill opened onto one of the side trails. Maybe the one we'd been following, maybe another.

From around the bend ahead, I heard yelps and stifled cries. Apparently they'd found her.

When I caught up to them, Lyle was already free climbing up the angled jumble of rocks, closer to the body. Jason doubled over, and Buster upchucked into the bushes. Rachel hung back, whispering *omigod!*

The sight of the poor dead girl made me stumble, and I echoed Rachel. *Omigod!*

Then I steeled myself and called to Lyle. "What are you doing? Come down before you fall!"

He'd reached the end of the split in the rock where he was scrambling and had only covered half the distance to the body. His face went pasty white, and he sank down into a crab-like crouch.

"You little punks!" He shouted down at us, as if we were somehow to blame for everything, including her death.

But he didn't move from his ledge.

"Omigod," Rachel said with a wail. "I didn't mean all those mean things I said about her."

Buster stood up, wiping his mouth. "Fanny's been gone from class such a long time. I thought she moved away."

I scooped both Rachel and Buster into my arms, trying to divert their view of the body. Some purple puffiness splotched her neck above the collar of her jacket. Was that natural? I was no expert in matters of death. Although there were some who would beg to differ on that. Of course, I didn't let my students know any more of my personal history than I had to tell them. Enough circulated already in gossip.

"Fanny's been gone because she switched to Kim's Karate," Jason said, leaning one arm against a tree trunk, as if he needed extra support. "Besides, you don't know it's her. We're too far away to see her good."

Rachel squirmed free from my arms and said, "Fanny has red hair, and pink is her favorite color."

That settled that.

Then Lyle moaned. "What's wrong with her face?"

* * * * *

A pair of open space rangers arrived and identified themselves as Rock and Oriana. I swear to God. Not so unusual for a place like Boulder. They'd already been in the area, they explained, checking up on reports called in about possible campers. Search and rescue wasn't far behind. Although, both the emergency and search elements were past. Rock and Oriana would take over for now.

As their names suggested, Rock was a stocky man, block-shaped, and all muscle. Oriana looked like a whisper next to him, hippie radiant and wasting-away thin. A dimple decorated her chin each time she smiled. I wasn't sure how she could smile so much at a death scene, but maybe she couldn't talk without smiling.

My students assaulted them with questions. Was the dead woman really Fanny? If not, then who was she? How'd she get there? How long had she been there? Was she really dead? How did she die? Why was her face swollen? They'd never seen a dead body before. How would search and rescue get her down?

Rock tuned out the questions and tromped over to the base of the Flatiron where he propped one boot up on the massive sheet of rock. He peered up its length, past where Lyle squatted. "Hmmm."

"If she was rock climbing," I said, peering up the slanted length to the cliff far above, "then where's her climbing gear? Where's her partner? Do you think she was climbing the Flatiron and then fell?" I shivered with horror, wondering if her bloating meant that when she'd fallen, she'd accidentally hanged herself. But then, where was the rope?

Rock shrugged. His voice rumbled in the baritone range.

"Not all of these formations require ropes. Whatever she was up to, it was a deadly mistake."

"Her first mistake was not having at least a spotter along with her."

"Maybe she did."

"Then, where is he or she?"

"Good question." Rock stared at Lyle and narrowed his eyes.

"It wasn't him," I said, following his gaze to Lyle, huddled up there, clinging to rocks. "He wasn't with her. He was with us."

"The whole time?"

"Well, no. He met up with us on the trail. He had a class to go to, so he couldn't run the entire distance with us." I bit my tongue. I didn't have to explain any of this to a park ranger.

But I *did* wonder if Lyle's story was the truth. I'd suspected that because Lyle wasn't in as good shape as the rest of my students, he'd wanted to drive to a closer access than the trailhead Buster had chosen. Now, as I looked at him crouching up there in the rocks, after the way he'd sprinted up the side of the hill, I realized that Lyle was in better condition than I'd thought.

Meanwhile, Oriana, the more personable half of the pair, stayed busy writing down our names and contact information. "In case someone wants to talk to you," she said, flashing her dimpled smile.

"We don't know anything," Buster said.

"Well, you never know. Have you seen anyone out here who looked like they're camping?"

"You think some campers have something to do with this

woman's accident?" I said.

"They're not allowed to camp in open space," Oriana said. "But maybe they saw something. Or, maybe she's one of them. Just sayin'."

"How do you know anyone was camping if they're not allowed to and you haven't seen them?" Jason asked.

"Some of the residents near the trailhead heard them and reported it. Someone was up here overnight, and I guess they were pretty noisy."

"Omigod!" Rachel said. "I heard them, too! My house is close to the trailhead. I thought someone was having a party up the street from my house. I didn't know it was coming from up *here*."

"Well, sound carries on the wind, and it whistles down and around these rocks," Oriana said, smiling.

I hoped this poor woman didn't fall because of some illicit overnight in the park.

Oriana asked us more questions about the specific time and location of our training run and took a few notes. She coaxed Lyle down from his perch and patiently listened to him and Rachel argue about Fanny. She refereed between us and the search and rescue team, once they arrived, and finally she told us we should go.

Released, we headed off down the trail, back the way we'd come, with Buster in the lead. He was determined to salvage something of our training run, and his pace was faster than the rest of ours. Suddenly he stopped and gasped. He held out his arms to either side, motioning us to stay behind him.

"What is it?" I asked, hurrying to his side.

"Don't move," Buster said.

As if I could.

Something coiled in a sunny spot in the middle of the trail. A snake, and its head lifted up, eyeballing us. Set to strike.

"Snake!" I shouted. Just because I'd grown up here in rattlesnake country, and just because I was supposed to be brave because I was a black belt, didn't make me any less terrified of snakes. Fear was irrational.

"Everyone hold still," said Lyle from somewhere behind me.

Then a loud crack split the air, ringing in my head. The snake shot into a barberry bramble. I whirled around. Lyle held a gun, pointing it at the sunny spot the snake had just vacated.

TWO

Time passed in a blur at Callahan's Karate. Images of the snake, Lyle's gun, and the redhead in pink with her swollen face tumbled through my mind. Swollen, because of her accident? Or maybe she'd been snake-bit. One brief report appeared in the newspaper about the deadly accident, but it hadn't mentioned anything about a snake. Nor the victim's identity.

I couldn't shake her tragedy from my mind. I kept wondering if Buster was right, and the dead girl really was the same Fanny who had been a student here at the studio. That would give her a connection to us, making her death feel personal, even to me. We were a team, my students and I, and to lose any teammate that way — even one I hadn't known — shattered the bond that held us all together. I could almost feel the poor girl's troubled ghost walk the floors with us here at Callahan's. Maybe I was taking this too far, but I felt as if I'd failed her.

And speaking of Buster, where was he? It wasn't like him to let a whole day slip by without coming in to burn off some energy, or at least to chat.

I hadn't seen Lyle, either, but that in itself wasn't so odd.

What *was* odd was the gun he'd apparently been carrying around in his running shorts.

During classes, I pushed all those issues to the back of

27

my mind and focused on my students. I stood in front of the mirrors, newly installed across the west wall of the workout floor, and studied my students — four gold belts and three orange belts, ranging in age from second grade to high school — as they practiced their upper-hand and knife-hand blocks that I'd just demonstrated. It was the after-school time slot, when distractions came easy.

The front door of the studio rattled and slammed shut. We all looked up, including the parents who observed their children from the folding chairs under the bay window. The studio occupied a hollowed-out 1920's bungalow, with some of the original features remaining. I kept waiting for the beveled glass in the front door to shatter, considering the way students banged through each day. So far so good. No tinkling sounds yet.

Instead, I heard light, scuffling steps, hoarse whispers, and thunking sounds. No one emerged into view from the foyer. Since my students were otherwise occupied with their practice, I edged sideways until I could see around the corner into the foyer.

Two skinny shapes hung in the shadows: my daughter Terra and Buster. I hadn't seen Buster since our trail run the day before yesterday. And what was Terra doing home this early? She always had some sort of band practice after school. She must've made sure to get home after school in plenty of time before Jason would show up for his mixed upper belt class, next after this one. She probably would have to doll herself up, or whatever it was that fifteen-year-old girls in lust did these days. Normally, she wouldn't give a thirteen-year-old boy like Buster the time of day. At fifteen, Terra had an image to keep up.

"What's going on out here?" I said.

They whipped around and gave me their cat-got-the-mouse looks that teenagers have perfected so well.

"Mom!" Terra said, glaring at me through the extra long wave of her bangs, carefully cultivated to look like they hadn't been brushed in a week. "Go back to your class. It's just me, home from school."

One of the benefits of moving into the apartment over the karate studio was that it was located close enough for her to walk home after school. When we lived in our fancy north Boulder home, I usually drove her, much to her mortification.

"You'd better get started on your homework, honey," I said. "Aunt Gillian is taking you out to dinner tonight."

Her braces positively gleamed. "Real food for a change," she said and darted up the stairs to our apartment, banging her saxophone case on every fifth banister post.

I turned to Buster. "You're way early for your class. Are you planning to stretch out, or are you going to hide out here in the shadows?" Upper belts liked to show off in one corner of a lower-belt class in progress. And Buster was my highest ranked student, so he could show off to everyone.

His chin slumped. His shoulders sagged. His backpack slipped to the floor with a thump. "I'm not here for class," he said.

Right. Then why had he come here today?

"You want to talk about it?" I said. Sometimes karate instructors had to be mom, too.

He peeked up at me with cautious hope written on his face. I took it as a nod of approval.

"Go stretch out anyway, while I finish this class. Then meet

29

me in the office."

After the gold and orange belts bowed out, I had a ten-minute break before the next class would begin. I pulled Buster's attendance card and carried it with me, leading him down the Hobbit-like hallway to the office, which used to be a kitchen back in the day. The karate studio had gone through several renovations since its bungalow heritage, but its sandstone footprint remained the same. The old living and dining rooms facing the street had become our workout floor, and the kitchen on the alley side of the house became my office.

The conference table, covered in linoleum and gleaming chrome, looked as if it had come straight out of an antique shop. It hadn't. I dropped into a chair and said, "What's up?"

Buster shuffled his feet, hesitating on the threshold, as if he was reluctant to come in. "It's just that," he finally said with a sniffle, "I've been talking to some of the kids on my street. They go to Kim's Karate, and they knew Fanny."

"Is that why you missed your class yesterday?" Normally, it was no big deal to miss a class, but at his level, this close to his test, it *was* a big deal.

He lowered his head and studied the checkerboard pattern of the linoleum floor. He mumbled something that sounded like "Sorry."

"Your belt test is just two weeks away." I bit off the rest of what the nagging mom in me wanted to say: *You can't afford to miss any classes.*

He looked up from the floor and sat down at the table with me. His eyes were red. He chewed his lower lip, grabbed a stray pen, and tapped it against the table.

"I'll let you make it up," I said, "if you can attend a lower belt class along with your regular classes. Think you can do that?"

He shook his head and spoke in a tiny voice. I could barely hear him. "Not because I don't want to."

"Why don't you tell me what's on your mind? Is it about Fanny and the way we found her out there on the Flatiron?"

He closed his eyes, but he didn't look like he was resting. His eyelids twitched, as if his eyes tracked something back and forth that only he could see in his mind. Something terrifying, from the way the rest of his face grimaced.

"It's just so hard to believe." His voice caught, and he paused to cough. He opened his eyes and gave me a feral look. I'd seen our pet ferret look at me that same way in a panic. "What happened to her, and all."

"I'm sorry you had to see that."

"I just keep wondering. I can't get it out of my head. What if someone pushed her from the top? There are trails up at the top, you know, above that rock where we found her."

I stiffened and watched him shudder. He was serious. "Deliberately?"

"Uh-huh."

"Where did you get an idea like that?"

He shrugged and clicked the pen some more. "I've been thinking. She didn't have many friends."

"That's hardly a reason for anyone to want to hurt her."

"Well, you heard what Rachel said about her. Or didn't say. The b-word."

I took the pen away from him and tossed it into a pottery pinch pot that Terra had made for me one Mother's Day. Softening my voice, I said, "That's still not a sufficient reason. Besides, as martial artists, we learn to work out our differences with others, rather than resort to violence. We still don't know for sure that the woman up there really was Fanny, but assuming she was, then she was a martial artist, right? It's more likely she was climbing where she shouldn't have been, and she had a terrible accident."

"See, that's just the thing," he said. "She *couldn't* have been climbing. Not Fanny. I mean, she was a wuss about rock climbing and heights and all that. Anyhow, we didn't see any ropes or anything. That's why I bet she wasn't climbing up from the bottom. I think instead she was hiking around higher up, and someone pushed her from up there."

"Is that what you decided, or did you hear someone else say that?"

He bounced in his seat with the impatience of a child trying to make a dim-witted parent understand. "What if whoever pushed her is going to come after *us*? You know, for finding her? That's why I didn't come to class yesterday."

He wasn't the only one who hadn't come. Rachel and Jason hadn't shown up, either. Nor Lyle. Alarm bells went off in my head. Were they all frightened by some newly created urban legend about a mystery mountain killer? "Do your parents know what you're thinking?"

"Well, actually, Mom's the one who told me to stay away from here from now on."

"Why didn't she come talk to me?" I sprang up from the table and wound my way through the labyrinth of file boxes stacked in the center of the kitchen — the residue of the filing mess my predecessor had left me. Atop the counter on the opposite side of the kitchen was a box of registration cards, and I flipped through them until I found the card containing

Buster's contact information. "I'll call right now and set up an appointment, so that we can talk."

"It's no use," Buster said. "She's at work."

"Then I'll leave a message." I grabbed the phone and punched in the numbers.

"She won't call you back."

I spoke into the phone, leaving my message for her to call me about the best time for a conference. Then I turned back to Buster. "Don't you want me to talk to her?"

"It's not that."

"Then what is it?"

Buster lowered his head and squeezed his fingers, as if he tried to wring out drops of blood. "Um, actually, she wants me to s-switch schools."

"WHAT?" Had I heard him right?

"S-switch over to Kim's. You know, that place across town?"

"Yeah. Kim's Karate. I've heard of it." Oh boy, had I ever. Where Fanny allegedly switched, too. Kim's was state of the art. With Callahan's budget, we couldn't compete with that. "But you're so close to testing. You'll have to start over if you switch schools now."

"Mom says they'll put me on a fast track."

"Is this something you want to do?"

"I don't want to quit karate, even if it means I have to go somewhere else to do it."

"This is all so sudden. Do you know why your mom wants you to go there?"

"She's just afraid for me if I stay *here*. She says it's not safe. First, there was all that stuff that happened to Mr. Valencia a couple months ago, and now there's *this*. I'm not supposed to be here now, and boy, am I ever gonna get in trouble when she finds out. She'll know, you know, once she gets your message. I better get home fast and erase it, before she gets home." He scraped his chair backwards and popped up.

"Just a minute." I sprinted around the file boxes and caught him by the arm. "If you do erase it, then you won't have a choice except to do as she wants. But if you leave the message in place, then maybe I can talk to her. I'll see if I can talk her out of her plan, if that's what you want me to do."

"I have some friends over at Kim's, so I guess it wouldn't be too bad if I have to go there. But..."

"Why the sudden change? Doesn't she support your goals?"

"She thinks they've changed. She's afraid the killer is going to get me if I stay here."

I sighed. "Did she actually say that?"

"Well, yeah, after that policeman came to my house. That's when she got the idea."

"Policeman?" Alarm pulsed through me. "What'd the police say?"

He shrugged. "I dunno. Mom wouldn't let him talk to me. I guess he must've told her about the killer."

A killer. Targeting Callahan's. Oh, cripes. Not again.

"Do me a favor, will you?" I said. "Did you bring your *gi* ?"

"Sure. I always carry it in my backpack."

That would account for his uniform's wrinkles, I thought. "Put it on, and go bow in the next class for me. I have to make a phone call. Then you can go home, if that's what you still want to do." Kim's had a full staff of instructors over there, but here at Callahan's, it was just me, with whichever student volunteers I could talk into helping me.

34

* * * * *

I waited until Buster agreed and left, disappearing back down the hall, and then I closed the door behind him. I reached for the phone again and dialed the police department. By this time, several months after my husband Max's disappearance, I knew the number by heart. I asked for my contact, Detective Rosenquist.

"Good of you to call, Mrs. Gannon," he said once I got him on the line. "You're just the person I've been wanting to talk to."

My blood always ran cold when he wanted to talk to me. Never mind that he insisted on calling me by the name I'd told him a thousand times that I'd never taken.

Rosenquist and his partner had been on my tail ever since last November when my husband, Professor Max Gannon, left our house to teach at the university, and then never showed up to his class. Once the investigation into his disappearance unearthed our marital quarrels, Rosenquist convinced himself that I'd done away with my husband.

"Really?" I said, lifting my voice to a chipper tone. "Why? Do you have news for me?"

"Are you expecting some news, Mrs. Gannon?"

I didn't understand why he was trying to get under my skin. I thought he'd revised his opinion about me last March when I helped him out on another case.

Evidently not.

"Has Max been found?" I said, knowing and dreading that such a day would eventually come.

"Isn't he still on that Caribbean island? When are you going down there to join him, anyway?"

"Never!"

"Good, then, maybe you'll hang around town and answer a few more questions for us."

My skin tightened, and my voice cracked. "About Max? I thought you closed the book on that subject."

"It's never closed until the missing professor shows up."

Scratching sounds came across the wire, as if he was making a move to hang up the phone. "Wait! Don't hang up. Can you put me in touch with the officer who wanted to interview Buster Novak?"

Silence answered me, which was better than a dial tone. Finally, he said, "What do you think I'm running over here? Match dot com?"

"I'd like to talk to that officer, since Buster is one of my students. Or maybe you can tell me what that was all about? You guys talk among yourselves, don't you? Why did they want to talk to Buster?"

Muffled sounds responded, followed by a clunk and more scratching sounds, as if he'd covered his receiver to talk to someone else.

"Hello?" I said. "Does the police interest in Buster have anything to do with the dead woman we found on the Flatiron?"

The phone line gargled some more at me, and then finally his voice came back. "That would be police business, and none of your business. Where are you calling from?"

"Callahan's, of course. It's where I work *and* live, remember?"

"I suggest you stay there. We're on our way."

Oh, joy. The park ranger had said there might be more

follow-up questions, but I hadn't expected them to come from a homicide detective like Rosenquist. It didn't bode well. Maybe Buster's mom was right about a killer on the loose.

* * * * *

By the time Rosenquist and his partner Hennessey arrived at the studio, Buster had left, presumably to erase my phone message to his mom. I put another talented student in charge of supervising drills on the workout floor while I showed the detectives to my office.

Rosenquist, a bear of a man, filled the narrow space that tucked between wooden cabinets and stacks of cardboard file boxes. Hennessey was his silent shadow, shorter and thinner. Ever present but detached.

"How may I help you, gentlemen?" I said, hoping that my forced pleasantness would coax them into giving me what I wanted to know: why the police visit to Buster's home had made his mom decide to switch schools. Callahan's couldn't afford to lose a talented student like Buster.

Rosenquist scowled, making his ruddy face throb with dark splotches. He had beady brown eyes, tousled black hair — what was left of his hair — and unshaven stubbles that peppered his jaw.

Hennessey, the sandy-colored fairer half, shrugged and shook his head.

I stifled my urge to babble, to fill the empty gaps in our so-called conversation, and watched Rosenquist pace between my stacks of file boxes. "You said on the phone something about answering questions for you, detective?" Being the only one talking made me feel itchy.

He stopped pacing and frowned at me. "You've been here, what? Two months? How well do you know your students by now?"

Alarm bells rang in my head. "Not all that well." The police could just leave my students out of whatever investigation they were conducting into Fanny's death. My students were my charges, and I would do whatever it took to shelter them. "Have you found out yet who that poor woman on the Flatiron was?" I asked, diverting their interest from my students.

"You'll read about it in the papers like everyone else. *After* the next of kin have been notified."

My stomach flipped. "The family hasn't been notified yet?"

"Look here," Rosenquist said, "we're the ones asking questions, not you."

I leaned against the counter and refrained from prompting him to go on.

"I told the family myself," said Hennessey, the sympathetic one. "Down in Denver."

Rosenquist shook his head and muttered under his breath. Had they disagreed about revealing any information to me? Good grief.

"Those poor people," I said. "My students thought she might have been a student here at Callahan's. But I never met her."

Rosenquist was all about drama. He paced through the narrow space of the kitchen office and tapped my file boxes as if counting them on his thick, stubby fingers. When he was good and ready, he continued. "We've gone over the reports you filed, Mrs. Gannon, and we only have a few questions to ask.

We won't keep you long."

My internal clock ticked off the minutes. "My name is Letterly. Not Gannon."

"One thing is troubling me, *Miss* Letterly."

Ms., not Miss, but I wasn't going to press my luck.

"How much time elapsed between when you saw the body for the first time and when you phoned in your report?"

"Just a few minutes."

"A few? Can you be more specific than that?"

"I'm sure it was no more than five minutes." But was I sure? Time had a way of slipping away.

Hennessey spoke up from his corner in his deadpan voice. "We're just trying to gather the facts, ma'am."

Rosenquist frowned at him and then turned back to me. "Why did you leave her and then come back again before you phoned in your report?"

"That's not quite true. I was trying to find a place on the trail where I could get cell phone reception. I phoned as soon as I could, and then went back the second time. I thought it was just a terrible accident. It didn't occur to me that it was a crime. Was it a crime?"

Evidently so, given the police interest in it.

A ruddy flush spread up and down Rosenquist's bull-thick neck. Maybe I'd pressed him too far. "Did you see anyone who might've been with her?"

"No. Did you find her climbing gear?"

"Who says she was climbing?"

"Why else was she there?" I was phishing for any information he had about a potential mystery mountain killer who might've pushed Fanny off the mountain, as Buster and his mom feared, but Rosenquist didn't bite.

"Why, indeed?" He would know about the reports of illegal campers, but if he couldn't connect the dots, then that was his tough luck.

We glared at each other as the second-hand ticked loudly in its sweep around the face of the kitchen wall clock.

"Lyle Sawhill is a student of yours?"

My heart beat speeded up at the sudden change in his direction of questioning. "Lyle? Why do you ask?"

A flicker of a smile twitched Rosenquist's thick lips. "How long have you known him?"

"Only as long as I've been working here. Two months. What do you want with Lyle?" I remembered how nuts Lyle had gone, especially when he thought the body was Fanny, someone he allegedly had a crush on. Someone, allegedly a student here. And now apparently murdered.

"I didn't see anyone out there in your class today that fits his description," Rosenquist said, waving his arm at the plaster wall that separated the kitchen office from the workout floor.

"That's because he didn't come in today."

"Why not?"

"How would I know? He's an adult, detective. He doesn't need a written excuse in order to skip a class."

"Where is he?"

"He left his contact information with the park rangers. Don't you have it?"

"Why are you protecting him?"

Was I? He was my student, and I protect all of my students, even those who carry guns when they shouldn't. "Should I protect him from something?"

40

"At the moment, you're the only one who knows the answer to that."

His ominous tone sent a chill through me. "I don't have any answers."

He grunted. Apparently, he disagreed.

"Are you suggesting that we need a lawyer?" I didn't have a lawyer. I hoped Lyle had one. I hoped he had permission to carry that gun, too. Even so, it wouldn't cover him in a city park.

Rosenquist thumped one of the file boxes on a counter. "What kind of information do you keep in here?"

"Records," I said evasively. "You know, that sort of thing."

"About your students?"

"We keep business and curriculum items, too." And who knew what else from the mess my predecessor had left and I had yet to sort?

"I want your student files."

I took a deep breath. "You'll have to speak to my boss about that."

Rosenquist pushed his cowlick around and let out his breath through gritted teeth. "You could save us time if you cooperated."

"I always cooperate with you, detective, but I can't authorize your request. You'll have to speak to Mr. Callahan."

I caught a flicker of a smile from Hennessey.

"C'mon, let's go," Rosenquist said, brushing past his partner. "But don't worry, Mrs. Gannon. We'll be back."

I bet they would. And I could hardly wait.

THREE

I stayed up half the night sipping herbal tea and worrying, but not about the threatened return of my police pals.

I kept tossing questions around in my mind. Was the victim really the same Fanny who'd attended this very karate school under my predecessor? Did Lyle have anything to do with her death, as Rosenquist implied? Or was there a mystery mountain killer, as Buster's mom suspected, targeting my karate students?

The answers, I felt sure, lay somewhere in the file boxes that Rosenquist was so keen on acquiring.

Long after my last students left, and long after I'd made sure Terra was in bed upstairs in our apartment, I went back to work, rummaging through boxes, searching for those answers. My only company was the distant thumping sounds of bass coming from someone's late night party across the alley. Living in the heart of off-campus housing these last two months had made me immune to the sounds of revelry.

My tea overdose must've fogged my mind. Nothing was making sense. I couldn't find any paper with the name of "Fanny." Although, that didn't surprise me, considering the sloppy record-keeping of my predecessor. And considering his history. Fanny could've been one of his women, someone he'd taken in as a student, in exchange for certain sexual favors.

I couldn't find any records of potential interest to homicide detectives, either. Not that I knew what they were looking for.

They must suspect that someone had helped Fanny fall from the top of that Flatiron. They'd planted the fear in Buster's mom's mind, and now she thought that Callahan's Karate was no longer a safe place for her child. Being the champion of my students, I would have to change her mind. I would have to prove that there was no mysterious mountain killer.

And that Lyle was not he. Rosenquist suspected that Lyle had pushed Fanny.

I couldn't believe it. I'd seen the way he'd broken down up there on the mountain. But then, I'd been misled before.

Anyway, even if he had wanted to kill her, why would he push her when he could've shot her with the gun he hid in his shorts? No, he couldn't have been responsible for that woman's death. On the other hand, what did I really know about Lyle? If he was carrying a gun, maybe he *did* want to kill someone. My mind kept turning in circles. My skin crawled at the thought that a loaded gun had been jiggling around in his running shorts in the midst of my students' innocent training run.

All that I found of interest in the file boxes was Lyle's home address. A number and street I'd never heard of. It must be a house in one of the new neighborhoods that mushroomed up almost overnight. I didn't know how a college student could afford such housing, but then, this town attracted lots of trust fund hippies. It was hard to picture Lyle as someone living off his family's wealth, but you never know. Even so, Lyle's address wasn't enough to trigger the detectives' desire for my records. They would already have that information from the park rangers. No, Rosenquist had to be looking for something completely different.

A distant voice caught my attention, shouting from somewhere down the alley that ran behind the karate studio. The thumping bass shut off in response and filled the night with a void of silence. All I could hear was the echo of questions spinning through my mind.

Maybe Lyle would come to class tomorrow and we could have a little chat at my chrome conference table. Then I could put all my questions to rest, like the party across the alley.

Right.

I switched off the lights and climbed the creaking wooden steps to our apartment above the studio. This second story was an add-on from one of the many renovations to this bungalow, and thank goodness for that. Saving on rent had saved my life.

My boss, Mr. Callahan, insisted that his instructor live on site as a caretaker to the place. To thwart against potential vandalism that off-campus merriment sometimes incurs. So I'd cleaned up the apartment after my predecessor the slob had left remnants of his unsavory partying, and Terra and I had turned our three rooms into downright cozy. Moving in here left our fancy house in the suburbs available to renters who could cover my mortgage payments until either Max released the house to me to sell or hell froze over. Terra had a different opinion, but what fifteen-year-old didn't?

I crawled into bed, thinking of the poor woman who'd lost her life. And what Oriana the park ranger had said about another party whose noise had floated down the mountain. Illegal campers, she'd thought. Had they had anything to do with the woman who'd died?

I tossed and turned most of the night, between all the

questions that didn't add up and too many tea trips to the toilet. Bleary-eyed the next day, I was halfway into my noontime round of stretches and strengthening exercises on the faded but well-scrubbed carpet of the workout floor when the phone rang. I bowed off the floor and ran down the hallway to the office.

"Um," said the person on the other end, and then he cleared his throat. It was my boss, Arlo Callahan. I recognized his hesitation even over the phone. Alarm signals pounded in my head.

"Yes?" I said. "What is it? What's wrong?" There I went again, assuming the worst. Negative thinking.

"Look," Callahan said, hesitating again. "Can you get over here right away?"

"Where's 'here'?"

"My office. We have a, um, situation on our hands, and you're the best person to handle it."

I did some mental calculations. "I should be able to make it in about half an hour."

His voice exploded. "Can't you get here any faster than that? Maybe do your ninja hustle?"

"I'll do my best." I didn't take the time to change but grabbed my purse and ran out into the alley where my ancient Volkswagen, a Karmann Ghia, was parked. I owed my boss big time.

Mr. Callahan usually stopped by the studio a couple times per week, unannounced, just to glow about his proud ownership of the place. He named the place after himself, even though we didn't actually practice karate. Our style was American Freestyle, a nontraditional version of Tae Kwon Do. Furthermore, he wasn't even a martial artist. He was a wannabe, a groupie.

When this studio came up for sale, he bought it with the help of his investor-friend's advice, kicked out the last instructor whom he didn't like, and chose me, for reasons I'd never fully understood.

But, hey. Who was I to complain? I desperately needed a job, any job, and all I had was an outdated resume. Looking back, maybe I should've chosen to be a working mother, but Max — I'd give him that — made it financially possible for me not to work outside of the home. And over those fifteen years, the world had changed. We secretaries had basically become outmoded. Everyone used personal computers anymore, and secretaries had had to morph into techie geeks in order to keep their jobs. I hadn't. All I was qualified to do was martial arts. That's what had kept my sanity in those last years with Max still at home.

Then I got lucky. Callahan offered me the job of head instructor at the studio he'd recently bought, and I jumped at the opportunity. It was either that, or lose the house. And then what? Where would Terra and I go? On the streets? No way. I was grateful to Callahan for providing me with a job and a new home — the apartment above the studio. I owed him. Big time.

Fifteen minutes later, I was still patrolling the downtown streets, searching for a prized parking spot. It was the lunch hour on the downtown mall, and my afternoon classes would begin in a couple more hours.

When I finally reached Callahan's office, I was out of breath and only five minutes late. He rented office space from a developer who'd converted an old church a few blocks away from the heart of downtown. Sharing office space made the rent, well, not cheap, but let's say more affordable. Callahan was all about affordability. Maybe that's why he chose me for the job as head instructor.

The center of the building was an airy atrium with skylights and vining plants. Terraced offices circled around the perimeter. Facing the front entry, the secretary/receptionist's desk created a modern slash of teak against a backdrop of brick and greenery. The air even tasted humid, a small miracle in a place like Boulder, where single-digit humidity was not uncommon. Maybe miracles still occurred in this former place of worship.

"Here you are, finally," Poppy said, looking up at me from painting her fingernails, anchored against the teak. Today they were purple for the Colorado Rockies. The nails, that is, not the desk.

One of the office doors behind Poppy's desk opened just then, releasing voices that drifted on the scent of wet leaves and captured Poppy's attention. Her painting hand jerked, and purple slashed from her nail down the side of her finger.

"Van!" she said. "See what you made me do?" Her lips, painted a matching purple, puffed out in a pout.

"Don't blame me, honey," said the man who sauntered out of the office behind Poppy's desk. "I can't make you do anything." Slick in his khaki slacks, pink Oxford shirt (open at the neck, no tie), and full head of black hair graying at the temples, he looked as if he could've modeled for a touch-of-gray commercial. He chuckled, smiling with his eyes, and clicked across the tile floor in his expensive loafers. He held out his hand to shake mine. "Van Orr, with the Orr Group. Are you here to see me?"

I let him shake my hand and then took a step backwards, putting more distance between him and me. "Actually, no." I turned to Poppy and skewed my face into a question. I didn't trust anyone who formed his own group.

He glanced at his sports watch with a quick flick of his wrist, then shrugged and gave me a sheepish grin. "Oh. Sorry. I thought you were my new client. She's a runner who wants to look at some mountain properties." His gaze swept across my stretch pants.

"I'll let you know when she arrives," said Poppy, who acted as secretary, receptionist, and general manager of most of the office tenants in this building.

"So." Van leaned against the edge of Poppy's desk and folded his arms across his chest while he studied me. "Are you interested in looking at some property? I can find something in anyone's budget."

Not in mine. "Maybe another time."

"She's busy, Van," Poppy said, and then turned to me. "You'd better get up there." Her carefully plucked eyebrows waggled upwards, indicating the general direction of Callahan's office on the second level. "He's got a couple of visitors in there with him, and they're hopping mad."

"Oh yeah?" Van said. "Who?"

I gave him an annoyed frown and wondered what did Callahan's visitors have to do with *me*?

Poppy shrugged. "Some man and some woman. They didn't come together, though. The man arrived first, like he had an appointment, only I didn't know anything about it, and later, the woman just barged in. Didn't ask me where his office is, or anything. She knew exactly where she was going. Didn't you get my texts?"

"What texts?"

Poppy sighed. "You'd better hurry. Mr. Callahan is sure

to have a stroke. And I can't afford to lose any of my people. I really need this job."

"Okay." I could relate to that. Anyway, a little more jogging wouldn't hurt my noon workout. I jogged up the stairs, taking them two at a time, and sprinted down the hall that doubled as a balcony overlooking the atrium. I turned back to give Poppy a thumbs-up — Van was still down there, grinning up at me. When I reached for the door handle to Callahan's office, the door jerked inwards before I could grasp its handle, pulling me off balance. I bounced on the balls of my feet to correct my upright position before tipping over into the angry woman who stood ready to plow me under. I blocked her way, which seemed to tick her off royally.

Her painted red lips curled into a snarl. "What the hell do you want?"

I kept my voice neutral and countered her hostility. "My boss." I extended my hand as a peace offering. "Nell Letterly, at your service."

That seemed to surprise her. For a minute I thought she was going to shake my hand. Her hand hung suspended in the electrified air that she radiated. Then she wagged a long-clawed index finger at me instead. It matched the fire engine red of her lips. I was willing to bet this angry woman's color coordination was less a fashion statement and more like war paint. "I know who you are. You're that Letterly daughter."

I bounced backwards a step, startled from her feint. A knot of indigestion formed in the pit of my stomach, feeling like a ball and chain. This fiery woman could just leave my dad the heck off of her war path. "Every woman is someone's daughter," I said craftily.

Her lips curled back in a sneer. "Including Francesca Denton. Ever think about that?"

She paused as if waiting for my reaction, but in true ninja style, I gave her none. Denton was a well-known name in the metro area, associated with big-time money grown from silver mines long ago.

The red-painted woman went on, blowing off a little steam of irritation. "Everyone accommodates the Dentons. You want my advice? See that you're not one of them, honey."

Actually, I didn't want her advice, but with her disposition, I gave her another neutral response. "Thanks for the tip."

She blasted past me, her high heels gouging holes into the carpet as she thudded away.

Sheesh. Who did she think she was? The Queen of Sheba? A transplant from the fast lane, no doubt. We had a few of that type rocketing around town until the mountains' soporific worked magic, calming them. I would give her a wide berth until then.

I tip-toed inside and closed the door softly against the wake vibrating from her anger. Men's voices floated out of the small conference room attached to Callahan's office. I followed the voices.

My boss wore his usual worried frown. The way he slumped into his swivel chair reminded me of a walking stick folded up into a space about half its size. At the head of the table, Callahan swiveled back and forth, burning off nervous energy, and tapped his pen against the pine surface. His visitor glanced at his wristwatch, a gold piece of jewelry that radiated beaucoup dollar signs.

You didn't often see three-piece suits in Boulder, where the usual dress code was biking shorts — yes, year-round. I figured the visitor wasn't from here, not only given the gray three-piece but also its lack of discount sheen. His round belly didn't fit well, either, in my hometown of health and fitness. He had plump cheeks to match, and they ended in the point of a cinder-gray goatee. He reminded me of a scowling, younger version of Santa Claus.

"This is my employee, Nell Letterly," Callahan told the visitor. I always knew something was troubling him when he forgot to say hello first. Callahan may be a bit absent-minded at times, but he was old-school when it came to manners. "She's the head instructor over at the karate studio that I operate."

I narrowed my eyes at Callahan. He didn't have anything to do with operations. I had free rein, pretty much. That was one of the bennies of working there.

I took my eyes off Callahan — we'd talk later — and extended my hand to the visitor. "Pleased to meet you." Actually, I wasn't pleased at all. But black belts were always supposed to remain even-keeled to life's little disturbances. That was a lesson I was still working on.

The scowling Santa handed me a business card instead of a handshake. Where had he been keeping it, up his sleeve? The card said his name was Alastair Lazar. His address was the exclusive end of the Cherry Creek neighborhood in Denver, and his identity was lawyer. Uh-oh.

"Sadly, I've used up most of my allotted time on this case by waiting for your arrival, Miss Letterly," Lazar said, steepling his fingers beneath his goatee. Miss, I noted, not Ms. I felt thirteen.

"I was in the middle of preparing for my afternoon classes, Mr. Lazar."

"Yes." Callahan piped in, pointing his pen to the ceiling. He nearly tipped his chair over backwards with his burst of enthusiasm and sudden unfolding. "And a darned fine job of them she's doing, I might add."

I was sure my jaw dropped. What had brought that on?

"Yes. Well." Lazar lowered his scowl to the pine table and shuffled some papers laid out before him. "I am here today representing my client, the Denton family. You know them, of course?"

"Not personally, no." But I had heard of the name, and not just half a minute ago in the doorway, being barreled over by the painted warrior woman. The Denton descendants, I believed, still lived in the fancy family mansion in Cherry Hills that their ancestor, the nouveau riche miner, had built over a century ago. The family was probably even more famous these days because they'd retained their fortune.

So if Lawyer Lazar worked for the Dentons, that explained his expensive watch, but a better question was what on earth could they possibly want with Mr. Callahan or me? I hoped it wasn't of the legal nature.

"Naturally you wouldn't know the Dentons personally," Lazar said. "You don't move in the same social circles, even if you also come from pioneer stock."

One of my unruly eyebrows lifted with surprise. Apparently he'd done some homework about me, although a bit faulty. I was third generation native, which was close but not quite official pioneer status.

"That woman who left here in a huff," I said, "mentioned the Dentons, too. Would someone care to tell me what's going on?"

Callahan shook his head and picked up a manila envelope. "She brought this over. It's an offer to buy the studio."

My heart lurched. I might be out of a job if he signed such an offer. Was that why he called me here? To break the news to me? "Are you..." I tried to speak, but my voice croaked. "Are you going to sell?"

"If he knows what's best for him," Lazar said, "he'll ignore her. That Phyllis Eberhardt is a vulture, waiting for the fall of the Dentons so she can pick them apart. And you, young lady, have given her the opportunity."

"Me? What did I do?"

"I understand that you're the one who found Francesca Denton."

"I found *who*?"

His lips twitched. He narrowed his eyes at me. "Francesca was the last of the Dentons, heir to the estate, and then the police paid a call to inform the family about her alleged climbing accident."

"Is it true that you're the one who found her?" Callahan said, dropping the envelope and leaning back to look up at me. He still hadn't invited me to sit.

I whistled. "That's who she was? Francesca Denton?" Oh boy. He was talking about the redhead's body hanging off the Flatiron. Our Fanny.

Lazar bent forward to peer at me. "Francesca's death is tragic, of course, but even worse, she was the last of the line."

"I'm so sorry," I said. "Please extend our sympathies to the family." Francesca Denton and our Fanny must be one and the same.

Lazar moved some papers around. "Indeed. The family,

54

however, requires more than mere condolences, Miss Letterly. You see, now the family fortune will most likely end up going to charity."

I didn't see at all.

"With your cooperation," Lazar said, "we can see to it that the estate will not be lost entirely but go to a cousin, instead. Sadly, he is not even a Denton, but rather the product of an unfortunate union."

I had no response to that. What could anyone say about such an attitude?

"My office drew up the papers exactly as the elder Mr. Denton, Deke II, requested before his death. You see, it was through his shrewdness that the family accrued their fortune, and he was not willing to see it squandered through the mismanagement of his own son, Deke III. The elder Mr. Denton stipulated that his two grandchildren — that would be Francesca and her cousin — were to jointly share in the inheritance. However, in the event of questionable circumstances regarding the premature death of either party, the entire estate would go to charity instead. Unless, of course, such questions are satisfactorily answered and the surviving party is deemed not responsible for said circumstances." Lazar paused, twiddling his thumbs while his meaning sank in.

"Now, Miss Letterly," he continued, "surely you understand why it is of the utmost importance that we clear up this matter immediately."

Right, but important for whom? The unfortunate cousin.

"Furthermore," Lazar said, "the family wishes no further embarrassment and requests that you purge all mention of Ms. Denton from your files. My staff is prepared to take charge of that matter for you, posthaste."

Excuse me? "I'm very sorry, but our records are confidential." Our files were becoming quite popular. I'd stayed up half the night searching through them, trying to find out why. The bags under my eyes attested to my late hours. And all I found was nothing.

That is, nothing about *Fanny*.

The lawyer sighed. "Very well. My people will assist you, then. It must be done, and the sooner the better, if we are to prevent the scandal sheets from muddying the family's name."

I wondered if the Dentons' embarrassment and what the police wanted to extract from our files could be one and the same. "Again, I'm very sorry, but we have to consider the privacy of our students."

"Justice is a matter much larger than that. I speak on behalf of the family, and rest assured, we will not tolerate any attempt to impede justice. Be informed that justice will be served."

"Justice?" I said, my voice squawking out of control. I glanced at Callahan for help, but he cradled his head in his hands. I turned back to Lazar. "Look, exactly what is it you're after?"

"I would hazard a guess that your records, if properly kept, will illuminate the name of the person or persons responsible for Ms. Denton's questionable death. You knew exactly which trail to choose in order to discover her body and stage your little, shall we say, charade, is that not correct?"

My mind spun. "We were on that trail because I was leading my students on a training run."

"Ah-hah. There you have it." Lazar gathered up papers and rapped them sharply together on the table.

"Have what?" I said. "Look, we had nothing to do with that poor woman's death."

This lawyer guy was nuts. On some sort of power trip. Looking for someone to blame for his client's loss. Heat spread through me, stiffening my spine.

"The young man in question will pay for this heinous crime."

"What young man?" But I knew the jerk meant Lyle. That's why Detective Rosenquist asked about him, too.

Mr. Fancy Pants stared down his nose at me, apparently stunned by my protest. I wouldn't let up. If he was going to make accusations, then he was going to have to be clear about them. "Who? I am responsible for my students, so I need to know."

His sigh sounded like a whistle through his clenched teeth. "If we knew his name, we would not have to trouble ourselves with this distasteful detour."

"Then, why are you so certain the person you want is one of our students?"

"Because in your quaint little studio is where all the trouble began. Ever since Ms. Denton first associated herself with your so-called school, she has been unceasingly harassed. Do not attempt any further pretense of ignorance regarding this matter."

"Let me get this straight: you think one of my students harassed her, which somehow has something to do with her fall on the mountain?" It was ridiculous.

Instead of denying the outrageous conclusion, Lazar slid the collected papers into a briefcase on the floor beside his chair, and stood up. With a curt nod at Callahan, he said, "we'll be in touch. No, no, don't get up. I can see my way out." Ignoring me, he executed an about face and marched to the door.

"Just a minute," I said, leaping after him. "Let's sit down and sort this out. You could've come straight to me to clear up your misunderstanding. You didn't need to trouble Mr. Callahan with any of this."

Lazar paused with his hand on the doorknob and spoke through gritted teeth. "If you wish to be successful in any endeavor, you must take your grievances to the top. You, young lady, are no one. You have my card. I suggest you be prepared to hand over your records to my office and our culprit to the proper authorities." He glanced at his golden wrist. "Shall we say, by Monday? We can be reasonable. Good day." Then he whisked through the doorway and slammed it shut behind him.

Or, what? I sank into a chair without Callahan's invitation. "Whoa. Did that man just try to suggest that one of our students killed that woman?" *Lyle.* He meant Lyle. I guessed that the family had given the detectives the same idea.

Callahan hunched low in his chair and clutched his forehead in the palms of his hand. "I'm ruined."

"He's wrong. Even if someone *did* push her to her death, how on earth could anyone think my students and I were the ones responsible?"

"Statistics," Callahan said with a moan.

"What statistics?"

Callahan spoke through his fingers. "The people who report an accident, which later turns out to be a crime, are often times the ones who did it."

"But that doesn't make sense. Not in this case."

"Right. It's not just any woman we're talking about. It's Francesca Denton."

My muscles tightened. Rage steamed from the tips of my toenails and worked its way throughout my body. "I'm sorry that she had to die, but just because she was born with a silver spoon in her mouth doesn't make her any more special than anyone else. No one has the right to blame us for her death just because my students and I happened across her body."

"You don't understand." He moaned.

"You're darned right I don't. Do such entitled people as the Dentons think they can find just anyone to be their scapegoat when some tragedy upsets their world? Francesca's death has no connection to us." Even so, now we had a fancy lawyer on our tail, in addition to the pair of detectives.

Callahan grasped his forehead and sank lower. "It's not you they care about."

"Darned right."

"It's me. They're going to run me into the ground until someone pays, so that they get to keep their estate."

"Good grief. Lyle doesn't stand a chance against them."

Sweat beads popped out on Callahan's balding crown. He reached for the envelope he'd tossed aside and opened it. "Maybe I should take this offer. Because the Dentons won't rest until they shut us down and take us apart, penny by penny."

"They can't do it," I said. "I won't let them."

No matter if all of my students were guilty, I wouldn't turn over any of them. I wouldn't let the lawyer intimidate us, either. But what was I up against, if his powerful client decided to ruin us?

FOUR

I stewed all the way home. Lyle was a bit odd, I admitted, but no way had he pushed anyone off the Flatiron. I was convinced of that. Never mind that I didn't really know him. I didn't have to. It just didn't make sense that he would harm the young woman he was supposedly crazy about. And now his rotten luck had gotten him in the way of the powerful Denton family. All that mattered to them was that someone paid for the slight to their empire. The injustice of it gnawed at me the rest of the afternoon.

I stewed the rest of the day, through afternoon and early evening classes. I snapped out curt instructions to my students. I liked my job. If Callahan caved in and sold, would the new owner keep me? And who would that be? Phyllis Eberhardt's client, presumably. She'd made the hand delivery of the offer for her client, and that must've been what ticked her off.

I stewed later that night, while Terra pointed out the inadequacies of my quick-serve casserole of leftovers as compared to her Thai dinner with Gillian the night before.

I was going to have to do something. I couldn't sit idly by and let the big boys railroad my boss, the kindest, gentlest man on the face of the earth. I couldn't believe that my goofy student Lyle was guilty of stalking anyone. Or of murder.

Lyle had a crush on Fanny. How could he possibly kill her,

even if she really was Francesca?

No, he was being framed. That had to be the answer. And I knew something about *that* business, after my run-in with the detectives a couple of months ago, didn't I? Since Lyle obviously hadn't done it, I would have to find out who had.

But my hands were tied until after Saturday morning classes let out, when my weekend officially began at noon.

After the last of the Saturday students left, and after I filed away the morning's attendance cards, I flicked off the humming fluorescent lights and padded upstairs. Sammy squeaked at me when I opened the door to Terra's and my apartment.

"Hi sweetheart!" I picked up Samurai Q. Ferret and scratched her behind her sable ears. Sammy was always the first to greet me as she bounced on her hind feet trying to see what trinket she might steal from me next. "Are you up, Terra?" I called to my daughter through her closed bedroom door.

The door opened. She rolled her eyes at me. "I've been up for *hours*. Cramming for finals. *You* said I have to pull up my grades, remember?"

What I'd actually said was that summer school remained an option. I shrugged. "Then I guess you won't be able to go exploring with me."

Sammy chittered as if to say "me, me, me" and twisted her neck, stretching in my arms to get a better view of my face.

"Oh, you want to go, too? You'd better tell Terra."

Terra's face flushed with interest under the glaze of teenage aloofness.

An hour later, freshly lathered up with sunscreen, we climbed into the Ghia, filling it with the scent of coconut, and took off. Exploring had always been one of our Saturday games.

We liked to wander aimlessly to see where new roads or paths would take us. Today's version wasn't exactly the same, since I knew exactly where I wanted to end up.

We chugged through town, winding through neighborhoods and back streets until we "accidentally" came across a dirt parking area for one of the trailheads leading up to the Flatirons. We hopped out and adjusted our hats. Terra's fanny pack twitched as Sammy squirmed inside, twisting around to poke her head out the zippered opening, zipped up to the edge of her neck, looking like her head stuck out of a noose.

I checked the map again. Lyle's home address that I'd pulled from the files at the studio should put his house not far from this trailhead's parking lot. Footpaths traced jagged lines from the residential neighborhood that lined open space, and they intersected with the main trail, which followed the gulch up into the mountains. Hmmm. This neighborhood had handy access to the Flatiron where Lyle had joined the rest of our group on our Tuesday training run. Where Francesca, aka Fanny, had died.

I was pretty sure that Lyle wasn't a killer. Which left my other option: he'd ducked out of sight these last few days because he was afraid of a killer. Or maybe he was afraid of the Dentons and their lawyer. Who wouldn't be? Either way, if I was going to help sort out this mess, then I needed to figure out who was the killer. I would start by examining the scene of the crime.

Terra and I slipped water bottles into the Velcroed loops of our packs and set off clanking along the gulch trail. I still hadn't told Terra about my mission. We enjoyed the moment. I wasn't ready to ruin it yet.

We trekked across an open area of scrub brush, working up a good sweat as the terrain climbed. By the time we reached an elevation where pines took over, my lungs worked at capacity, leaving me feeling invigorated with a natural high. Up here, the air smelled thick with pine as the trail tunneled through giant lodgepoles. A trio of young women thudded down the slope towards us, tripping over their hiking boots in their haste.

"Hello," I called out, but their return of the usual greeting exchange sounded breathless.

"Watch out..." said the chunkiest hiker. She paused to gulp air. "There's a rattlesnake back there."

"A *snake*?" Terra screeched. "Oh my *God*."

My skin tightened. "Where, exactly?" I asked, remembering the snake on the trail a few days ago. By my calculations, the location of that encounter was straight down the side of the mountain from us, as the crow flies. Or fell.

"We didn't see it," said the tallest hiker over her shoulder as the trio disappeared around a bend, "but there's a woman, about a mile up the trail, says there's a snake out here somewhere."

Terra and I exchanged glances. Of course there were snakes out here. Somewhere. Disappointment coursed through me. It wasn't necessarily the same snake, I told myself. Then again, maybe it was. Sammy ducked back inside the pocket of the fanny pack.

"Let's get out of here, Mom."

"Don't be silly. We'll be fine, as long as we stay on the trail and keep a lookout."

She rolled her eyes in disgust. "You go first, then."

As we hiked farther, I scanned the brush alongside the trail and listened hard for rattles. A couple of times I thought

I heard the ominous warning sound but then decided it was a ringing in my ears. Terra crept along behind me, sticking close to my shadow.

No one lapped us on the trail. We lapped no one. That was odd for a gorgeous spring day, and on a weekend to boot. But we kept seeing hikers coming the other way, opposite the direction we were heading. My skin prickled when I heard a few of them mumble about snakes. Were snakes even out this early? Of course they were. My students and I had seen one just a few days ago. I hadn't seen a snake on a trail for about twenty years, not since Boulder's population exploded with outsiders looking for the good life here in the mountains. And now there were two snakes in the same week.

Finally we came to an overlook. Somewhere along here was where Francesca had fallen, leading to the crevice way below that had caught her deadly fall. I wanted to go closer to examine the area, to see if there was any evidence of what had happened to her. Evidence of a scuffle, maybe. I didn't know what I was looking for, but somehow, I would find something to exonerate Lyle. Maybe the killer had left a clue behind, something the police hadn't found yet.

Right.

Instead, a woman sat on the exact rock I wanted to check out. I edged toward her, through an archway of boulders, and studied the terrain.

It was a sheer drop-off. I stood poised at the top of a sheet of rock. One wrong step, and anyone could've stepped into thin air. This flat rock sloped at a slight angle about six hundred feet down into treetops. Goosebumps prickled the back of my neck, and I swayed, feeling light-headed and a bit winded. From the climb. From the vista. A panorama of plains spread out endlessly, far below.

"Careful, honey," said the woman on the rock beside me. "You don't want to fall here."

I took a step back and turned to face her. From the red splotches on her freckled face, she seemed to be crying, not admiring the view. A basket sat on a flat piece of ground beside her rock. The faded green of a backpackers pack tucked under some bushes that sprouted out between rocks farther up the slope. What had she been doing? Camping and gathering wildflowers? Both were highly illegal. Where were Rock and Oriana when I needed them?

My civic duty burned within me. "Gorgeous day, isn't it?" I said, moving closer to her rock. I peered into the basket. It was almost empty except for a layer of grass clippings. Picking grass wasn't illegal.

The woman sniffled and swished her frizzy black curls as she watched me. The emerald green of her eyes reminded me of a cat's, except they sparkled with tears. "It's awful purty," she said, wiping her face with a curled fingernail painted blue. Mascara smeared. "I come straight up here soon as I got to town, and I declare, I still cain't hardly breathe." She gulped and patted her ample bosom. A gold chain as thin as a thread clung to her neck, and whatever dangled from the end tucked inside the low-cut neckline of her tangerine tank top. "How on earth do you folks breathe up here, a whole mile high?"

Wrinkling my face into a frown of concern, I dropped down into a squat beside the tourist woman. Terra stayed upright behind me. Alert. "You get used to it when you live here a while. It takes a few weeks for most outsiders to adjust. You have to

take it easy in the meanwhile. Until you adjust to the altitude."
I checked out her flimsy flip-flop sandals and short-shorts. A
bit too lightweight for this trail, and definitely too optimistic
for May. Heck, only a couple years or so ago we had a blizzard
in May. This newcomer wasn't wearing a hat, either. But then,
how could a hat stay on top of her head with all those frizzy curls
poking out like sprung springs? "There are plenty of other,
easier hikes you could try over there on Flagstaff." I jerked my
head backwards, in a northerly direction. We Boulderites can't
help ourselves. We love to recommend local attractions to the
tourists.

"Thanks for the advice," she said. A shy smile tugged at
the corners of her full lips, sparkling hot pink. The clash of her
colors made my eyes hurt. "I got me plenty of time, I reckon,
seein' as how I'm gonna be stayin' here for good from now on."

"Oh. You're not just passing through? You're actually
moving here?"

"That's right. I'm gonna be livin' with my honey from now
on. That's how come I come up here, up north, to look for a
place for us to live. We ain't got much, but I reckon we can
manage to buy ourselves something cheap."

Not in this town. She'd find that out soon enough.
"Welcome, then. I thought you were one of the summer tourists
we usually get. A lot of Texans come here in the summer. To
beat the heat."

"No'm, I'm more south than that. My sweetie is too. He
come up here first, a few months ago, checkin' things out, gettin'
us all fixed up with a place."

"If you need any help getting settled in, just give me a call.
Let me give you one of my cards." I stood up and dug through

my jeans pocket. One used tissue. I slipped my daypack off my shoulder and riffled through a pocket.

"Mom," said Terra, lowering her voice to a whisper. "You'd better tell her about the you-know-what."

"Right," I said, pulling out a card and handing it to the woman.

She glanced at it and did a double-take on me. "This is *you*?"

"That's right. I'm Nell Letterly." I stood up straight, trying to reach all five feet of my height.

"But it says here you're some sort of karate instructor."

"Uh-huh. Come check out our studio sometime. We give two introductory lessons for free."

"Maybe I will, honey. I mean, ma'am. That's what people are supposed to call you, ain't it?"

I nodded. Apparently, she'd had some exposure to our martial arts culture somewhere.

She went on. "I'm Jasmine Mayotte, and I'm pleased to make your acquaintance. Folks sure are friendly around these here parts."

"We try to be —"

"Mo-o-om, don't forget the *snake*!"

Jasmine's shoulders straightened from their slump. "Clara?" Her voice lifted. "You seen her?"

"Clara? Who's that?"

"My pet snake."

"Your snake?"

"Sure. I couldn't leave her behind, y'know? She used to get along real well with my honey. And besides I thought Clara would like it up here." Jasmine reached over to pat the basket.

"This is where she sleeps. She rode up here all the way in this, and I thought now that we're finally here, she'd like a breath of fresh air, but when I took the lid off, she up an' run off. I don't know what to do."

Terra and I glanced at each other. So that's why all the hikers were hurrying away, the other way. "If it's a pet, it must be a little garter snake," I said. I hoped. Not a rattlesnake, as the hikers had told us. Or worse, a python.

"He-yell no, she's a rattler. Poor baby, must be scared to death out there by her lonesome."

Poor baby, indeed. Clara wasn't as scared as all the hikers that had fled the area. "Isn't that kind of unusual to have a rattlesnake for a pet? I mean, don't people usually have snakes that don't bite? Or, that is, not 'have' but take care of. That's what I mean."

I kept forgetting. In Boulder people didn't own pets. We were guardians of pets.

"You don't have to worry none. Clara won't hurt you. I keep her venom all milked out."

What a relief. "She still bites, doesn't she?"

"Sure, but they're just love tickles. They don't hurt none." Jasmine held out her left arm and pointed out several puncture wounds. "No worse'n a cat bite. I'll bet that little critter of yours bites, too." She nodded at Terra's wiggling fanny pack. "Whyn't you take that thing on out of there and set it down? I'll betcha it could call Clara for me and tell her to come back."

"Ferrets don't talk," Terra said.

"Sure they do, honey. All animals talk. Not like you and me talking out loud. They talk in your head."

Terra shrank away from the overlook where Jasmine

perched. "Oh yeah, I just remembered, Mom. I'm supposed to meet Lindsay today, 'cause her mom said she'd help us with our geometry. We got to go. *Now*."

This was absolutely not true. I knew for a fact, through the parental network I'd taken great care to establish over the years, that Lindsay and her family were going to the zoo today. "In a minute, honey. First we have to look for what we came here to look for."

"You lookin' for something, too?" Jasmine said. "Maybe I seen it while I been callin' for Clara."

"How long have you been here?" I asked, eyeing the pack tucked under a bush.

Jasmine flushed. "Long enough." She opened her mouth as if to say more, and then bit her lips, clamping her jaw shut.

"More than a day?"

Her chin dipped, as if she was getting ready to nod her head yes, but then she stuck out her lower lip and said, "How come you want to know?"

"There was a woman who had an accident here four or five days ago," I said.

Terra sputtered. "I read about that online. Is *that* what this is all about? Mom, you're not holding out on me again, are you?"

I shook my head at Terra and frowned, a signal that we would talk later. Then I turned back to Jasmine and erased my frown. "She fell off this cliff. From somewhere around here."

Jasmine flinched. "Was she hurt bad?"

"Sadly, she didn't make it. I thought you might've seen something that would help the investigation. That is, if you've been up here a while, looking for your snake." My gaze shifted to the pack.

"I ain't camping, if that's what you think." She turned her back on the backpack, as if trying to block it from my view. "Me and my honey, we had a fight, so me and Clara had to go somewhere, didn't we? What are you, some kind of cop, too?"

"Heck no." I scrambled through my mind for an evasive answer. "I'm just sort of helping out the family. They're connected to the, um, karate studio, and they want to know what happened to their daughter. Did you happen to see her? Maybe Monday night?"

Jasmine narrowed her green eyes at me. "What'd she look like?"

"Long red hair, pink jacket, college age."

Something flickered across her face. Recognition? I held my breath. I couldn't believe my luck. Had I stumbled across a witness? "So, did you see her?"

"Hmmm, Monday, you say? That would've been the night I rolled into town. Sorry, I cain't help you."

"You said you came straight up here."

"Nope, I never said that."

I took a deep breath, releasing the tension from my own face that would reveal I knew she was lying. "There was a group of hikers up here that night," I said, refraining from calling them campers. If Jasmine had been up here then, she would've heard the campers' noise, too. Maybe she was one of them. "Did you happen across anyone hiking at night?"

"Honey, I seen lots of hikers and what have you." She sprang to her feet and grabbed the snake's basket, as if preparing to leave. But then she stopped and pressed one of her blue-painted nails across her upper lip. "Wait a minute. Now that you mention it, maybe I did see them. There was a man, and he was looking for his girlfriend. Said she got lost. She was wearing a pink jacket, and she had red hair, too, he said. He wondered if I'd seen her."

How convenient that she suddenly remembered this. "A man?"

"Well, more like a young man, I reckon. Short. Skinny. Horn-rimmed glasses. Black hair that stands up in spikes."

"Lyle?" An alarm pulsed through me. She'd just described my student, Lyle.

"Yeah, Lyle. That's what he said his name was." She fluttered her mascara-ed eyelashes at me. "He was awful upset. About losin' his girlfriend. Y'know?"

I couldn't believe a word she'd said. Talking snakes and crazy stuff. But she had pulled Lyle's description out of the blue. I hadn't given her *that* information. Only his name. How had she known what Lyle looked like?

She would know because she'd seen him up here.

FIVE

We had to hurry, because that night was going to be Date Night with Dad. The rules I'd set up back when I was still in school and Mother died from breast cancer gave Dad the right to choose the time of day or night and the activity. Since I'd started working at Callahan's, Dad had always chosen a time that didn't conflict with my teaching schedule.

"Okay, Mom, *give*," Terra said as we thumped our way back down the mountain to the trailhead.

I was accustomed to giving my daughter and my dad edited versions of the interesting situations I sometimes found myself in. She deserved an explanation after the way I'd hijacked her up the mountain. Anyway, she and Dad would probably hear gossip about the death of the young woman, or read further reports about it in the newspaper. Sooner or later, Terra and Dad were going to find out that the victim was possibly a former student at Callahan's, so I might as well confess.

I told her about it as we drove over to Dad's farmhouse, seven miles east of town. The spicy smells of take-out Chinese saturated my Karmann Ghia along the way.

Date Night with Dad wasn't always dinner. More often, we played gin rummy or read books in front of his wood-burning stove while Terra went through the stacks of yellowing music

73

books on the upright that Mother had insisted my brothers and I grow up with. Occasionally we all watched his favorite sit-com on the telly, although lately there didn't seem to be any that he liked. Whatever. It was his choice.

Tonight, he wanted to sit on his front porch and puff on his pipe, blending the woodsy smells of tobacco with the country air of hay and cows. Comfort smells of home.

Creaking in his rocker on the porch, Dad always liked to tell stories about the constellations. Only the brightest stars shone, even out here, seven miles away from city glow. The longer days of late spring made twilight hang in the air as if reluctant to give the day up to night.

Terra's music wafted out the windows while Dad told me about the Roman twins who'd loved each other so much that they'd been put in the heavens as the stars Castor and Pollux, together for eternity.

His voice rumbled on as I looked for the twinkling pair of stars Dad pointed out. I didn't find anything that looked like twins, but it didn't matter. Being out here, the lulling sound of Dad's voice soothed my soul and filled me with a sense of peace. The world was all okay in the presence of my dad. The monsters were held back at bay. My contentment almost blotted out the images that kept tumbling through my mind.

A blaze of red hair hanging down from the dead girl on the Flatiron.

The shadowy shape of a killer — Lyle? — peering down from the drop-off at the top of the mountain.

Rosenquist and Lazar scowling with suspicion.

I shivered, and not just from the cool night air. Dad's voice had stopped, I suddenly realized.

"Nellie?" Dad poked my arm.

"Sorry, Dad. What did you say?"

"Never mind what I said. Something's troubling you. Are you going to spit it out or not?"

I sighed. I never could keep anything from my dad, not for very long. If I ever tried to, he dug in like a terrier and wouldn't let go until I confessed. I'd become pretty good at editing special versions for him.

"I was just thinking about twins," I said lamely.

His rocking chair squeaked once and then stopped, telling me that he'd stiffened in his chair, giving me his full attention. "Go on."

"And relationships like that."

"Uh-huh. What's his name?"

"Who?"

"That new someone you met, that's who."

"I haven't met anyone. That is, not like *that*."

"I'll tell you what, Nellie. Maybe it's about time you did. These last couple of months, with your new job, and now that you've got renters in your house, why, I've never seen you happier. You deserve someone new in your life, now that you finally got rid of that no-good —"

"Hush, Dad."

The piano music died.

I leaned close to him and whispered. "It's not what you think."

"Then what is it?"

Dad was usually spot-on, but this time he was off-base. I had to quash it fast. "I was out running with my students a few days ago," I said, raising my voice to start in on the edited version of the training run that I'd practiced on Terra in the car on our way over here. I'd learned the hard way that Dad always found out whenever I had anything to do with the news.

The piano music started up again.

I told Dad my story, but I left out the gruesome part about Francesca's facial swelling. Too much information.

Although I did tell him about the snake on the trail. But I left out the parts about Lyle's gun and the police visit. No point in alarming him needlessly. I wrapped up my story with the lawyer's threatening visit to Callahan.

Dad grumbled under his breath. His rocker resumed creaking, sawing a furious rhythm.

"So now the Dentons think my student Lyle is somehow responsible for Francesca's death," I said, "just because we happened across her body. It's so unfair! How can they implicate the studio just because it was our bad luck to find the body?"

"They're trying to throw their weight around."

"Mr. Callahan thinks they're out to ruin him financially. It's so stupid. So pointless. So not fair." I bit my tongue. Black belts didn't whine. But dammit, I wanted to. Besides, if I couldn't whine to my own dad, then...

We didn't curse, either.

I settled into a good grump. Why did people who had so much want to take away from people who had so little?

"You know life isn't fair," Dad said. "Sometimes folks will just try to run right over you, if you give them half a chance. It's all about control. That's what you do in that studio of yours, isn't it?"

"Not exactly. We learn to control ourselves, not others."

"And now someone's trying to control you. Is that what you're worried about?"

I wasn't worried. "I just wish I'd happened along sooner. Maybe I could've helped her."

He snorted. "You can thank your lucky stars you didn't get there any earlier. You want to repeat March all over again? You already found one dead body back then. Isn't that enough?"

The scar on my leg throbbed at the reminder of those events. "That was different, Dad."

"Not so different. It's all about who you are, Nellie. You always got to do what you got to do." Dad spoke as enigmatically as Master Hwang. Sometimes I thought both of them could read my mind. It was so embarrassing.

"I can't let them shut down Callahan's," I said. "It's not just my job. I owe Mr. Callahan. Without him, where would I be?"

I knew the answer to that: I would be living in Dad's guest room, because my house would've been foreclosed by now, had I not been lucky enough to find renters. Either way, I was out of a home. Mr. Callahan had saved me from humiliation when he hired me on. I could never repay such a debt. How did you put a price on your pride?

"I just want to see you happy before my time's up," Dad said. "That's all."

"I *am* happy."

He grunted. He didn't believe me. "And settled, too."

"Been there, done that." Being settled wasn't part of the equation to my happiness.

We listened to a train wail in the distance, rushing somewhere, while time stopped for us here on Dad's porch. Finally, he grunted. "Look," he said, breaking past the conversation killer of my happiness. "Anyone can join your studio who has the money to pay, can't they?"

"Right, Dad. But once my students come under my guidance, I am responsible for their actions."

"You're taking this too far. No one can blame you for what they do away from your class."

"I teach them a way of life. It's all about positive attitude. It's a way of thinking. If they fail to uphold the black belt way of life that we value, then I haven't done my job well enough."

"You've been at this teaching gig, what? Two months? Give yourself a chance. You've always been too hard on yourself. You can't expect to turn anyone's life around in only two months."

"That's just the thing. I don't really know my students at all. I just don't want to believe there is a connection between that girl's death and Callahan's Karate."

"If there is, then you'll find it. Just remember, Nellie, I helped you back in March, and I might be able to help you again. Don't forget."

Oh, boy, did I ever remember. "That was different. I had to clear my name back then."

"And now you have to keep your studio's name clean, so what's the difference?"

I sighed. "Not much, I guess. I've got to do the right thing for Callahan's. I have to."

"Darned right, we do," Dad said.

"Not 'we'. Me."

Dad snorted, apparently not willing to stand down.

Before I could persuade him not to get involved, my cell rang. Just about the only one to ever call me on my cell was Terra, but it obviously wasn't her. Through the window I could see her silhouette, swaying over the keyboard, sending out a medley of tinkling music, one tune after another.

"Excuse me, Dad."

Even in the shadows, I could see annoyance glitter in the whites of his eyes as he bit down on his pipe, watching me fish the phone out of my pocket. I stood up and wandered down the steps of the porch onto the springy turf of new grass.

"Nell?" said the familiar voice on the other end of the line. Gillian Gannon, my soon-to-be ex-sister-in-law. Max's half-sister, one of the trust-fund hippies who flooded my hometown, drawn here by the good life. "Where are you?"

I started to fill her in on my whereabouts, but she cut me short. I held the phone away from my ear and listened to her steady stream of chatter. It was something about wanting to buy some mountain property and would I accompany her to some open houses the next day on Sunday? She didn't want to make herself vulnerable, and surely I understood about the dangers of a single woman all alone, and yadda yadda. The only time I was ever useful to Jill was when she needed me for back-up for whatever crazy new enterprise she entered into. I cut her off, giving her the name of Van Orr with the Orr Group. He was looking for new clients. I promised to call her back later.

I climbed the steps back to the porch and perched on the railing. "What are you looking at now, Dad?"

"Nothing anyone can see," he said. "Your snake story reminded me of the snake up there, hiding beneath the lion."

"If you can't see it, how do you know it's there?"

"That's what snakes are like. They hide until they strike. Just like that woman who's trying to get me."

"What woman? What do you mean? Is someone bothering

you?" I could feel my defensive hackles rise. Anyone who troubled my dad would have to go through me first.

"Look over there." Dad pointed to Kansas. "You see it coming up?"

"I don't see anything."

"You will, just hang around until it gets a bit darker."

"It's getting late. I've got to get Terra home and into bed. What am I supposed to see, and what woman are you talking about?" Conversations with my dad often went that way. Come to think of it, conversations with my sensei were equally mired in metaphor.

He sighed, exasperated with my slow wit. "Can't you see Arcturus rising? You better get your eyes checked, Nellie. Now I'll grant you, you can't see the rest of Bootes, but he's there. He's the farmer. Like me, out here in God's country."

"Okay." I saw a bright point of light that was either a plane landing at Denver's airport or the star he referred to. "What about the woman?" He was trying to distract me from something unpleasant that he needed to tell me. I could tell.

"We won't be able to stargaze much longer," he said as he puffed thoughtfully on his pipe, making it glow in the darkness.

"Why not? You going someplace?"

"Of course not, Nellie, don't be a danged fool. Only way I'll leave this place is in a box."

I shivered. May by day might act like summer, but by night it was winter cold. "You know I don't like for you to talk like that."

He chuckled. "Stop your worrying. It's not my time yet. Even though that danged woman thinks it is."

"Enough of this, Dad. What woman? Is this something I

need to take care of for you?"

"Heck fire if I know who she is. Stopped by here today. Wants to buy my farm. Said something about a new subdivision going in across the street. That's how come we won't be able to stargaze much longer, not if they bring the city out here."

"Buy your farm?" Interest pricked through me. "Well, wait, let's not be too hasty. You ought to think about it. This old place is too much work for you. Since Hugh and Zack moved away, I'm the only one of us sibs who can help around here, and I'm not much help. Maybe it's time to think about finding a smaller place, someplace that's less work for you."

The ends of his mouth turned down as he hunkered in his rocker. The bowl of his pipe glowed as he sucked on it. He was sulking. "I don't know. I can't let your mother down. She'd turn over in her grave if she thought anyone wanted to dig up her orchard and cement it over."

"All I'm asking is that you think about it."

He grunted. "She wants me to call her back."

"Who?"

"That woman. She left her card on the table by the front door."

I stood up and walked into the warm light filtering through the stained glass globe of the hall lamp. Sure enough, there was a business card dropped onto the wooden surface of the antique table, next to a pile of junk mail. The crisp white card displayed the logo of a realtor's office. I picked it up and angled it closer to the light. "Jimmie Condo," it read. What kind of woman had a name like that?

SIX

I wasted no time. The next morning I breakfasted alone and left Terra home in bed. I still had some free time before I needed to account to Gillian my whereabouts for her open house venture, so I climbed into the Ghia with the business card I'd pilfered from Dad's mail. No one was going to mess with my dad.

Jimmie Condo's office was a couple blocks from downtown, not too far from Callahan's, in a small unit of offices and condos, built in the early modern style, probably from the '70's. The place looked like a square cruise ship.

Her office was on ground level, opening onto a courtyard where a helmeted, backpack-clad young woman fumbled with the padlock connecting her bike to a rack.

"Morning," I said, striding past the biker to Condo's office door.

"Closed," the sign read. Through the glass window of the door, I could see that the office was dark. Dang. I glanced at my watch. Another hour before I'd promised to call Jill. Theoretically, I needed to be on sister-in-law duty soon. I didn't have all morning to wait around for Jimmie Condo to open her office.

"It's closed," the young bicyclist told me. As if I couldn't read.

"Yeah," I said. "I hoped she might come in early."

A single burst of laughter erupted from the young woman, sounding like an explosion bouncing off the courtyard walls.

"I take it," I said, "she's not an early bird?" Although, in my book, eight wasn't so early.

In this town it was. Boulder yuppies usually didn't get up until mid-morning, and then their first stop was for a latte. Like Gillian's routine. At this hour, it was mainly service workers and church goers who were on the prowl.

The biker shrugged. "Only if they're out to excoriate someone."

That made me pause. I studied her carefully. Using a big word like that, along with the bike and the backpack in this town probably made her a student at the university. "I gather," I said, choosing my words with equal care, "you've had some encounters with her?"

"Not me. But some neighbors on my floor..." Her voice faded away with a sniff and a sigh. She wiped the corner of her eye where a tear glistened. "Trust me, you should find another realtor."

"I'm not here looking for a realtor."

The biker recoiled, as if I'd surprised her with a backfist to the head. "I can't believe you're friends with those jerks. You seem too nice."

I snorted. "I'm not her friend. I have a, er, business issue to discuss with her."

She snorted back. "I can guess it's nasty. Are they suing you, or something?"

"Something like that."

The young woman frowned and narrowed her eyes. "Well,

you're in luck. Here comes one of them now. Too bad, I have to go." Her mouth curved to one side, giving me a look of sympathy. Then she jumped on her bike as if she couldn't get away fast enough.

I waved to the biker and then followed her gaze to get a good look at the woman named Jimmie Condo who'd been bothering Dad. To my surprise, I recognized the woman who was rattling a key ring while making a beeline for the office door. But her name wasn't Jimmie Condo. It was Phyllis Eberhardt. She'd nearly taken my head off at Callahan's office after she'd delivered her offer to buy the studio and put me out of a job. Was there an epidemic of buy-outs going around?

I scurried over to intercept her before she succeeded in disappearing inside. "Excuse me, remember me? I'm Nell Letterly — "

"Well, well, look who's here," Phyllis said. "I was expecting you, but not at this ungodly hour."

"Do you work with Jimmie Condo? That's who I'm looking for. She left her card with my dad. Is she going to be in to the office soon?"

"Honey, that wasn't Jimmie. That was me. And don't you let Jimmie catch you calling him a 'her', either, you hear? He sent me out to your dad's place because he had another obligation. He's a busy man."

"What kind of name is 'Jimmie Condo,' anyway?"

She grunted. "It's better than James Colondoski. He made up the name to go with what he does best, develop condos. Everybody remembers Condo."

"He wants to build condos on my dad's farm?"

"Is your father ready to sell yet? We may have a client lined up, and we wouldn't want to lose out. It's going to be a big project when it's all said and done, but it won't go anywhere without your father's piece of property."

"Dad said something about a development. Is that already in the works? What do you know about what's happening? That might make a difference whether or not I can help you."

Phyllis assessed me with a thoughtful gaze as if she was considering whether or not to tell me more. She must've realized that I was a major influence in Dad's business decisions, because she smiled and invited me in. She unlocked the door, flipped on a light switch, and motioned me to a chair on the visitor's side of a steel desk loaded with precarious piles of papers. Never taking her eyes off me, she slipped her jacket from her shoulders, ringing its clunky silver buttons against the metal side of the desk. Her hips kept on swaying as she moved toward the back of the office.

I lowered myself down to the indicated chair and couldn't help but notice a sheet of paper on the desk, on account of all its red marks. And because it had been singled out, lying to the side of the various stacks. Alone, it lay in the center of a cleared area of workspace. It looked like a print-out of a list of properties, each with a thumbnail photo. One property was circled in red. In the margin, an asterisk and the name "Denton" were scrawled in red. I tried to read the paper upside down while Phyllis busied herself in the back, hanging up her jacket and filling a coffee pot. When I deciphered "Mountain" in the header, I interpreted the address of the circled property and made a mental note. Pine Nugget Lane. It was located up one of the canyons of the foothills just outside of town.

That reminded me. Gillian was hot on some scheme to

buy mountain property. Any minute now, she would probably interrupt me with a phone call. I silenced my cell.

Phyllis returned from the back of the office, sank down into her chair with a loud squeak, and snatched the paper away, stuffing it into a drawer. "Your dad is a stubborn man, Ms. Letterly."

"You can say that again."

"Maybe you can help all of us by changing his mind?"

"Whose help precisely are you talking about? What exactly is your role in the project you mentioned?" I glanced around the notebook-cluttered office.

"If you're hoping to talk to Jimmie," she said, dancing around my question, "you can forget it. He's a busy man. You'll have to talk to me, instead. I handle the front office. Now, how soon can we expect to get your father to turn over possession?"

"It's not likely that he'll move anytime soon."

Phyllis ticked her tongue. "He's not getting any younger. He ought not to be living alone on a farm like that."

"I happen to agree with you about that, but he loves living in the country the way it is. He doesn't really farm anymore, except for keeping the horse and a small garden. It's peaceful, y'know?"

"Don't worry," Phyllis said, "he'll come around."

Was I worried?

"I've seen a lot of clients like him," Phyllis went on. "They protest loudly, but then in the end, when reality hits, they come around. I'll give him a week to change his mind. Maybe two, since he's a tough old nut."

I snorted.

"You don't believe me, honey? Of course not. You haven't

been around like I have. You haven't had to fight for what's rightfully yours, and then watch as someone else steps in and takes it all away from you."

Um, actually... Max came to mind.

"We won't sit around for anymore of that, will we?" Phyllis said. "If your dad doesn't do the right thing now, he'll end up losing his property anyway to eminent domain. You don't want to see that happen, do you?"

Even with my doubts, my heart thudded in my chest. This was Boulder, after all, where changing a light bulb on your front porch required a dozen permits. Jimmie Condo couldn't pull off a thing like eminent domain. Phyllis had to be exaggerating. She was just trying to intimidate me.

I hoped.

I hoped there wasn't a project already in the works that Dad and I didn't know about yet. "He'll fight to the end," I said. "It's no use trying to persuade him to sell. He doesn't want to."

"That piece of property he's sitting on just gets in the way of development," Phyllis said. "He can't stand in the way of progress. Life keeps going forward, whether he likes it or not."

"You make it sound as if there are already plans for development." That would ruin Dad's peace for sure. "What do you know about any plans?"

"I know that the time is right for him to sell. It's never going to get any better than this, neither for your dad nor for your boss. Be a help, and —"

"Callahan?"

"Who else?"

The offer to buy the studio, I realized, would've come from Jimmie Condo. Not Phyllis's client. Phyllis was just Condo's courier. "What's Condo up to? Sounds like he wants to buy up the town."

She grinned. "Just about. It's about time someone else made himself known around here."

"Why does he want to buy Callahan's Karate?"

Phyllis shrugged. "He has plans. He might sweeten the deal if you help convince your boss to agree to our terms."

"Mr. Callahan has other things on his mind at the moment," I said. "For instance, that girl's death. You must've heard about it. The co-ed on the Flatiron?"

Her gaze shifted away from me. "A terrible tragedy. But it shouldn't affect our negotiations."

"Maybe it does. It seems the young woman who died had been one of our students."

"So?" Phyllis said.

"Her family wants answers."

"Honey, her family always thinks that everyone should jump when they snap their fingers."

I sat up at attention in my chair, stiffening my core. She knew who the victim was. "Has her identity been made public?" I didn't remember that the newspaper article released the victim's name.

"Hah. The Dentons can't go anywhere without making waves in the public. It's about time that tragedy knocks them down a rung or two."

Yikes. My skin stung from the bitter vibes this woman radiated. "Sounds like you've had a bad encounter with them."

"In a manner of speaking. They built their wealth and fame on stolen property. That's why I'm here to help prevent that from happening again. I trust that I can count on you to do the right thing?"

She kept saying that, but I wondered what the right thing was. Her idea and mine were likely not the same. I changed tactics. "While I'm here... My sister-in-law is looking for a realtor to help her buy some mountain property. I couldn't help but notice that you have a list of some properties." I gestured at her closed drawer.

She squeaked her chair, shifting. Or squirming? "We're not really doing much real estate anymore. Jimmie is more of a developer, and I specialize in property management."

It sounded like she was trying to get rid of me. "Okay. Then maybe you can recommend another realtor who *will* show us those properties?"

"Those places you're referring to," she said, "aren't available. They're foreclosures. Banks own them, and they're going to auction. You've got to have a lot of cash on hand for that."

"Oh, my sister-in-law has plenty of cash." Daddy Gannon's cash.

Phyllis leaned forward in her chair. I could almost see her salivate. "You know what she wants to do? Is she into flipping?"

"Um," I said, stalling. "I think she's more interested in the investment. Not for herself. For the family. Back east. You wouldn't believe the investments they've made."

Yeah, like what Max did. Somewhere in the Caribbean.

Phyllis plucked a business card from a dispenser on the desk and slapped it down in front of me. "You just give her Jimmie's card. Tell her we'll make an exception for her. We'll take her around."

"She's only interested in one place in particular." I recited the address I'd seen of the red circled property.

Phyllis jerked back and narrowed her eyes. "Not that one.

It sold already."

"Already? Really?"

"They go fast, honey. You've got to be quick in this market."

Like Phyllis was quick, I thought. Quick, getting to Callahan's office. Even quicker, making her way to Dad's farm.

Her gaze bored into me, as if she was trying to read my mind. And heck, maybe she was. I could almost feel the back of my mind pinch.

"You've got to do your research," she said. "We'll be happy to show her something else."

"I'll pass along the information," I said.

"And now, if you'll excuse me, I have an appointment to get ready for." She eyeballed the door, and I got the hint.

Just as well. I felt my cell phone vibrate, tickling my hip. I slipped Condo's business card from the desk, thanked her for her time, and backtracked to the door.

Back outside in the cool morning air of the courtyard, I pulled the phone out of my pocket and studied it. I'd missed Gillian's call. Darn.

But the phone and the card in my hand reminded me of what else I needed to do. I sat down on the sandstone bench beside the rack of bicycles and pawed through my purse until I found the card that Mr. Alastair Lazar had kept up his sleeve. I phoned his number. I had some information for the family, I told him (almost true — I could stretch what I'd learned at the scene of the crime — or I could make it up). I implied that I might be able to accommodate his Monday deadline. Could Mr. Lazar kindly get me an appointment to meet with the family?

SEVEN

Lazar must've thought I intended to cave in to the family's demands and divulge Lyle's whereabouts, because he produced.

I was expected for tea later that afternoon.

I didn't personally know anyone who did tea here in the west, but then, my stock came from the service sector who serviced the suppliers who supplied the miners who struck it rich. That made me far enough removed that I never got a peek behind the ten foot stone walls that surrounded the private estates cloistered within Cherry Hills, a ritzy suburb of Denver where a lot of those folks who struck it rich from the wild west went.

The gatekeeper was skeptical when I drove up in my dented Karmann Ghia, but he phoned the house, confirmed my claim to an appointment, and admitted me to the grounds. Suddenly I felt as if I'd driven into an old favorite story of mine, *Rebecca*. The winding drive didn't lead through woods, but graceful poplars and oaks lined the drive as a symbol of wealth and luxury. Trees weren't indigenous to this dry, hostile land, except for cottonwoods along streams in the flatlands — hanging trees from the wild west — and pines in the high country. At the end of the row of extravagant trees stood a mansion. Your fairly typical mansion with sprawling wings and towers anchoring the corners and a massive double door in the center, upheld by stone pillars. It reminded me of a stone fortress, and it made me wonder what this family's dragons were that required them to live behind such thick walls. By the time I pulled up in front and turned off the engine, someone was opening my car door for me, some sort of valet, I supposed, judging from his monkey suit. He greeted me and waved with a flourishing arm toward the massive front door, in case I'd missed it, where he passed me off to another monkey suit waiting for me.

Our heels clicked across the marble floor as he led me past sweeping stairs, down a side hall to a door at the back of the house, and into a room that could've been a stage set for Downton Abbey with its brocades and leaded crystals and bouquets of pink roses.

Pink, Francesca's favorite color, according to my student Rachel.

People lived like this? Here in Denver? Cripes!

A life-size portrait of a young red-haired woman hung in a gilt frame above the pineapple-rimmed fireplace. Francesca? She wore a flaming pink tank top and a rose pencil skirt that showed off her lanky thin figure. With the right training, I bet she could've had one powerful roundhouse kick with those long legs. The artist had captured melancholy in the downturn of her gray-green eyes and combined it with haughtiness, appropriate for the heir apparent to this estate. Her chin tilted up, her shoulders squared back, and she ignored a fluffy dog playing at her heels.

But Jeeves didn't give me a chance to inspect the portrait any closer. He folded open some French doors that led out onto a patio beside a pool that overlooked terraced gardens. Someone swam laps — a woman, judging from the swim cap. She stroked overhand, face down, and kicked up a churning spray behind her. Jeeves picked up a folded towel and marched to the edge of the pool where her lap aimed, so that when she got there, coming up for air, meaning to turn for another lap, she saw him.

"The young lady is here for tea, madam." He held out the towel for her.

I glanced over my shoulder, but I didn't see anyone else. He must mean me. I was forty-two and technically, I was classified as a senior, but only in tournaments. Certainly not "young lady." I couldn't wait to tell Terra, so that she could modify her opinion of my oldness.

The swimmer pulled herself up out of the pool and took the towel that Jeeves extended to her. She wrapped it around her toothpick thin figure that would've been considered frail had I not seen the power of her swimming arms and legs. Said legs were riddled with varicose veins. She walked over to a chaise near where I stood, switched the towel for a terrycloth robe, and skinned the skull cap off her head. A mane of silver hair shook free.

"Please. Have a seat, Mrs. Letterly." She indicated a cushioned wrought-iron chair beside her chaise.

Ms., not Mrs., grrr. "Please. Call me Nell."

She evaluated me silently for an awkward moment — awkward for me, that is, and then told Jeeves, "We'll have our tea out here, Richard."

Wasn't it obvious? Nearby, a poolside table was draped with white linens and set for four.

"Very good, Madam."

"Where is Tucker? Why isn't he here?"

"I do not know, Madam. I will show him out here myself, as soon as he arrives with his guest."

"Yes, do that."

Jeeves, aka Richard, turned on his heels and left. The swimmer studied me with the frostiest blue eyes I'd ever seen. As if she demanded to know why I hadn't yet taken my seat. What was the point of that? They were going to throw me out as soon as I told them to lay off Callahan and my student. Let the police handle the investigation before the family railroaded innocent victims. She sank into her chaise, and I remained standing over her.

"How good of you to come today," she said, turning my request for an audience into her summons. "You have news for us, I presume?"

I didn't have Lyle to hand over, if that's what she meant, and I was pretty sure that's what she meant. So I would distract her. "Thank you for inviting me, Mrs. Denton."

"Oh gawd, no. Not *Mrs.* I'm Cybil Denton, Francesca's aunt. You may call me Ms."

I let a silent beat pass, and then said softly, "Please accept my condolences for your loss."

She laughed, but I didn't see the humor in Francesca's death. Or Fanny's, either. "We lost Francesca long ago," Ms. Denton said, "considering that I seem to be the only one who ever looked out for that girl. Certainly, my brother's wife never did."

"Your brother's wife?" I asked. "Is that Francesca's mother?"

She snorted. "Gawd, no. That bitch walked out long ago."

I wished Lawyer Lazar had filled me in on the family

dynamics, other than Deke the elder's financial eccentricities. It wouldn't have hurt Lazar to forewarn me about the existence of this aunt. But I was getting the picture. Ms. Denton, the prim and proper aunt, had either raised Francesca in place of the absent biological mother, or else she'd interfered in the raising of Francesca. Maybe both.

Ms. Denton went on. "I was referring to the one he married after that, when Francesca was a budding teenager."

Terra's category, although my daughter had moved past buds and into sprouts. Francesca's mother, then, was a female version of my good old husband, Max. My heart went out to Francesca, and my attitude towards Francesca's aunt improved a notch or two. I finally eased down into the cushion of the wrought-iron chair where she wanted me to sit.

"Will Francesca's father be joining us?" I asked, nodding at the table for four.

Aunt Cybil tittered. "No, no. Tucker, my son. Francesca's cousin. I'm afraid that Francesca's father has, shall we say, other interests at present."

"Other interests besides his daughter?"

"That is correct. And his current other interest is young enough to be his daughter, I have pointed out to him time and again, but will he ever listen? Gawd, no. They're in Cancún this week. I shall have to delay the memorial service, consequently, and speak on behalf of the family. Do you have family, Mrs. Letterly?"

Oh boy, did I. "In fact, that's why I'm here. To clear up your misunderstanding regarding me and my family." I included all of Callahan's Karate in my definition of family.

"There is no misunderstanding on my part," she said,

swinging her long legs from the chaise as if in preparation to kicking me out. "You are the one who found Francesca's body, are you not?"

"Correct, but that doesn't mean —"

"Someone must be held accountable for Francesca's death." Aunt Cybil sprang to her feet and paced beside the pool.

"Unless it was an accident," I said, feeling dizzy from watching her movement.

"It was no accident."

The certainty flowing through her words chilled me. She spoke as if she'd witnessed the fall. "How can you be so sure?"

"The police were here to tell us everything we needed to know."

"But the police aren't sure what happened." Or were they? Rosenquist always did his best to withhold information from me.

"She would not have found herself in her unfortunate circumstances had it not been for that horrid place where you work. That *karate* school." She paused her pacing and twisted her lips, as if the words put a sour taste in her mouth.

I stiffened, feeling my arm hairs bristle, and ignored her misconception. "What unfortunate circumstances did Francesca find herself in?" Whatever it was, it ended with her death, accidental or not.

Aunt Cybil laughed again, tilting her head back and flicking her wrist in the air. Then she pounced towards me, stuck her finger in my face and hissed, or maybe she was whispering a secret. "It's in places like that — your *karate* school — where one is exposed to persons of less than desirable backgrounds."

"On the contrary," I said, feeling my neck muscles tighten

into ropes of steel, "martial artists are the best people you'll ever meet." I could name a few exceptions, but I wasn't going there.

Her mouth opened as if to say something, and then it closed, wordless. Her finger dropped down to the sleeve of my Sunday best tee-shirt. She flipped the cotton with a disgusted frown and resumed her pacing.

"Do you know for a fact," I said, "that Francesca met one of your so-called undesirable types in my studio?"

Cybil Denton's bias reminded me of Gillian's. While I was motivated to change my sister-in-law's opinion on account of our family connection, I had no interest in convincing Aunt Cybil of her mistaken beliefs. It wasn't my mission to change her. She wasn't my aunt, thank goodness.

Cybil finally recovered her voice. "Of course Francesca met her killer there. He happens to be one of your karate hoodlums."

That ruled out any of *my* students. I didn't know about previous students, though, during my predecessor's tenure.

She went on. "Hear my words: places like that should not be allowed to exist. They promote violence. Do you understand? See what's happened?"

I didn't want to egg her on. Sometimes the best defense in martial arts is knowing when to hang back. Let your opponent use up all her steam. I could wait her out. I shrugged and said nothing. I ran through a mental catalogue of my students that Francesca might've known from class. Lyle, with his alleged crush on Francesca, came to mind. Was Aunt Cybil referring to Lyle? Lyle wasn't a hoodlum. He was certainly nerdy. But was he violent?

Well, he *did* carry a gun.

"You look decent enough," Aunt Cybil said. "How can you

associate yourself with a place like that? I urge you to reconsider your position. You have a responsibility, after all, since you are the one who found Francesca's body."

I wasn't following her logic, but I could understand that grief might warp the logical process. If only this entitled woman would allow herself to grieve.

The French doors opened just then, interrupting her lecture, thank goodness. Out stepped a young man who appeared to be in his twenties. He sauntered across the patio towards us, and Jeeves trailed along behind, carrying a silver tray of tea things and clinking china.

"Tucker, how good of you to make an appearance," Aunt Cybil said. "Mrs. Letterly wishes to have a word with us."

"Please call me Nell." I rose and held out my hand, which he took in a limp shake, without meeting my gaze. He looked distractedly around the garden. Birds chirped and the spring sunshine warmed us.

"How's the water, Mother?" he said, as if I wasn't there.

"Passable. Do sit down. Where is your guest whom you insisted on bringing today?"

"In the study, making a few phone calls that couldn't wait. He said we should go ahead and start without him."

"How good of him," Aunt Cybil said, maintaining her frosty gaze without blinking. How did she do that? "Richard, give us ten more minutes."

"Very good, Madam."

When Jeeves left us alone, Tucker turned to me and flashed a winsome smile. "And what is that word you wish to have with us, Nell?"

I felt myself warming inside under the power of his smile.

I stifled my warmth, remembering my purpose here. "Some questions have been raised regarding the role of Callahan's Karate in your cousin's death, and I —"

"That place Francesca frequented?" Tucker said. His smooth eyebrows, delicate for a man, knit together into a rumpled sock line.

"Tucker," his mother said, "Mrs. Letterly works there. Against better judgment."

"Ah-h-h-h." Apparently he understood the secret language flowing unspoken between them.

"Excuse me," I said, jumping in. "But Francesca hardly frequented my studio. I never met her. Furthermore, I found no records of enrollment in our office for a Francesca Denton." I didn't volunteer that my students had insisted Francesca, aka Fanny, had trained at Callahan's under my disorganized predecessor and then switched schools.

Cybil sniffed. "Obviously, her records were destroyed."

"Or she might've used another name," Tucker said. "She sometimes did that. When she went out in public."

I could be equally snotty. "If you persist with your lawyer against Callahan's," I said, "you will need to produce evidence of her enrollment there. Otherwise, you have no case."

Cybil's lips twisted into a sneer. "I wrote the check myself."

I gaped at her. If she was feinting, it was working. I couldn't follow her contradictions.

Tucker nodded, smiling at me. "We are not short on evidence. You see, Mother is guardian of our trust funds. Francesca's and mine. Until we turn thirty. We always have to go through Mother when we want a little extra allowance."

"But why would you pay for her martial arts lessons," I said, "if you don't approve of them?"

Cybil sniffed. "At the time I thought it was a better alternative than her other little adventures."

"Francesca was always wanting more money," Tucker explained to me.

"Not only Francesca, dear boy," said Cybil. "You've been known to need a little extra, too, from time to time."

Tucker shrugged. "The money's there. Why not use it?"

"Someone has to protect the family's interest," said Cybil, "and that someone is me. I will not see it squandered in one generation. Francesca's father has already squandered enough. That's why our father bypassed him completely and entrusted me with the estate. You will thank me one day, Tucker, when it all becomes yours."

Tucker laughed. "Mother, Mother!" He gasped for breath and wiped the corners of his eyes. "What would you say if I told you I know how to double our worth?"

Cybil narrowed her frosty eyes. "I would say to watch your tongue. You are being very rude to talk of such matters in front of our guest."

"Well, Mother, you're the one who brought up the matter of money. How much did you spend on Francesca's foray into fighting?" He threw a few ill-formed punches as an illustration. "And penny-pincher that you are, why didn't you tell her to take up something less costly, say, running?"

"She was afraid, Tucker. That psychopath stalker was threatening her. She wanted to learn self-defense, and I thought why not? It couldn't hurt. Little did I know that it would only bring her more readily available to her killer."

I jumped into their verbal match. "Excuse me, but let me

point out that if there really is a psychopath at large, then she could've met him or her anywhere, not just in my studio."

"Are you doubting my word?"

Bingo.

"And," I added, "she wouldn't have enrolled in a specific self-defense program at my school because we don't isolate that piece of it from our overall curriculum. You must have Callahan's confused with another school." Like Kim's Karate, my fancy competitor across town. They offered a self-defense program for anyone off the streets. Not that I was going to name names. I would settle for extricating Callahan's from the lawyer's targeted assault.

Cybil turned her unblinking stare on me and added a frown. "I assure you, I am not the confused one in this family."

But someone else was, I wondered? Without Francesca, Tucker stood to inherit the whole enchilada. But only if the questions surrounding her death could be answered. And if someone played the part of scapegoat. Someone, like Lyle. That's why they were so eager to get their hands on him.

"We are fortunate," Cybil continued, "that our good Mr. Lazar is demanding justice on our behalf. He will see this distastefulness through to the end, until the appropriate person or persons pay for their crime. We will not rest until justice is ours."

If she meant to frighten me, she did. Her bias was set in stone, and I didn't see any way that I was going to persuade her to stop blaming Callahan — and me. We were the responsible people she was looking for. In good martial arts fashion, I masqued my fear and switched tactics.

"Would you excuse me while I find the ladies' room?" I said.

Cybil sighed, sounding annoyed. She reached for a cell phone sitting on the table beside her chaise. "One moment, while I call Richard out here again. He will show you the way."

"Please don't bother him. I can find the way myself. Back through the room he brought me through, I assume?" I had already leapt halfway across the terrace before she could summon Jeeves.

"Behind the stairs in the foyer," Tucker shouted at me and then burst out laughing.

I ducked into the Downton Abbey room and pulled the verandah door closed behind me. The room smelled cloyingly sweet with roses. It was as if some floral shop had emptied its stock into this room. Quickly, I fished my cell phone out of my purse before Jeeves could intercept me, switched it to camera mode, and zeroed in on the portrait of Francesca hanging over the fireplace. *Click.*

I dropped the phone back into my purse as footsteps echoed across marble, announcing the arrival of Jeeves.

"This way, miss," he said with a frown as he escorted me to a narrow door under the main staircase.

Cherubs decorated the faucets in the bathroom. I kid you not.

On my way out a few minutes later, I looked both ways down the entrance hall, but did not see Jeeves waiting for me. I ducked behind the stairs and peered around the edge. A man's soft voice echoed, bouncing across the marble. It seemed to be coming from one of the rooms that opened onto the hallway. I tiptoed over to an open door and peeked around the corner.

A man stood with his back to the door. At least, I presumed it was a man. He wore what might've been a suit, except the jacket was a garish lime-green plaid that hurt my eyes, making me blink. The trousers were starched white, and the shoes were white with little flaps. I had never seen a man's suit like that before. Maybe it wasn't a man. Except, his build was stocky, like a man's. Brownish-gray mutton chops bloomed from the sides of his head.

"I don't care what he told you," said the garish man, whom I supposed was Tucker's guest for tea, into a telephone receiver. His low voice cinched it. He sounded like a man. "He's bluffing. I won't offer him a penny more, and that's final. Don't worry, he'll give in."

At that moment he swiveled around, faster than I could duck out of sight. He had to have caught sight of me. So I scooted onward, making like I owned the place and had not paused to eavesdrop. I kept on heading for the pool and didn't stop along the way.

Tucker and his mother glowered at each other, apparently not noticing the brilliance of the spring day. Spring days were rare along the Front Range. They were so ephemeral.

I steered the conversation to my purpose. "Maybe you could tell me something about Francesca, since I never met her." I kept emphasizing that part. "I was hoping to find out from you something about her so that we can figure out what really happened."

And remove Callahan from their line of fire.

I would divert the family from their warpath by finding out who really was responsible for Francesca's death.

Cybil bought it. "Well," she said with another sniff. "I can tell you exactly what happened. And, mark my words, none of it would've happened if she hadn't gone to that wild party school in the first place. No, I'm not talking about your little *karate* school. I'm talking about your university."

It wasn't my university — Max the AWOL jerk's, maybe — but I let it pass.

"We thought Francesca would have been better served at a smaller, more dignified university back east. Someplace where she wouldn't cross paths with all of her strays. She used to always bring home strays when she still lived at home. I tried to tell her that it was not her mission in life to take care of every homeless person in the world, but would she listen to me? I tried to explain to her that it would only get her into trouble, that people would take advantage of her, especially when they found out how fortunate she was. Alas, it has come to pass."

"No, Mother," Tucker said, "they're not strays but opportunists. They completely brainwashed her."

"What sort of opportunists?" I asked.

"For instance, the young woman she invited to move in with her in the condo, rent-free."

"Where was she living?"

"In one of the family-owned properties up in Boulder. One of our investments." Tucker recited the address, and I made a mental note.

"The roommate was a problem from the get-go," Cybil said. "Always scheming."

Scheming sounded like that would make the roommate a likelier candidate for blame than Callahan's Karate. "What sort of schemes?"

Cybil rubbed her fingers together in the universal symbol of money. "Those strays were always trying to get their hands on Francesca's money."

"Like the time she wanted to buy that derelict place in the mountains." Tucker snorted. "Remember, Mother? What a piece of junk. The roommate brainwashed our Francesca into thinking it would be a wise investment, some sort of historical relic, I suppose, but really, there was no potential at all. It was an idiotic idea."

"Did she buy it?" I asked.

"My brother was here at the time," Cybil said. "Fortunately, he had enough of his wits about him to support my denial of her outrageous request."

"When was that?"

"Let me think." She squinted at the flowering tree. "If my brother was here, then it must've been sometime between his ski trip to the Alps and his yacht in Antigua. That would've made it early to mid February."

According to my students, February was the last time Francesca came to the studio as her public persona, Fanny. Her request had been turned down by her family, and then she left Callahan's Karate, according to my students. "How did she take the rejection of her request?"

"You have to understand that she was very strong-willed. She always had to have her way. Usually her father let her wheedle until she had whatever she wanted, but not that time."

"Do you know why not?"

"It was too outlandish, of course. To think that she could save a place like that from being demolished."

"Save it?"

"It was already half fallen down from the elements, but one of those historical preservation groups thought it had some sort of value, I suppose."

The French doors opened again, and out stepped Jeeves with the tea tray.

Cybil frowned. "Richard, I clearly told you we must wait for our guest, did I not?"

"Madam, he had to leave suddenly. He begged your forgiveness and asked me to present his card."

"What audacity," Cybil said. She grumbled and snatched the card that Jeeves held out to her. "Who are these friends of yours, Tucker?" She read the card. "Who is this Jimmie Condo?"

EIGHT

Next morning, I left home shortly after Terra left for school and headed downtown, to the address Tucker had given me. It was one of the Denton family properties, a condo investment a couple blocks off the downtown pedestrian mall. I found a place to park several blocks farther away and walked the rest of the way. When I got there, I stopped dead in my tracks, staring up at the back side of the square cruise ship building. Francesca's complex turned out to be right around the corner from Jimmie Condo's office, where I'd chatted with Phyllis only the day before. Those offices and Francesca's condo shared the courtyard, where I'd met the disgruntled biker co-ed.

I found Francesca's unit on the third floor, which smelled of frying bacon. Lifting the knocker, I wondered too late if I'd arrived too early. Or if her roommate was still in residence, now that Francesca was deceased.

I should've thought this through before barging over, but as usual, I hadn't. I was still reeling from the impact of how small my hometown really was. Francesca's living space was conveniently close to the warrior woman's stomping grounds.

Footsteps shuffled to the door, and a woman's soft voice called out, "who is it?"

"My name is Nell Letterly," I said, trying not to project loud enough to wake the neighbors. I could feel her examination needling me through the peephole.

The door yanked open, and a pixie-tiny woman, even shorter than me, stood in the doorway. A butterfly tattoo peeked out of the neckline of her oversized tee shirt. She rubbed her sleepy eyes, and then massaged her tousled blonde hair. "I need another week," she said. "It's crazy this time of year to find another place to stay."

"Um... I'm not here about that."

She leaned against the door, as if she was too tired to hold herself up. She frowned at me. "You're not from that lawyer guy's office?"

"No, I'm here about your roommate. Francesca Denton."

"My roommate is dead." She started to shut the door in my face. "And anyway, that's not her name."

I stuck my foot in the doorway. "This was the address her family gave me for her. Maybe you knew her as Fanny Dent?"

The blonde fuzzball stopped closing the door and blinked at me.

"Please, may I come in?" I handed her one of my cards that had my name and address printed on it, as a sort of verification that I wasn't lying.

She did a double-take on the card. "You do karate, too?" she said, opening her eyes wide, finally coming awake.

"Yes, and Fanny was a student at my school. Please, I really need to talk to you. It won't take long."

"Oh, okay, I guess." She pulled the door open wide and stood aside for me to enter.

The tidy room was furnished with student basic. It could've been a showroom for Ikea, except for the posters of men who scowled at me from white walls, trying to look like studs in their spread-leg poses. They looked more like gangsters to me. They could've been the same celebrities whose posters decorated Terra's walls. This reminded me of how close in age Francesca had been to my daughter, and a chill rippled down my spine.

"You're a student at the university?" I asked, circling the room, keeping an eye on the frowning men eyeballing me.

"Uh-huh. I'm Abby. Abby Quinn. But I didn't ever do karate with Fanny. I only went with her a couple of times to observe." She glanced again at my card. "I don't think it was called Callahan's, though, and I don't remember seeing you there."

"I understand she switched from my school to Kim's Karate."

"Kim's! Yeah, that's it. So, what do you want to know? I've got to get ready for class soon."

"Abby, I'm so very sorry for your loss. You must've known Fanny well, and this has to be a shock to you, losing her this way."

Tears welled in the corners of her big blue eyes, glistening like marbles. "She was just about the best friend I ever had. Except, she couldn't even trust me enough to tell me who she really was. I didn't find *that* out until the cops came."

"Were they the ones who broke the news to you about her death?"

"Yeah."

"Wow, that must've been a terrible shock." I looked around the open space, a sweeping L-shape that included the dining area and a kitchen shining of chrome. It wouldn't have surprised me to see Rosenquist smirking at me from the table, but he wasn't here. Instead, a vase of wilted roses sat on the table.

"I thought maybe they had the wrong apartment, like the girl who died up there on the Flatiron wasn't my Fanny but someone else. But the cops made me go with them and identify the body." Abby shuddered. "There was something creepy wrong with her skin, but I could still tell it was her. Except they said she was really Francesca Denton, from some rich family down in Denver. I had no idea. This whole thing is like a bad dream. I keep thinking I've got to wake up soon. I've just got to."

"Why do you think she kept her identity a secret?"

Abby shrugged. "Who knows? But that explains a lot, in retrospect."

"Such as?"

"Well, for instance, the obnoxious woman in the fur coat who came to visit last January. Are you kidding me? Real fur? This is Boulder, hello? She only stayed long enough to write out a check and hand it over to Fanny."

"Did Francesca — I mean, Fanny — tell you who the woman was?" I could guess.

"Nope. That's just the thing. I asked, too, and all she said was that she was some crazy old friend of her mother's."

Aunt Cybil.

"But she wouldn't say a word about the check," Abby said. "That's so like Fanny. She never talked about money. I mean, for the rest of us, going to school, it's always a struggle to have enough money. So far, with my loans and scholarships and part-time jobs here and there, I'm staying current on tuition, but I'll tell you, there's not a dime left over. But Fanny? She never asked me for rent or grocery money."

"She let you stay here for free?"

"Right."

"When did you move in?"

"At the start of the school year, last August. The place where I was going to stay? That deal fell through at the last minute. I was going to be a part-time nanny in exchange for room and board, but the woman I was going to work for got transferred over the summer and didn't even bother to let me know. Can you believe it? I got to town in August, after hitchhiking from California, with no place to stay. I had to couch surf for a while, and when I met Fanny at some party, she said I could move in with her."

"Just like that?"

"Yep. We hit it off right away. She said I could pay her back later if I insisted, but in the meanwhile, it was more important to her to have the right roommate, instead of no roommate at all."

"But she didn't need a roommate to split any expenses," I said, thinking aloud.

"Oh, she needed me, all right," Abby said with a grin. "Wait, don't get me wrong. She's not like that. Gay, I mean. She always has — I mean, *had* — " the grin slipped away, "a string of boyfriends. She just always needed someone around her. Like she was afraid to be alone."

"Is there a current boyfriend?"

"I'm pretty sure there's someone new, but she wouldn't say who he was, not even to me. It was obvious, the way gifts started showing up. Roses, fruit baskets, that sort of thing."

"Like those roses?" I said, pointing to the glass vase of dead stems. I wandered over to the dining room table to get a closer look. The filmy residue from evaporated water suggested the bouquet had died a while ago. The card tucked into the dried leaves read *Bulbs & Bouquets*, one of the fancier florists in town.

"Yeah, I should've dumped them." Abby whisked past me, snatching up the vase and carrying it into the kitchen. "I just kept waiting for her to come back. I thought I would enjoy the flowers in the meanwhile, because she always threw them away as fast as they arrived."

"Sounds like the guy was more serious about her than she was about him."

Abby nodded as she upended the vase of dead roses over the trash can. "These last few months she seemed so, I don't know, so...not all together, y'know?"

"You think she was preoccupied about something?" Or about *someone*. The new guy. Lyle?

"Definitely. Especially since spring break."

"Is that when the roses started appearing?" I asked.

"No, they first showed up around the time she broke off with Innis. Last February. That's why I was sure there was someone new. Innis never gave her anything except a hard time."

"February must've been a tough month for her," I said. "Her family told me that's when her dad turned down her request to buy some fixer-upper place in the mountains. Did she tell you about that?"

Abby turned her back on me and clunked the empty vase into the sink. "Nope, not a word. She never let on that she had enough money to buy anything more expensive than jeans. But it doesn't surprise me. She was real interested in historical preservation, so I guess if she had the money, that could translate into real estate."

"After her dad turned her down, she apparently switched

schools, from Callahan's to Kim's. Do you know why she did that?"

"I'll bet it was on account of Innis. He always treated her like he owned her. Even after she broke up with him. He never got it, that it was over between them. He thinks he's still the only one, but he's like so wrong. He kept bugging her all spring, kept wanting to hang out with her."

"Do you think she took up with him again?"

"She went out with someone, but I'm pretty sure it wasn't him. Innis doesn't care anything about history, not like Fanny."

"I'd like to talk to him. Do you know where I can find this guy?"

"He's Greek. You know, as in frat boy? He's some dude she met in a bar at the beginning of ski season, and all winter she was like all ga-ga over him. Then they had that big blow-up fight, and now he's history. Sorta'."

"Do you know what the fight was about?"

She shrugged. "I'm guessing it's because she finally wised up and didn't like the way he was treating her. Does it really matter?"

"It could, if someone helped her fall off the Flatiron."

"You think he did *that*? He's a creep, but I can't believe he would've done that. It's more likely he would've got in a fight with the new boyfriend, whoever he is. Maybe that's why she kept him so hush-hush. All along, I thought it was because she didn't like him."

"Do you know where I can find Innis?"

"You should try Flaky Jake's if you still want to talk to him. That's where she and him always went out. Real regulars there. She could always get in there with her I.D."

Swell. A bar. Not my kind of entertainment. I would have to get Gillian to take me there. She would know her way around bars. Not me.

"Do you think Fanny was afraid of Innis?"

"Yeah, maybe. Innis wasn't the first one who bothered her. She had this talent for hooking up with abusive boyfriends, and no wonder! She used to do some pretty wild things, like she told me how she drove to Mexico for spring break last year, all by herself. After that, she decided she needed someone around. Like me. Safety in numbers, that's what matters more, she always said..." Abby's voice drifted away, lost in thought.

"And this year?" I asked. "Did you go with her to Mexico for spring break?"

"That's just the thing. She told me she was going home. Like, really? She didn't even go home for Christmas. I had to stay here and work, anyway, and when she came back, she was all tanned and depressed at the same time. I think the new boyfriend took her to some fancy beach, maybe Cancún, and she found out he's not as much fun as Innis."

"You think maybe the new boyfriend was abusing her, too?"

"Yeah, maybe." A tear slipped down her cheek, and she sniffed. "None of this would've happened if I'd been there for her, but she wouldn't let me in."

"It's no good blaming yourself," I said. "Whatever happened to her wasn't your fault."

Abby sniffled some more.

"We can help best now," I said, "by finding out what happened to her, and why. When's the last time you saw Francesca?"

"She was Fanny to me." Abby's lips quivered. "It was a week ago Saturday. Fanny was on her way to some meeting with the Pioneer Society. Y'know, that grassroots historical preservation group? She was doing some volunteer work with them. Anyway, we were supposed to go out clubbing together after that. I kept texting her, but she never replied. The cops were like all interested in that."

I did a quick mental calculation. Francesca disappeared two days before she fell off the Flatiron. Was she already dead before she fell? "Where do you think she was all that time?"

Abby shrugged. "Off with the new boyfriend, I guess, in some secret hideaway. The cops asked me that, too. But really, I have no idea. It wasn't like her not to text me back."

"You think maybe she *couldn't* text you?" Because she was dead. Or otherwise incapacitated.

Abby wailed. "I don't know. The cops didn't believe me that I don't know."

I took her in my arms as she shuddered with sobs. After we cried together for a while, wetting each other's shoulders, patting each other's backs, I felt as if I'd known Abby all my life. She certainly didn't seem like the conniving money-grubber that Aunt Cybil and Tucker had tried to paint her as, taking advantage of Francesca.

"We'll figure out what happened to her," I said when our tears finally subsided and I let her go. "When the police took you to the morgue to identify her, did you notice anything...I don't know...different about her?"

"Other than being all puffy?"

"Well, you know, like was she wearing her own clothes or someone else's?"

"Hmmm." Abby tapped her upper lip with a nail-bitten finger and thought. "She was wearing sandals, so that tells you she hadn't meant to go out there rock climbing. Anyway, she wasn't a rock climber. And she was kind of afraid of heights. But there was something else, now that you mention it. She wasn't wearing that necklace she always liked to wear."

"Necklace?" I pulled out my phone and thumbed up the photo I'd taken of Francesca's portrait. I pinched the photo to enlarge it, and sure enough, there was a necklace painted round her throat. "Is it this?" I showed her the photo.

"Yes, that's it!" Abby brightened. "It had some special meaning to her, like it was the only thing of her mother's that she had, or something like that. She always wore it. Never even took it off to shower or sleep. I thought it was kind of tacky, but she liked those pink crystals. Rose quartz, she called them."

"Maybe the clasp broke," I said, "and she had to put it away somewhere, like in the pocket of her backpack. Was her backpack recovered with her body?"

Abby looked as if she might cry. "The cops didn't say. You think maybe her necklace is in there? I wonder if someone tried to steal it, and they fought..." Abby's voice caught. "And that's why she fell."

"A random someone?" I asked. "Or someone who specifically coveted her necklace?"

Abby thought. "She mentioned something about a cousin who was always jealous that she'd inherited the necklace instead of her."

"Her? Or was it a male cousin?" I was thinking of Tucker.

"She never named names. I just assumed. Why would a guy want a necklace?"

"Perhaps for the value."

"Oh, I don't think that necklace was worth anything. I could be wrong, I suppose."

I wondered how wrong we all were in our suppositions. Who would've guessed that an ordinary co-ed like Fanny was worth a fortune? "Do you know of any enemies Fanny had," I asked, "or anyone she argued with? Maybe had a problem with?"

"Y'mean, other than Innis and the guy who sent the flowers? Nope. Everyone loved Fanny."

Clearly, not everyone. My student Rachel had invoked the b-word about Fanny. "Someone must've frightened her, since she switched schools to learn self-defense at Kim's."

"That was on account of Innis. She wanted to know how to protect herself from him in case he came on too strong to her. Wait a minute... There's our neighborhood Nazi. No one gets along with her, though, not the way she yells at people for letting their cats out or playing music, or chaining up bicycles to *her* railing. I don't think she had it in for Fanny anymore than anyone else, though."

"She?"

"Yeah. She works in one of the offices across the courtyard."

"Sounds like Phyllis Eberhardt."

"Is that her name?"

It was hard to imagine a professional like Phyllis wanting to steal a cheap necklace, no matter how warrior-like she was. "Maybe Fanny just didn't wear her necklace that day when she went to her meeting," I said. "Have you looked here, among her things, to see if she left it behind?"

"Well, no, I hadn't thought about that, although it's unlikely. C'mon, let's take a look in her jewelry box."

I followed Abby into the first bedroom off the hall. The

room contained an eclectic mix of what looked like garage-sale specials. Abby flicked on the overhead swag, a Chinese paper lantern dripping with gold tassels, and a rosy glow lit the bookshelves and folding tables and heap of fleece throws spread across the mattress on the floor. Abby marched over to a dresser painted magenta and popped up the lid of a lacquered box. Her fingers dug through the assortment of chunky chains and beads.

"I don't see it," she said.

I held my breath while she searched. The missing necklace must've had something to do with Francesca's death.

Abby kept pawing through a tangle of jewelry. "But wait, what's this?" She plucked a small piece of brass out from under the costume jewelry.

"It looks like a house key," I said.

"But what's it doing in here?" Abby said. "Fanny always carried her keys on a ring hooked to her backpack."

"What do you suppose this key works? Is it an extra key to the condo?"

"It doesn't look like it, but let's find out." Abby charged back to the front door and poked the key into the lock. It didn't fit.

"You should turn that key over to the police," I said. "It might help them with their investigation."

Abby frowned. "I suppose I'll have to, but when could I do that? I have a ton of finals to study for, and a couple of them will make a difference to whether or not I get to keep my scholarships." She sighed. "I don't really have a chunk of extra time right now."

"I could turn it over to them for you. Would that help?"

Her face lit up. "Really? Do you think you could? That'd be

super! You don't mind?"

"Not at all." It would give me an excuse to badger Rosenquist again. Maybe in the meanwhile, I could even find out what door this key unlocked. I tucked it into my jeans pocket, wished Abby well, and headed out.

NINE

My Monday deadline would expire today. So far the world hadn't ended. If Lazar showed up with his goon squad, at least I would have Francesca's secret key to bargain with. Sure, I'd turn it over to Rosenquist, as promised, but I had some other things to do with it, first.

Luckily, I still had a few hours before reporting to duty for my first class.

I headed back to the studio, steering the Ghia carefully around the potholes that riddled the alley behind our row of centurion bungalows. From this view, from the alley side of the studio, yeah, maybe I could see why Aunt Cybil and Tucker thought Callahan's a trashy place. Trash cans lined the alley, half of them turned over by the wildlife that rules this town. But that's another story.

We had two parking spots behind our studio, one for me, and one always reserved for Mr. Callahan. He drove a dented Subaru, our town's mascot of the roadways. Now, a shiny Lexus, fire engine red, straddled across our two spaces. Fortunately, my Ghia only needed half a space. I pulled in beside the Lexus. Its owner was not in sight. Maybe it belonged to a guest of Mr. Callahan's, and my boss was showing his guest around the place.

More likely, not.

I pulled one of my business cards out of my purse and

scribbled a polite note on its back side, informing the Lexus driver that this was a reserved parking space. Finding a parking spot in Boulder was like winning the lottery, and we jealously guarded our prized parking spaces. I tucked the card beneath the offender's windshield wiper and headed across the flagstone stepping stones to the back entrance into the kitchen office.

I jabbed my key into the lock and then paused. I pulled Francesca's secret key out of my pocket and turned it over in my palm. I held it up to the light and studied its jagged teeth. Did it work the locks here at the studio? After all, Francesca had been a student here at one time. My students argued that Francesca only came here because she'd had the hots for my predecessor.

And then she'd met Lyle here.

I wondered if Francesca's admirer who sent her roses could've been Lyle. From the talk among my students, it sounded as if Lyle's infatuation with Francesca had not been reciprocated. Abby said that Francesca threw the roses away, but she also thought that Francesca went skiing with the new guy over spring break. How reliable was gossip? Maybe Francesca and Lyle had been seeing each other on the sly, trying to keep their relationship hidden from the Dentons. Was that why the family had their shorts in such a knot over Lyle? Furthermore, if Lyle knew anything about her death that he was trying to keep to himself, maybe that accounted for his having ducked out of sight.

Abby also said Francesca'd had a string of boyfriends. My predecessor's undoing was the way he womanized. Maybe Francesca had been one of his women, and so he'd given her a key. That would explain why I hadn't found any records of her in the student files. His women were "off the record," so to speak.

That could also explain why she would've suddenly switched schools, if they'd had a falling out, a misunderstanding, a lover's quarrel when the next woman appeared in his line.

I slid my key out of the lock and held it up to compare against Francesca's. The teeth traced different patterns, but I tried Francesca's key anyway. Dad had changed these locks for me when I moved in. It didn't work, of course.

I stomped inside, crestfallen, and hung up my purse on a hook behind the door into the basement... But wait.

There was the basement. More like a dungeon, really. I stared down into the narrow chute of a stairwell that led into the dark underbelly of the bungalow. Cast-offs from the house's history were sent down there. Maybe that's where Dad had stashed the old locks. It was worth a check, even though the basement dungeon creeped me out.

I flicked on the light switch that illuminated the wooden steps and started down, brushing my fingers across the splintery siding where a railing should be. Another job for Dad's handyman skills. It was a miracle I made it all the way down without stumbling on a wobbly slat and breaking a leg to go along with the scar that was already there. There I went again, being negative.

Stop it, Nell.

The pool of light from the stairs reached far enough to see my way across the dirt floor to a pull chain hanging down from the overhead beams. I yanked it, but the light bulb up there among pipes and floor beams remained stubbornly dark. Swell. I should've brought a flashlight. There were a lot of things I should've done.

I glanced around at the shadowy shapes of boxes and

mechanical tanks. A soft gray light filtered in through the postage stamp square of a high-up window, encased in a window well outside and covered in layers of grime and cobwebs inside.

A shadow moved past the window.

Maybe a squirrel. Maybe a branch moving in the breeze. Maybe a killer.

I laughed at myself and took a deep breath to quell my jumpy nerves. My eyes slowly adjusted to the dim light, and I made out the rough stone walls and some storage shelves. The place smelled of damp dirt. Was that a drip I heard? Swell. Just what I needed. A flood.

Stop it, Nell.

I made my way over to the shelves and poked around, managing to fluff up a handful of sticky cobwebs. This was useless. I needed to either change the light bulb or fetch a flashlight. Either way, I would have to go back upstairs. No problem. I headed to the lit stairs, looking like a rickety ladder from the perspective down here, feeling like a moth attracted to light, when all of a sudden, the floor boards above my head squeaked. Someone was walking across the floor upstairs. But the studio wasn't open. I'd locked the kitchen door behind me, hadn't I? Maybe.

Heels clicked across the floor above, and then a woman's voice called out, "Hello-o-o?"

I darted up the steps and leapt into the kitchen, in time to catch a glimpse of the backside of a tall woman disappearing down the hall, heading in the direction of the workout floor. "Here I am," I said, shutting the basement door behind me.

My visitor wheeled around, spinning her long, crimped hair in a move I recognized from sparring matches. Maribeth, my sort of friend who worked as a part time instructor over at Kim's Karate. I couldn't really call her a friend, because I only saw her when we competed in tournaments or performed in demos. So far, we hadn't inflicted serious damage on each other, so that made us friends, I guessed. She was the closest thing I had to a friend since my best friend moved away a few years ago. I'd never cultivated serious friends as a faculty wife. One of these days, I was going to have to work on developing a few new friends, now that Max was out of my life. But making friends took time, and extra time was something I never had. What was the point of investing time in shallow relationships?

She marched down the hall, frowning at me. "Good lord, what happened to you?" When she came close enough, she reached for a lock of my limp hair and gave it a flick. "Ewww," she said, extracting a cobweb from my hair.

"What brings you over here, Maribeth?" I handed her a tissue and shook my hair. Cobwebs, I didn't mind, but tag-along spiders were another matter.

"Just making my rounds." She scrubbed her fingers and threw the tissue in the basket beside my desk. Then she slipped a backpack from her shoulder and pulled out a pack of flyers, banded together with a rubber band. She smacked them down onto my desk. "Here's some information about the block of runners Mr. Kim is organizing for this year's Bolder Boulder. He wants us to have a massive block of karate kids running together. You think you'll have anyone from Callahan's who could participate?" She looked doubtful.

"Of course we do. We've been training to run the race, but we were planning to run it together as our own team. I'll ask my students and see if they're interested in joining your group.

It might be fun." Or I might lose more students to Kim's, the larger studio across town that periodically sucked students away from me.

She smiled, taking in my so not state-of-the-art office, and said, "You know, you really ought to re-consider Mr. Kim's offer about coming to work over at our place."

I shook my head. Kim had made the offer last March, but that would've meant leaving Callahan's, and I couldn't do that. "How about a cup of tea?" I said instead, trying to divert her curiosity about my motivation for staying here.

"Sure. I've got a few minutes." She sat down gingerly at the chrome table, as if expecting her chair to collapse at any moment, while I busied myself with the mugs, tea basket, and microwave.

She settled on healthy green tea, while I chose black. I needed caffeine.

We chatted about spring, and the dangers of spring fever messing with the necessary dedication we martial artists constantly monitor in order to achieve our goals, and the wonderful way that the Bolder Boulder provided a pick-me-up in the midst of spring malaise. Eventually I led her to the topic of the body on the Flatiron. Rock-climbing was a different sort of athletic achievement from ours in the martial arts, but it took conditioning and strength, just like ours did.

"I understand that she'd been one of our students," I said of Francesca, "but she switched to your school to concentrate on self-defense, since Kim's offers that separately."

Maribeth made an "o" with her lips and leaned back in her chair. She raised her eyebrows. "She might've been one of our students. Why do you ask?"

Why was she being evasive? "Because the police think that her fall wasn't an accident."

"You mean, they think it was murder?"

I shrugged. "They're not telling me what they think, but I think that's what they think. Apparently Francesca was afraid someone meant to harm her, and that's why she wanted to learn some self-defense. I just wondered if you knew her and if you have an idea who she was afraid of? That information could be helpful for their investigation."

"But why do *you* need to know? Are you working for the police now?"

"No." I sipped my tea and shrugged, trying to appear cool and detached. "Her family has been asking some questions, that's all."

"Then, you should let the police answer them. Why don't you?"

Good question. But I could be evasive, too. "I have a stake in protecting the reputation of this school. The police aren't interested in doing that."

"I don't get it. How does it affect your school's reputation if Francesca switched to Kim's and then died?" Maribeth waggled her shaggy brows. "Oh, wait, now I think I see. Do the police think you're knocking off your students in retribution for leaving your school?"

"No, of course not."

"Someone else is knocking off your students?"

"Not in general. At least, not for leaving Callahan's." I hoped.

"You're worried about losing your students, aren't you?"

"Well, sure, but —"

"Look," she said, "you shouldn't get involved. Take my advice. Have you forgotten already? About that lesson you learned last time?"

She was referring to all the trouble I got into a couple months ago regarding my ill-fated predecessor. "This is not so different. That time I had to clear my name, and this time I have to clear the school's name." I glared at the analog clock face hanging on the wall above the sink. Time was running out. If Lazar showed up here, what would I tell him?

She tipped her head sideways and frowned at me. "Well, I still don't get it. You have your rating, don't you? What does that have to do with this girl's death?"

I sighed and decided I needed to be straight with her, if I wanted her to cooperate with me. Or at least, more straight. So I told her about Lyle. "Francesca's family thinks he's guilty," I said, finishing up my confession, "apparently just because of his infatuation for her. And because Francesca met him here, the family is determined to shut us down. Since they're an important family, financially and socially, they matter, at least as far as the police are concerned. That family can make life tough for the rest of us. I need to clear things up, so that we can get back to business. Mr. Callahan is sure to have a stroke over all this. If word gets out, he's afraid some of the students will decide to leave, that it's no longer a safe environment here. That could ruin us."

Maribeth nodded and ticked her tongue with a sympathizing sound. "Your boss is so excitable. So unlike my boss. You ought to re-consider Kim's offer to come work at our place."

"I like it here." She seemed determine to side-track me from my questions. "Look, do you or do you not know anything about someone bothering Francesca?"

She tapped her upper lip with a pearly pink painted fingernail, either helping her to think or showing off her manicure. "I think I remember her, now that you mention her. Red hair, top heavy, skinny as a stick everywhere else, right? Wore lots of flashy jewelry?"

"I never knew her, but one of my students mentioned that Francesca always liked to wear pink." I showed her the photo on my cell phone. "Is that her?"

Maribeth squealed and grabbed my phone away from me, turning it this way and that. "Oh, I remember her now! Came in Friday evenings with her entourage. A little blonde girlfriend sometimes, and other times her little puppy dog who followed her around and let her beat him up. I didn't like the way she treated her friends. She's not very nice. Francesca, that is. I bet there are plenty of people who wanted to pay her back one way or another."

"Puppy dog? She brought a dog to class?"

Maribeth laughed. "Figuratively. It was some guy, reminded me of a puppy dog the way he was so devoted to her. Hey, I wonder if he's your Lyle guy?"

I jumped up from the table. "Come with me," I said, leading her into the hall to the workout floor. Respectfully staying inside the taped-off area, I headed for the bay windows on the street side of the school. That's where the parental units sat to observe classes, and that's where I'd hung a bulletin board with announcements and photos. I scanned them now and found a group photo of one of the orange belt classes. I found Lyle in it and pointed him out to Maribeth.

"That's him!" she said with another squeal. "The puppy dog!

He's not one of our students, but he usually showed up just as Francesca's class was getting started. She would drag him off the sidelines and insist that he had to be her partner because the only thing he was good at was getting knocked down. Then she laughed at him every time she took him down."

"Sounds like she was a bully."

"Exactly! I wanted to slap her myself a few times. Maybe find a reason to spar with her. But the best part? I didn't have to spar her, because one time the puppy turned vicious and knocked her flat on her butt."

My eyebrows shot up. "Lyle did that?"

Not only was he a closet sprinter up mountains but also he seemed to know how to defend himself. He must've gotten knocked down one time too many. And then he decided to fight back. No wonder the cops thought he killed Francesca.

TEN

I didn't usually frequent bars and nightclubs. After six straight hours of teaching classes, I'd rather spend the rest of my evening at home with my daughter's company and our ferret's entertainment. Also, by the time the nightclubs opened, I was usually in bed. I didn't even know where they were hidden — downstairs in cellars, off alleys behind sketchy businesses, sometimes on rooftop porches. But Gillian Gannon, my soon-to-be-ex-sister-in-law, knew them all.

Flaky Jake's squeezed between a bank and a bakery, then mushroomed backwards off the street in a labyrinth of added-on rooms. We found a table in one corner between the gleaming oak bar and the swinging door to the kitchen. Upside down wine glasses hung above our heads, and we were in the way for the bartender and each wait person pushing in and out of the kitchen. Any minute now, I expected one of them to dump one of their trays laden with dirty dishes onto our laps.

"Thanks for coming with me, Jill, on such short notice." She'd agreed to meet me here after my last class let out. I had to shout at her just to hear my own voice over the background roar of voices, laughter, clinking dishes, and scraping chairs. Television screens overhead flashed a Rockies game, gone to extra innings, which kept pulling my eyes away from Jill, even though I wasn't especially interested in the game. Not tonight. From another room came the sound of someone's voice over the microphone, going on about something impossible to hear.

"It's about time you got out, girl." Gillian's designer make-up sparkled, and she wagged her French manicured index finger at me. "You have to get over Max. Like I've been saying all along, you have to move on."

Right. I swallowed some beer, pretending to enjoy it, while I let her observation, flawed as it was, roll past me. "Thanks, too, for taking Terra out to that Thai dinner the other night. She loved it."

"Sensible girl," Gillian said. "She's a Gannon, after all."

I didn't count as being part of the Gannon family, and maybe that was partly my fault, for never taking their name. I was plenty proud of my own, thank you very much. But not being warmly welcomed into the Gannon inner familial circle was one of the issues I'd had with Max. I kept my mouth shut about that. I had long since moved on. Another mission controlled me now. My job, my *lifeblood*, was at stake if I didn't divert the Dentons' suspicions that Callahan's studio played a role in Francesca's death.

And how was I going to do that? Now that I was beginning to believe they were possibly right?

Lyle most likely had pushed Francesca off the Flatiron in a moment of rage. Deep down, I hoped that this Innis character would change my mind.

"I'm just the person to help you move on," Gillian was saying. "Coming here was a good idea. This place was a great choice, tonight of all nights, when they do trivia. If your guy's a regular here, he won't miss trivia. This is going to be more fun than looking at real estate any day."

My cheeks burned. "Sorry I couldn't make it on Sunday. Something came up."

"Something more important than your own family? Never mind, you don't have to answer that."

I pulled the card Phyllis had given me out of my purse and slapped it down on the table. "I found a contact for you, though. Someone who's eager to show you some properties."

"Too late," she said. "I've already got a date with Van. What a hunk!"

"Date?" I reached to take the card back.

"Okay, it's an appointment." Gillian snatched the card away before I could touch it. "I like to keep my options open." She squinted at the card. "Jimmie Condo? Why does that name sound familiar to me?"

I shrugged and scrutinized the faces of servers whisking past me, customers jammed around tables, new arrivals wandering in and out, and thought it would be impossible to find Innis, Francesca's ex-boyfriend. I didn't even know what he looked like.

Gillian patted her perfectly coiffed hair. Her jade eyes glittered, anticipation written clearly across her face.

"Don't get the wrong idea about coming here," I said.

She waved her fingers in the air. "There's no age limit on having a little fun. You could benefit from that piece of advice."

A server, an over-worked young woman with wisping strands of hair escaping from her ponytail, stopped by our table. "Can I get you another one?" she asked, out of breath.

Gillian dropped her fingers from the air, onto the rim of her pint glass. "Check back in another five or so."

"Excuse me, miss," I said as the server turned her back on us and started to rush away. "I understand that Innis Wood is one of your regular patrons, and I wondered if you know him?"

"Guinness Innis? He's hard not to notice."

I sat up straighter, pleased with my sleuthing skills. I was making progress. "Great. Is he here tonight?"

"It's way too early."

"Can you point him out to me when he comes in?"

She tipped her head sideways, as if considering what was in it for her. Dutifully, I opened my purse and slid out a five, which I tucked under the dish of unidentifiable crunchies.

"Funny that you should ask about Innis," she said, snatching up Mr. Lincoln and tucking him in the pocket of her apron. "You're not the only one looking for him."

"Really?" Gillian sat up taller, swinging one of her shapely legs across her knee.

I pulled another five from my wallet and hoped that Callahan would reimburse me. "Who else wants to know about him?"

The server laughed and pointed at the far side of the room where trivia was going on. Two people stood in the center of a crowd, chugging beer. I recognized one of them — the one who upturned his pint and dumped the contents over his head. It was the open space ranger.

"Oh my gosh, I can't believe it's him," I said, barely loud enough to hear my own voice over the surrounding din.

Gillian heard. "Honey, where have you been keeping him?" She sprang to her feet, grabbed the server's towel from the tray of dirty dishes that she balanced, and said something that sounded like "...introduce me..." as she rushed away, drawn like a magnet to the action.

I glanced at the server, hoping she might rescue me from having to rescue Gillian, but she only shrugged and pushed on through the swinging door into the kitchen. That left me no choice. I picked up our purses, unwilling to leave them unattended, and followed Gillian.

By the time I squeezed past people and caught up to her, she was mopping beer off the bullish ranger. He probably never noticed the salsa stains on the soiled towel, not the way Gillian fussed over him. His attention was fixed on her performance. Gillian was good at the siren bit, I'd give her that. He didn't notice my approach, either, but Gillian did.

"Here you are, finally!" she said, dabbing her confiscated towel behind his ear. "Are you ever going to introduce us?"

Her words forced the ranger to glance my way, and when he saw me, his jaw tightened. "Do I know you?"

"No, not really," I said.

"Sure you do, honey," Gillian said. "You told me all about him, the way you met while out hiking somewhere near the Mesa Trail, remember?"

Recognition awakened in his face, pulling his eyes open wide in his beer fog. His body stance tensed, on alert. "The woman in charge of the kids," he said. "Where are they?" He looked around the melee, as if expecting munchkins to converge on him.

"Home in bed," I said. "Martial artists need plenty of rest."

"Yeah? And what about you? How come you're here, and not home in bed?"

"Same reason you're here. Looking for Francesca Denton's boyfriend."

"Hello?" Gillian said. "If Nell isn't going to introduce us, then I guess I'll have to do it for her. I'm Gillian Gannon, but honey, you can call me Jill. And you are...?"

The ranger turned back to Gillian, ready to glare at her, but when he saw her crooning over him, his face softened.

"C'mon, honey," Gillian said, snuggling up close to the ranger, "let's get you out of that wet shirt."

He and Gillian faded away through the crowd, leaving me there alone in the center of beer chuggers, holding two purses. I slunk back toward my table in the corner, slouched behind my unfinished pint and watched people mill, under the influence of their bottled spirits, while I waited for Gillian to return. I wasn't sure she would, not even for her purse. She was unpredictable around men who attracted her, and lord knew why the ranger did. She had a keen ability to choose losers. But then, so had I. Not that I was looking. Max had burned any interest out of me.

Servers whisked past me, glancing with disapproval at my unfinished beer. I scanned the crowd for a glimpse of Gillian's blonde locks. No such luck. My ponytailed server returned, breathless, and plunked down a check.

"Whenever you're ready," she said. "No rush." Apparently she'd given up on me.

I was about to give up on both Gillian and finding Francesca's boyfriend, Innis, when Gillian dragged the ranger to the table. He wore a dry tee-shirt, brand-new and creased with folds, displaying a cowboy image of Flaky Jake holding a beer stein. The ranger's coarse black hair, slicked down behind his ears, shone from the golden lights of the swags above us.

"So..." he said after the server snatched away the check and replaced it with fresh pints of beer. "I hear you want to meet up with Innis Wood."

"That's right," I said. "And so do you. Why?"

Ranger Rock shrugged and chugged. He wiped foam from his mouth with the back of his hand and blinked hard, as if clearing his vision. With all that beer, he must've seen wavering images of me. "What's it to you?"

I explained to him about the police suspicion of my student Lyle and the family's threat to close the studio unless we handed him over. I didn't want to lose my job. Maybe the ranger could understand that. I left out what I'd learned: that the woman with the lost snake had placed Lyle at the scene of the crime; that Maribeth had confirmed his short fuse and consequent capability to push Francesca. Instead, I told the ranger what I hoped: maybe Innis knew something that could tell us the truth. Maybe he knew someone who had a better motive. Like Innis himself, if Abby's information had been correct that Innis was an abusive boyfriend who couldn't get the concept of "goodbye." Had Innis participated in the illicit camp-in?

The ranger listened to my story as he polished off his pint and asked for another. No wonder his girth was almost as wide as his height, giving him the shape of a muscled cube.

"Now it's your turn," I said. "Why are you looking for Innis?"

"He has something of mine," Rock said.

When it appeared that Rock had told us all he cared to reveal, Gillian glanced at me with a mischievous smile and snuggled closer to the ranger. "Maybe we can help Rocksie Wocksie get his lost thingie wingie back?"

He grunted and tipped his empty pint glass up over his lips to lick up the literal last drop.

"Why does he have something of yours?" I asked, narrowing my eyes at him. "Did you know each other before Francesca's death brought you two together?"

"You might say that," Rock said. "That fraternity Innis belongs to was assigned to us in open space for a community service last fall. The brothers were supposed to help us restore some trails that had fallen into disrepair. Then I hit pay dirt. Lucky me. I got Innis Wood assigned to me." Rock paused to shake his head, disgust written across his face at the resurgence of some memory.

"I take it he wasn't very helpful?" I said.

"That's putting it mildly." Rock grunted again.

"You said he has something of yours," I said. "Did you give it to him then?"

"Nope. He stole it from me a couple months ago. My henna kit."

I frowned at him, struggling to find the significance of this. Struggling to keep from blurting out "so what?" Instead, I said, "Is that a big deal? I mean, why is it so important to you?"

"Hey, it's my stuff."

"Okay. But how do you know he's the one who stole it?"

"'Cause he told me so. Said he was borrowing it. Said he had to use it to lavalier some girl who was getting too big for her britches and he needed to rein her in a notch or two. Nothing like getting a promise of marriage to do that trick."

Gillian and I exchanged glances, a bit unsure of Rock's thought process.

"Excuse me," I said, "but what does this have to do with Francesca?"

"He lavaliered her all right. He tattooed his Greek letters right across her bikini line with my henna kit."

"How do you know he's the one who did it?"

"Who else?"

"Well," I said, "what do you hope to gain from meeting him here tonight? He can't give it back to you now."

"Maybe not the henna he used, but he can give back the rest of the kit. And tell me how she took it. Was that why she jumped off the rock?"

"If he frightened her, why would she let him do that to her?"

"Why, exactly." He rapped his empty glass against the table.

"You don't think she volunteered to let him henna her?"

"I think he has some explaining to do."

"How do you even know about the tattoo in the first place," I said, "if it was in such a private place on her body? She was fully dressed when we found her. Wearing pants and that pink jacket. And sandals."

He twisted his mouth into a scowl as he scanned the room and twirled his fingers in the air over his empty glass. "I've got a buddy in the police department, and he keeps me informed."

"Really? Who?"

"You wouldn't know him. We both rent rooms in the same house."

"Can't he get in trouble for telling you stuff like that?"

Rock shrugged. "We talk. Seeing as how I was the first to respond. Sometimes information slips out when we're off duty. We're both professionals."

"You sure are, honey," said Gillian.

"Speak of the devil now," the ranger said, his thirsty gaze focused on the front door, where a bottleneck of new arrivals pressed before the bouncer checking ID's. "He's late." The ranger bumped his chair backwards, scraping it along the tile floor. He sprang to his feet and waved his arms, although as short as he was, I wasn't sure if he could be seen over the milling crowd. Never mind, because he must have given off an aura of command that made several heads turn. A young man squeezed through the crowds, heading toward us. He looked young enough to make Lyle appear mature.

When he reached our table, his cheeks were flushed, and bloodshot streaks riddled his eyes. He'd already been drinking, I deduced. He wore a sweatshirt with Greek letters emblazoned across the front, and he puffed out his chest as if trying to compensate for his lack of muscular solidness. He looked like a tall, skinny version of a macho Rock wannabe.

"Hey man," he said pointedly at the ranger, completely ignoring Gillian and me. "What're you doing way over here in the corner? How come you're not over there where the action is?" He jerked his tousled head backwards, indicating the make-shift stage where the game of trivia and beer chugging was going on.

"Better over here," Rock said, nodding at Gillian and me. "We got ladies here. You going to say hello or keep being a jerk?"

The kid assessed us with a wary look and shut up, the way my students do whenever I walk in on them when they're acting out.

Gillian flashed her winsome smile at him, but it didn't win him over or even seem to penetrate whatever fog he operated under.

The ponytailed server breezed up. "I see you found him," she said. "Looks like you got a reunion going on. Need any refills?"

"It's about time you showed up," Rock said. He gave her his orders while I covered my nearly full pint with the palm of my hand.

The kid pulled an unoccupied chair over to the table, even though someone's jacket hung over the back. He placed the confiscated chair in the traffic path to the swinging doors to the kitchen. He was an accident waiting to happen. Rock enlightened everyone on our names, although the newly arrived kid, Innis Wood, didn't appear to pay attention.

He spoke to the ranger, again as if Gillian and I weren't there. "They took me in for questioning, man."

"Who did?" Rock frowned, or maybe he pretended a type of fatherly concern.

"The cops. They think I killed her. Why would they think that?"

"'Cause you left your stamp on her," Rock said, "like a dummy."

"Why did the police let you go?" I asked.

Innis turned slowly to stare at me with a look that read, "Who the hell are you, lady, and why are you interrupting me and my pal?" He shook his head, and said instead, after chewing for a while on his words, "They just asked me some questions. I know what they're thinking, though. I'm not so dumb."

"What sort of questions?" Gillian said.

"Like where I was last Monday night. Did her and me have some sort of fight. You know. That kind of thing."

"And where were you?" I said.

"You think I can remember? That was a whole frigging week ago."

"What about the fight?" Rock said. "Maybe that's what tipped off the cops."

"We didn't fight, man, lay off."

Rock frowned. "You saying she just let you henna her with

my kit, all lovey dovey?"

"I didn't kill her!" Innis lurched to his feet, as if poised to run away.

I jumped up, too, and laid a restraining hand on his arm. "We just thought you could tell us why Francesca was out there, on top of the Flatiron."

"Why do you keep calling her that? My girl was Fanny."

"She never told you her real name?"

He shook my hand off his arm. "That *is* her real name. Was, I mean."

I let the name go. "You probably knew her better than anyone. You were out there together, weren't you? Monday night?"

"Yeah. I did." He sniffed and fell back into his seat. "Know her best, that is. And yeah, I guess that's what night it was. Monday."

"Maybe you saw something," I said, reseating myself. "That would help the police find out what happened to her."

"I didn't see nothing. She ran off, and..." His face glazed over, either thinking about what he didn't see or else he'd had too much beer. "I let her go."

When he didn't elaborate, I went on, softening my voice. "What was she like?"

"Sexy as hell and just as stuck up. Drove me nuts."

I made a mental note to find out if she'd been sexually assaulted. Was that why she'd been up there in the mountain park after dark? Dragged up there to be assaulted? By a frustrated boyfriend? By Innis?

Or Lyle.

"Do you think it's possible she was rock climbing?" I said

when his silence drew out too long.

"Never. Is that why you think she was out there?"

"Not me. It was mentioned as a possibility. But she had no equipment. Not even the right shoes. Just little thin sandals. And no one was with her. At least, no one that stuck around."

"Maybe there was someone," Innis said, "and he went off for help."

"He?"

"A metaphor. You know."

I guessed Innis wasn't an English major. "So you think Francesca and some male friend were rock climbing without ropes and something went wrong?"

"Isn't that what you think?"

"I have no opinion. I never knew her. You're the one who knew if that was likely behavior for her."

He scratched his head to help him think about the mire he was sinking into. "Naw, probably not. Rock climbing was reckless enough with ropes. But without? No way. She worried about everything. 'Lighten up' I kept telling her, but would she? Never. She worried about everything. Too much snow, not enough snow, killer flu at the bar, botulism in restaurants, listeria in her organic foods, bikers with no helmets, drivers texting, you name it. They were all out to get her, too."

"And one person in particular," I said. "Apparently, that's why she was taking self-defense. To protect herself from someone who frightened her. That was you, wasn't it?"

"Hell, no. It was that old pervert, The One and Only Great Jimmie Condo."

"Jimmie Condo?" Gillian asked with a gasp.

I sputtered, struggling to find my voice. Everywhere I

turned, Condo's name cropped up. "I take it you don't like him."

"He's a slime ball, if that's what you mean."

"So you know him?"

"Only third hand. I had to listen to Fanny go on and on about him, like he was one of her Greek gods or something, and how great he was. But no, I never met him, not in the flesh, that is. He's the reason we split. Fanny and me."

My eyes popped open wide. "She was dating Jimmie Condo?"

"Hell no, he's old enough to be her old man. He was the father figure she never had."

"But you and Francesca had a fight about him?"

"Me and Fanny. And no, not exactly. We had a difference of opinion, that's all. She thought he was the next greatest thing to online chat rooms."

"But you disagreed."

"You bet. I saw him for exactly what he is."

"And what is that?"

"I already told you. It's all about him."

"Okay," I said, "so you wanted to win Francesca back, and you thought if you took her someplace crazy, maybe camping in mountain park, you could make it into a magic moment, and lavalier her."

"Except it didn't work out the way you planned," Rock said, "and she ended up jumping off the rock. Is that what happened?"

Innis's eyes flew open wide, and his gaze whipped back and forth between Rock and me. He settled on me, studying me like I was a nuisance ant that he was getting ready to crush. "We weren't camping. And anyhow, how'd you know about that? No one's supposed to know. About us being out there, I mean.

Who are you again?"

Patiently, I explained my story again for his benefit. When I mentioned Lyle's name, Innis's face flickered with recognition. I pursued that angle. "Do you know Lyle?"

"Not personally, no, but I know about that freak. He was bugging the hell out of my girlfriend. He was even spying on us from the bushes."

"If you weren't camping," I said, "then why were you out there? Watching the moon rise?"

"Trails close at sunset," Rock added.

"Something my house made me do." Innis clamped his jaw shut, as if he meant to tell us no more.

Rock laughed. "You idiot. You and your stupid games."

The server brought a tray of beers and placed them in front of the other three. I'd had no idea Gillian could drink so much beer. She was a California wine sort of gal.

I let a beat go by while they sampled their beers, and then I prodded again. "Was it some sort of scavenger hunt that your house sent you on? Is that why you were in the mountain parks after dark?"

Innis choked. "Something like that."

"And Lyle followed you?"

"He tried to stop me from stealing her from some stupid party."

"You mean, you *kidnapped* her?" My voice rose before I could control it.

"It wasn't like that."

"It's all part of the game, Nell," Gillian said with a knowing smile.

Innis blinked at her, as if seeing her for the first time. "I thought we shook him, but man, that dude's like a leech."

"So you ran up into the mountains to hide, and he followed you?"

"No, not hide. We wanted a little privacy, y'know?"

"But what happened after that?" I said. "What made her run off? Did you two have another fight?"

Innis sampled his beer and choked, either on the drink or on my words. When he finally found his voice, he glared at me. His eyebrows twisted into the angry shape of the letter "M." M for murder?

"Where'd you hear about that?" he said when he finally found his voice.

"So you deny it?" I said.

"I never hurt her," he said. "Even if we disagreed a couple of times."

"What'd you disagree about?" I said, not willing to let him off. "Jimmie Condo?"

"I don't know that it's any of your business," he said.

"Answer her," Rock said with a snort. "We all want to know. You cooperate, and I might get my bud the cop to go easy on you. If not, I could tell him you got my henna kit."

Innis thought about that a while, and then he slowly nodded.

"Maybe if we all cooperate," I added, "we can figure out what happened to Francesca."

"You should ask that freak what happened. He probably saw it all. Hell, he probably even did it. Yeah, I bet that's what happened. She told him to take a flying leap, and instead of him jumping off the mountain, he pushed her off."

A sinking feeling weighed in my gut. Because I thought he was probably right. Innis and Francesca had argued, she left, and Lyle was waiting. Except, she took out her anger on him. Yes, I could see it now. Her snotty attitude. His fragile ego. Something snapped in Lyle's mind. And then she fell to her death.

ELEVEN

I walked Gillian home after the bar. It wasn't far, only a few blocks, and she sang all the way, apparently as pleased with her conquests that evening as I was feeling depressed. Her condo, a piece of Gannon family property, tucked between downtown Boulder and the mountains, a few blocks to the west. The location made her easily accessible to the bar scene by night and mountain activities by day.

Penelope, the golden retriever that Gillian was guardian of, greeted us at the door with a wet nose brushed against my upturned palm and other body parts. Penelope seemed to know this song and dance. She led us down the hallway, swaying her silky hair and clicking her toenails against hardwood, to the den in back. Gillian sank down into one of the stiff wing-backs her interior decorator had chosen for her, while I flicked on the gas fireplace, poofing away the chill of a spring evening. A bar countertop separated the den from the kitchen, where I headed to start a pot of chai. From the kitchen, I could also keep an eye on Jill.

"I just don't want to believe that the Dentons are right," I called out above the sounds of clinking porcelain mugs. "It looks like Lyle is the guilty party."

Gillian yawned. "Don' be so hasty."

"A whole week has gone by since Francesca's accident," I said. "That's not hasty. I've already talked to half a dozen or so people, and each one I talk to makes the case worse for Lyle."

"Tha' many? Who? Any more hunks?" Gillian perked up, straightening from her slouch.

"Sorry to say, no hunks. There's Tucker, the so-called incompetent cousin. Not my term, but the lawyer's, and I have to agree with him on that. Poor thing, only has half a brain. Can't think for himself. Tucker believes whatever Aunt Cybil feeds him. So Tucker thinks Lyle is guilty just because the family believes it. They don't seem to have any hard evidence, just their bias that anyone hanging out at a karate studio must be ready to throw people off mountains."

"Withou' Francesca, that little rich boy gets all their money now, doesn't he?"

"Down, girl," I said, and not to Penelope. And while I was reminded of Gillian's enthusiasm regarding money and men, I added, "you're not seriously interested in either of those men you met tonight, are you? I'm not sure we can believe a word they say. Besides, Innis is way too young for you, and Rock is too —"

"You're no fun. All you want to do is sleuth."

"The rest of the people I've spoken to are women," I said. "Sorry, no hunk material for you there. Phyllis has some sort of ax to grind with the Denton family, and I'll bet she would've liked to push Francesca off a mountain if she'd had the opportunity. Problem is, no way could she ever climb that trail to the top of that Flatiron in her pencil skirts and three-inch heels."

"Y'know where she shops?"

I ignored that and went on. "Then there's Abby, the

152

roommate. The family thinks she's after Francesca's money, but I don't believe that. She seems like such a sweet kid. Anyway, even if it's true, she would've needed Francesca alive in order to keep reaping her financial benefits. Now that Francesca's gone, Abby has to find another place to live. Another way to buy her groceries. No way would she give up her free ride. Nope, Abby couldn't have done it."

Gillian made no response, and I kept thinking aloud. "Then, there's that woman who lost her snake. Jasmine. Not that she's a suspect. She didn't even know Francesca. Why would she want to kill her? But she did confirm seeing Lyle at the scene of the crime. Out of all those people, Lyle keeps turning up as the most likely suspect. I just don't want to believe it, but after tonight, after hearing what Innis had to say about the way they went into the mountains, and Francesca ran off... Assuming we can believe him. But what *does* hold up is his claim that Lyle was there, waiting. Jasmine confirmed that he was there, too. And we know Lyle was capable because Maribeth described how he snapped that time over at Kim's in a burst of anger and knocked Francesca down. Yeah, I'm beginning to believe maybe it's possible. Maybe Lyle *did* do it."

No comment came from Gillian, and I wondered if she'd dozed off.

"On the other hand," I said, "Jimmie Condo's name keeps popping up, but —"

"Gotta meet Jimmie." Gillian's sleepy voice sang, but so did the tea kettle.

By the time I carried the tea tray around to the glass-topped table, Gillian was snoring softly. "Forget the chai," I said, "let's get you off to bed."

"S'okay. When can I meet Jimmie?"

* * * * *

After I tucked Gillian in and took Penelope out for her pee, quick before any roaming mountain lions could find her, I locked up behind me and drove the mile or so up the hill to my place. I'd only had a few sips of beer a couple hours earlier, not enough to impair my driving. Unlike others, sad to say, who were out and about in this wee hour after the bars closed. The flashing lights I saw a block or so off my route reminded me how vulnerable I was to drivers stupidly driving under the influence. I kept to the side streets and breathed a sigh of relief when I pulled in safe and sound to my parking space. Sliding my house key into position, I unlocked the car door and followed the path to the studio's back door.

The door stood ajar a couple inches.

I'd locked up before I left to meet Gillian in the bar. I was sure I hadn't forgotten. Some would even call me anal about safety.

I wasn't so sure about Terra. I would have a talk with her in the morning, lecture number five hundred sixty-one since we'd moved in here.

I tiptoed inside, flooding the place with light, and bolted the door behind me. Floorboards creaked as I trod softly up the stairs. At least I found the apartment door securely locked at the top of the stairs. I checked on Terra, sleeping soundly in her bed, nestled amongst her stuffed animals, a routine that hadn't changed these last fifteen years.

All seemed quiet downstairs. The unlocked back door had

just been an innocent oversight. Still, I chained the apartment door and mentally reviewed our emergency escape plans. Out the window, down the maple tree. I climbed into my own bed and tossed and turned for what felt like the rest of the night.

It wasn't the first time I'd been wrong. I listened to the coyotes yipping in the distance. I listened to every piece of gravel crunch in the alley out back — my college neighbors kept late hours. I listened to the creaking pipes inside. What tales could they tell about the history of this house?

None of it made sense. But even if Lyle had killed Francesca, I still couldn't believe it was anything but an accident. I'd seen the panic on Lyle's face when we found Francesca's body. The poor kid was probably terrified. That's why he hadn't shown up here at the studio in almost a week. That, and the fear of God put there by lawyer Lazar.

And thinking of Lazar, I realized he was all bluff. Nothing more. His deadline had come and gone. All that huff and bluff — it went along with his attitude.

No matter if Lyle was guilty, I wasn't ready to turn him over to the sharks. I would turn him over to the police. Just as soon as I reported my conclusions to Callahan.

* * * * *

But the next morning, after lecture number five hundred sixty-one and Terra's protests of innocence, my elusive boss was nowhere to be found at the other end of a phone line.

What now? If we had a killer in the school, should I even try to fight the powerful Denton influence to keep the studio open?

After Terra left for school, I spent the morning taking the

studio apart, searching for evidence of a night-time intruder. I found none. Once again, I'd left my duffle bag downstairs, but nothing was missing. It still held my practice chuks and kamas and the clothes I'd worn the day before.

I headed into the basement, searching for the old lock. I could swear that the secret key in Francesca's jewelry box would fit it. Mindless activity kept my mind numb as I searched. The lock had to be here somewhere. Dad wouldn't have thrown it out, would he? He'd spent his life guided by the belief that everything was fixable. He could scavenge something from anything. Maybe he'd taken the old lock to his farm.

Because it wasn't here.

I needed to hear from Lyle his account of what had happened Monday night before I decided which sharks to throw him to. The police, Lazar, or Callahan. On the other hand, maybe I shouldn't give Lyle a chance to explain.

I really needed some inspiration to tell me what to do.

At times like this, I needed advice from Master Hwang.

I changed out of my jammies and drove to his studio way out east, a long and narrow unit in the center of a strip mall, anchored by a tire store. I'd spent years here, training for black belt, and the Ghia knew the way. It took exactly twenty-seven minutes from my door.

Master Hwang always made himself available to his students for private consultation over the noon hour, when he went through his round of exercises. I pushed through the swinging door to the sounds of weights clanging softly and locker-room smells of sweat and used shoes. The place brought back mixed feelings for me. Copious amounts of my blood, sweat, and tears had been spilled into Master Hwang's green indoor/outdoor carpet. I took off my shoes and dug my toes against the springy pile.

Master Hwang's wiry figure lay prone on a bench press as he lifted an obscene amount above his bulging muscles. Respectfully, I waited until he and his spotter were done. He wiped himself off with a towel and slipped an orange silk *gi* on over his tee-shirt. Then he blinked at me in acknowledgement and turned on his heels to the back room, a big empty room the size of a ring, empty except for pads and carpet. I knew the drill. I was supposed to follow. The spotter was not.

He stood rigidly at ease in the center of his private workout space, folded his arms across his chest, and waited silently for me to initiate the usual greetings and get to the point.

"What do you do," I said, "when you find out you're wrong about something you knew for sure you were right about? And you're no longer sure. You're no longer sure of anything." Well, that didn't come out right, I thought. It sounded like my usual doubts.

I tried again. "What I mean, sir, is this: how do I fight a powerful opposition that is threatening to ruin the school where I work?"

The Dentons had already pushed Francesca away from them, forcing her into a relationship with an abusive boyfriend she didn't really want. Francesca was just trying to get away from the family's rejection of her. I wondered if the Dentons were behind my over-achieving student's mom's wish to switch him to Kim's. How far would they go to shut down Callahan's?

Master Hwang's pencil-thin eyebrows arched, and his mostly hairless head dipped slightly in a nod, telling me that he was processing my request for advice. Then he unfolded his arms and waved to the floor. "Fifty push-ups," he said. "Go now."

Oh rats. You'd think I'd learn. Having doubts was one thing. Expressing them to my sensei was quite another. I fell to the floor into position.

After my first ten push-ups, he started to speak. "You no see truth because you are weak. You must strengthen."

He was right about that. My muscles already burned at twenty.

"You are never wrong if you follow the path of truth," he said. "You must keep going forward, seeking the truth, until you are one with the truth."

My back ached at thirty, but I kept going.

"Once you gain enough strength," he said, "then you see the truth."

At forty, my dips shortened. Either that, or I would crash onto my nose.

"Truth is way you master yourself on the floor," he said. "You never give up. Never admit defeat. Only then will you see truth."

As I polished off my set of fifty, I tried to decipher Master Hwang's cryptic message. Did he mean that as I'd adjusted the dips in my own push-ups in order to persist and finish the proscribed fifty, I would also have to adjust my own actions in order to see the truth?

I thanked him for his wisdom and bowed away.

I wasn't sure what I had learned there, but at least I had achieved part of my own daily workout. I could've done that on my own floor, but somehow, I felt an inner glow of peace which I always gained from Master Hwang.

* * * * *

All the way back to town, I processed Master Hwang's advice. He meant, I decided, that I couldn't give up my search for justice, even if it meant changing my mind about things I didn't want to believe. As for example, Lyle's guilt.

I couldn't delay any longer what I had to do. There was still another hour or so before drop dead time of going on duty at the studio, so I headed over to the police station. Being a gorgeous spring day, and the lunch hour to boot, several employees picnicked outside. Detective Hennessey's bushy hair stood out above the rest. I parked the car and headed over to his wrought iron table. Luckily, his partner, the ornery Rosenquist, was nowhere in sight.

"Good afternoon, Detective," I said, approaching him. "Mind if I have a word with you?"

"Not at all, Ms. Letterly. Have a seat."

He was as polite as his partner was rude. We sat there in silence together, admiring the views of snow-covered peaks in the distance and soaking in the warmth of the sun. He waited for me to tell him what was on my mind. I dug into my jeans pocket for Francesca's key, but my pocket turned inside out. Empty. My eyes widened and my voice choked.

"I know it was here," I said.

Hennessey was a man of few words, which probably made him a good complement to Rosenquist, who was all about bluster. Where was he, anyway? I was grateful that he wasn't around, since he always succeeded in winding me up.

I was pretty wound up already. Francesca's key was missing.

Just like her necklace.

Maybe Sammy had stolen it to add to her collection of shiny treasures.

I journeyed backwards through my mind, remembering having tucked the key into my jeans pocket, later changing into my uniform, leaving the jeans in my duffle bag, and the bag in the studio, and...

The open door the night before hadn't been an accident. Someone had jimmied the lock open, broken into the studio, taken the key from my pocket.

Someone had known exactly where to find it.

Not Sammy.

"It was a key," I said.

Hennessey let me do most of the talking, but I could tell the way he glanced askance at me that he thought I was an idiot and my theories were lame. The non-existent key, I told him, worked the studio's old lock, and I told him why. Francesca must've had a relationship with my womanizing predecessor. They both held track records for that sort of stuff, after all. I also told him my conclusion that Lyle must've accidentally caused Francesca to fall. I could tell Hennessey was listening, on account of the way he interjected a solemn frown and an occasional nod.

"Well, I won't bother you anymore on your lunch break," I said finally, standing up. "I have to get to work soon, anyway. I'll go look some more for that key. I must've misplaced it." Not. "I just thought you should have it, in case it might tell you anything about what happened. Finding out the truth of what happened is most important."

"Thank you, Ms. Letterly. I assure you that we will follow up with the proper questions as soon as the doctors allow us."

"Doctors? What doctors?"

"Lyle Sawhill's doctors. You see, he was struck on his bicycle early this morning on the streets downtown. A hit and run." Hennessey paused a beat while my jaw gaped open and I felt the warm rush of blood draining from my face. Then he added, "They took him to the hospital with a bullet wound, but they tell me he's going to pull through okay."

TWELVE

Holy moly. Lyle had been hit with a bullet *and* a car. Maybe it wasn't just a drunken driver who'd hit him. If there was a bullet involved, maybe it had been intentional. That would explain why the driver ran away.

And I had just started thinking that Lyle was the killer. Accidental, but still. I had been hasty to judge him without a trial. Regardless of his guilt or innocence, he was still my student and would remain so until a jury settled the matter.

Now, someone else had tried to kill him.

Who would've deliberately tried to do such a horrible thing? Maybe the real killer. Maybe the real killer suspected that Lyle had seen him — or her. Lyle could identify him, and so he would need to be eliminated. Innis was pretty upset at the bar the night before. And drunk. Could he have done it? But what about the gun? Lyle had a gun. Had he wounded himself, trying to protect himself from the driver?

I stopped at the hospital on my way back to the studio. It turned out to be the wrong hospital. But when I finally tracked down his location, the nurse on duty barred my way. He was in X-ray, could I wait?

Actually, no. After running back and forth across town, it was now time to get back to the studio for my first class of the day. My visit would have to wait until after classes let out later that night. The nurse frowned. Why not come back in the morning and let the poor boy get some rest overnight?

There wasn't much else I could do about it now except get back to the studio and my job. Who knew how long I would have a job?

* * * * *

Later, when I was in the middle of teaching the green belts, the front door blew open and Rosenquist thudded inside. He looked mad. His partner, the sane polite one, Hennessey, followed like a silent shadow. An emaciated shadow, by comparison to Rosenquist's heft.

Rosenquist's tie flapped from side to side as he strode across the workout floor, shoes on, absolutely no regard for the respect of the floor. He was waving a piece of paper, either trying to get my attention, or lifting the paper triumphantly. Either way, he got it. My attention, that is.

"Rachel, you're in charge," I said, backing away from my students whose forms had stopped mid-form while they craned to look at the interruption.

Rachel squeaked. "Me?"

"Don't forget, you're testing soon. Call this a practice run."

She gulped. "Okay. I mean, yes ma'am."

I bowed off the floor and waved Rosenquist to the strip of taped-off area where shoes were permitted. Hennessey lurked by the door, grinning. Rosenquist remained oblivious. He marched through the workout floor toward the arched doorway leading back to the kitchen office, as if it had been his idea all along to make Hennessey and me trail along behind.

He rattled the paper like some tour guide holding a flag aloft to corral his group.

"What's this all about?" I said once we reached the kitchen.

But he didn't answer. Instead, he grabbed the first file box within reach on top of a stack, flung it to the floor, and ripped off its lid. "What's in here?"

"What do you think you're doing?"

He rattled the paper again. "Search warrant. You can go back to your class and let me and Hennessey get to work."

"What are you looking for?" I asked.

"We'll know it when we find it. Go on, now, get out of here."

Instead, I marched over to the phone and punched in Callahan's number. Poppy said she hadn't seen him all day but would have him call me back ASAP. I watched the detectives paw through boxes for a while. I couldn't stop them. So I gave up and slunk back to class.

Rachel stood helplessly to one side of the group of green belts and watched them stumble through their moves. Relief flooded her face when she saw me emerge from the kitchen office.

"Can I talk to you?" she said, the whites of her eyes shining.

"Well, we can't talk in there," I said, nodding towards the office where the two detectives ransacked my files. "Let's go to my back-up office." I led her to the entrance hall where the detectives had just stormed through. "Looking good!" I told the students who diligently plowed on through their forms. "Keep it up!" I cranked the music on my way past the stereo. Standing in the entrance hall, I could watch the students work while giving Rachel the sense of privacy. We stood in front of the stairway to my apartment upstairs, facing the possibility of Terra's return home from band practice at any moment. "What's up?" I said to Rachel.

"Isn't there anything I can do to make sure I pass my belt test?"

"What do you mean? I've watched you and I think you're ready."

"Well, I don't know. Out there trying to lead the others just now? I couldn't remember anything. How am I supposed to remember my own stuff if I go blank like that?"

"Just keep practicing until it becomes second nature to you and you can go through the forms in your sleep."

"No, you don't understand."

What was she trying to tell me?

"I mean, what if I freeze up? You said you've already seen me, so can't you, like, just go ahead and pass me anyway? You said I know it already."

"Knowing your form and mastering it are not necessarily the same thing," I said.

"Huh?"

"Putting it another way: passing a belt test is the traditional way to advance through the ranks."

"But why does the belt test have to be in *front* of everyone?"

"It's a team effort, a time of celebration of one's progress. Family and friends like to share that moment with you."

"Well, I don't have anyone who wants to see me, so can't we just bypass all that? Can't I just, like, do my stuff in front of you?"

"You want a test in private?" Sometimes, in rare circumstances, that happened. But it was very rare, since the point of the test was to perform under pressure.

"How much would it cost?"

"Cost?" My voice raised a decibel. Students on the workout floor turned to look at us. I lowered my voice. "The cost of a belt test is factored into your tuition. You know that. You've been through three tests already."

"And each one keeps getting harder," she said. "Can't I just pay you a little extra to have a private test?"

"As in 'bribe'? Rachel, I'm shocked. This is not the way we run things here. I am striking you from the list of testers. You will have to wait until the next test before you are eligible for promotion to the next rank."

Her face took on a look of desperation. Her eyes widened. She leaned close enough that I could smell the taco she'd had for lunch on her breath. Beads of sweat dotted her forehead. "Look, can we just forget the whole thing? Forget I said anything, okay?"

"We'll forget it, and we'll move forward."

"So can I still test?"

"Not this time. You'll wait until next time."

"Just because I asked you for a simple favor? That's so not fair!" She stomped over to the shoe rack, scooped up her things, and stomped out the front door.

"Rachel, wait!" I called after her, watching her run along the sidewalk, dropping a trail of socks and sweater and papers from her opened bag as she ran. I picked up her stuff and sighed. Lucky for me, she'd dropped this much. She'd have to return now, if she wanted to reclaim her things. Maybe she'd calm down by then.

Rosenquist pushed past me, carrying an armload of file boxes.

"You can't need all that, can you?" I shouted with frustration. He was walking out with my student records. How could I track my students' progress without my materials?

Hennessey followed behind him with another stack of boxes. "Have a good day, ma'am," he said.

"Wait! When do I get that back?"

"When we're done with them," Rosenquist said with a grunt. He slammed the boxes in the back seat of his unmarked black sedan parked illegally. Of course, in this neighborhood, most cars were already parked illegally. It was the city's effort to discourage the ownership and operation of cars.

"But they're my records! And I have a test coming up soon. I need to have access to my records for the test."

"It's police business, ma'am," Hennessey said, adding his pile of boxes to the back seat of the car. Rosenquist had already flounced into the passenger seat, waiting for Hennessey to chauffeur him to their next point of business.

Hennessey paused before swinging around to the driver's side and gave me a look of sympathy. "Rock told me about your chat last night."

"Rock, the ranger? Then, you must be the one? His buddy?"

He nodded. "I thought you might like to know."

"I appreciate that, Detective."

Rosenquist rolled down his window. "Hennessey, are you coming? Or are you going to stand around and shoot the breeze all day?"

I watched them drive away with the school's records. They hadn't taken all the boxes from the kitchen office, though. I wondered what they'd left behind. Nothing useful, no doubt. This was the thanks they gave me for doing the right thing and trying to hand over Francesca's key. I hadn't, but at least I'd told Hennessey about it.

I felt like I had been run over, too, the way the cops had breezed in and out, taking my files with them.

I made it through the rest of the day's classes and waited until the next morning to go to the hospital to see Lyle.

But when I got to his room, I found someone else in his bed, an elderly woman. I did a double-take of the room number. Check. I found a nurse and asked if Lyle had been moved to another room.

"He checked out yesterday afternoon," the nurse said cheerily.

"But..."

"Nothing was broken, so he could go home."

Swell.

I headed back to the studio to look up Lyle's address. Luckily, when I'd pulled his card last week during my search of the file boxes, I'd scribbled down his home address on another slip of paper and tacked it to the message board. Hopefully, the cops had left me my bulletin board. I remembered the name of the street, but not the house number.

I could tell right away that someone was upstairs in my apartment, on account of the way the ceiling creaked. I tiptoed up the stairs. The front door to my apartment stood open, and Terra's favorite music drifted out the door.

Then Terra appeared in the doorway. "Here you are," she said. "Where've you been?"

"Never mind me, why aren't you in school?"

"Early release today, don't you remember?"

This early? Why bother to go in to school at all? If my

daughter was ditching today, which wasn't so uncommon on a beautiful spring day, then I would soon find out with a text message. Bottom line, she was safe. With me.

"I guess I've been too preoccupied with Francesca's death, and I just forgot," I lied. "Since you're home, you get to do errands with me."

She rolled her eyeballs at me as I whisked her through the door and locked it behind us.

THIRTEEN

I would start by confronting Lyle to demand whatever information he had that would clear everything up. If he wasn't going to stick around in the hospital for me to visit, then I would go to him.

I felt guilty dragging my daughter away from her music. Maybe it was selfish of me, but I needed her support as much as my students needed mine.

"Errands? What errands? Can't I just like stay home?" Terra complained the entire way across town. When our route retraced the way to the trail access we'd used last weekend, she bounced against her seatbelt and raised her voice to the pitch I recognized as her uncontrolled enthusiasm. "I would've brought Sammy," she said, "if I'd known we're going into the mountains."

"Who said we're going into the mountains today?" I turned off into a side street that zigzagged around a ridge.

"Mo-om! This way just goes into some boring neighborhoods."

"You think? I have some students who live around here. I wonder if they live on this street? Let's find out."

"So what?" Terra huffed and bounced in her seat, shaking the entire car. "Like who?"

"Well, Lyle, for one."

"You ought to find some new friends."

As we coasted a couple more blocks, I tried to explain to her about my responsibility to my students. How learning karate was different than book learning at high school, because karate was all about controlling oneself, and that included one's lifestyle. Being sensei to my students was more than just teaching them karate moves. I was also their lifestyle coach. And if one of my students was ever in trouble, then I had to be there as support and a guide for that student's journey through his or her trials.

"Whatever," Terra told me.

Some "trial." Someone had run Lyle over. Someone could've *killed* Lyle.

His house on the other side of the ridge was a bi-level in need of paint and a lawn. Then again, maybe they cultivated river rocks and thistle weeds in order to discourage deer from stopping here to lunch. Maybe they discouraged other visitors, too, since there was no doorbell. I pounded on the door and waited. Terra waited, lurking on the sidewalk. I pounded again.

Footsteps thudded inside the house, and a muffled voice said, "Whaaaat?"

The door swung open, and a tousled young man stood there, rubbing his eyes. Bushy brown hair stuck out in all directions, and he wore only an undershirt and boxer shorts with buffaloes on them.

I took a step backwards. "Good morning," I said cheerfully. "Is Lyle —"

"Christ, what time is it?" the man said, pulling his fists away from his eyes and cracking one of them open to a slit.

I glanced at my wristwatch. "Half past eleven. I'm looking for Lyle Sawhill."

The man relaxed into a slump and opened his eyes to half lids, although that could've been as far as they went. The exposed half showed red in the whites, and he focused them down on me for the first time. "Who?"

I repeated the name.

"The astronomy dude?"

"That's him. Can I see him?"

"Naw, I don't think he's here."

"But you're not sure? Where else would he be?"

"Have you tried the lab where he works down at school?"

"He was just in the hospital. Shouldn't he be home, resting?"

"Hospital?"

"You didn't know about the hit-and-run accident he was in?"

"News to me. He pays his share of the rent, but he comes and goes. Like me. We're on different schedules." He stretched his arms behind his neck and yawned, showing me his armpits and tonsils. "Do I know you, lady?"

"Not unless you've been to the karate studio with Lyle."

"What karate studio?"

"Didn't he tell you he's training in the martial arts?"

"News to me. What's that got to do with you?"

"I'm Nell Letterly." I handed him one of my cards. "And I'm Lyle's instructor."

Buffalo man squinted at my card for a full minute, and then scanned me up and down, all five feet of my featherweight build. "No way. I mean, sorry. Want me to go look in his room and see if he's here?"

"Please. Do you mind?"

"I guess not. You and the chick want to wait inside?"

"I'll come in. My daughter prefers to wait outside."

"Oh, all right, I'll come along," Terra said, sauntering down the sidewalk towards us.

The man held the door, waiting for Terra. He stood aside and waved us up the half flight of stairs to an arrangement of barbells, bench press, treadmill, and stacks of blinking electronics that furnished the living room. I felt like I was climbing up onto the bridge of a spaceship. Not that I had any personal experience with that.

"Cool," Terra said, taking it all in.

A few minutes later, our charming host padded back into the room. He'd covered up his boxers with a pair of baggy camouflage shorts that hung down to his knees, weighted down by bulging pockets that revealed the tips of more gadgets. "I was right," he said. "Lyle's not here. You want to hang around and wait for him?"

"You think he might show up soon?"

"No idea." His head swiveled around, following Terra, who strolled past the equipment on her circuit of the room.

"I'm sure we can't wait long," I said. "My daughter has —"

She whipped around, piercing me with her steely gaze, cutting me off before I could say the uncool word "homework." Instead, I said, "Do you have any idea where else Lyle would've gone?"

"Not a clue. Like I said, we got different schedules."

"Do you ever see him very much? When's the last time you saw him?"

Lyle's roommate shrugged. "I dunno. Two or three days

ago, what difference does it make?" He shifted on his bare feet, growing restless, apparently, but hesitant to kick us out. I decided to take advantage of that.

"I just wanted to check in and see how he's doing. But aside from that..." I made it up as I went. "As part of Lyle's progress in the karate school, we need to complete a character reference for him. Did he ever tell you about that?"

"Huh-uh." He scratched the back of his head.

"Do you mind answering a few questions about him?"

"I guess not."

I wished I'd brought a notepad and pencil from the car. No doubt, Terra would remember any data for me. "You're Lyle's roommate?"

"Well, housemate, but yeah, I'm one of them. There's a chick, too, Chandra, but she's not here, either. So I guess you just got me to talk to, huh? The guys call me Ham."

"Ham?"

He flushed and glanced at Terra who appeared to ignore him in favor of the blinking equipment. "It's short for Hamilton. Hamilton Yeager, that's me. My folks back east bought this house, and my job is to rent out rooms. We could still take in one more, if you know of anyone. Maybe someone from your karate studio?"

"I'll pass that along. When did Lyle move in?"

"Last January. I haven't seen much of him since then. What's it been? Four months? I don't know how much I can help you with your — what'd you call it? Character reference?"

"That's right. Did you know each other before you decided to room together?"

"Naw. I put up a bunch of notices on bulletin boards around

campus, and he was the first one to text me. There were a few others, too, but they changed their minds."

"What did he tell you about himself when you interviewed him about the room?"

"What interview?"

"Didn't you interview him before you let him move into your house?"

Ham shifted some more and folded his fists into his armpits. "Not my house. Dad doesn't care who rents as long as he gets his money, and the dude looked all right. Except... Oh well, he pays his rent money each month. That's all that matters."

"How much is it?" Terra asked.

"What, the room?" Ham told her, and my heart did a flip. I hoped Terra wasn't thinking ahead to the time when she would move away. She would be calculating how much money she'd need.

I felt time slipping away and steered Ham back onto topic. "Except what? You were going to say something else."

"Well, he's a little strange, but then his head is all wrapped up in black holes and what not. That'd make anyone a little strange, don't you think?"

I gave him my noncommittal, impassive, ninja gaze. "Why do you think Lyle never mentioned to you that he's training in the martial arts?"

"Beats the hell out of me, but it doesn't surprise me. One, because he doesn't talk much, at least not to me and Chandra. Two, because he's always working out when he's home. And three —"

"You should get Mr. Callahan to buy one of these, Mom," Terra said, running her fingers along a handlebar of the treadmill.

Really. My gaze shifted over to the workout equipment. My students were responsible for their own conditioning outside of class. But Lyle deliberately kept his conditioning a secret from me. I remembered how easily he'd scrambled up the side of the mountain last week, even though he'd claimed to be out of shape. How could he expect me to help him with anything if he wasn't going to be forthright with me?

"And your third reason?" I said, prompting Lyle's housemate. "Why aren't you surprised to learn that Lyle's training in the martial arts?"

"He's paranoid."

"Paranoid?" My voice rose.

"Sure. Haven't you ever noticed? You ask me, it's all about a woman. But I'm just guessing. You probably shouldn't put that in his character reference."

Terra glanced over her shoulder, giving Ham her special haughty look, and I felt one of my eyebrows twitch. My student Jason had taunted Lyle on the trail about wanting to be buff for Fanny, aka Francesca. Maribeth said Lyle was Fanny's puppy dog, and Innis agreed that Lyle had been pestering Fanny. Was Francesca the reason Lyle had signed on at Callahan's? "Do you know if Lyle is seeing anyone?" I said.

Ham snorted. "Want me to hack into his Facebook page?"

"That won't be necessary. How about other friends? Do you know if there's someone he *does* talk to?"

"*Can* you hack in?" Terra asked. "You could see who his friends are."

"Absolutely not," I said. "I won't condone anything illegal. Besides, I'm only interested in friends that he communicates with in person."

"Oh, I get it," Ham said. He contorted his face in an obvious wink and curled his fingers into air quotes. "For his character reference, right?"

He didn't believe me.

"Look, this is serious," I said. "He's been hurt. And before that, he skipped his last two classes, so now I really need to talk to him. About his dedication." And a few other things, like what he knew about Francesca's death. And why he carried a concealed weapon. And did any of that have anything to do with his getting shot and run over? Etcetera, etcetera.

Ham stroked the beard prickles dotting his chin. "Sorry. I don't know what's up with him. But I do know that lately he's been hanging out with some crowd doing volunteer stuff. Something to do with historical preservation and what not. As if he doesn't have enough stargazing to do. You ask me, that's where the woman is."

I startled and tried not to telegraph that. I felt winded with surprise, the same way when someone lands a sneak upper cut to my ribs. "The Pioneer Society?"

"Is that what it's called?"

"My friend Bri?" Terra said. "Her mom does that. Maybe she knows this guy you're looking for."

My daughter, my informant. I wanted to hug her right there, but I figured she'd drop dead with embarrassment.

"Weird, huh?" Ham said. "See? It must be about a woman. Otherwise, why would a science nerd care about dead stuff?"

Why, indeed. And speaking of dead, that reminded me of my most worrisome question that I'd slowly been building up to. "Do you know anything about the gun that Lyle carries around with him?"

Ham frowned. Apparently I hadn't surprised him the way he'd surprised me. "That little 22? It's too small to do any real harm. Good thing, as paranoid as he is. He swears someone keeps following him, like someone wants to kill him or something. Hey, do you suppose that has anything to do with that accident you mentioned?"

I struggled to control my flutters. So much for my attempts at ninja impassivity. "Do you have any idea why he thinks that?"

Ham shrugged. "And all along, I thought he was just excessively paranoid."

I bit my tongue to keep from sounding like a parrot, took a deep breath, and then went on. "If he thought anyone wanted to hurt him, he should've gone to the police about it."

"Yeah, that's what I told him to do, but I don't think he listened."

So instead, he decided to take matters into his own hands and carry around a concealed weapon. And now someone *had* hurt him. Lucky, he hadn't been killed.

I wondered if Lyle had dropped out of sight because he was afraid of a killer or because he was a killer on the lam?

FOURTEEN

I let Ham go back to bed and Terra back to her music, while I went through my noontime round of exercises on the workout floor of Callahan's Karate. Tomorrow would be another training run, helping our students to prepare for the Bolder Boulder, and without Buster around anymore to plan our practice, I'd have to draft another student. Lyle was out of commission who knew where, and Rachel had left the day before in a huff.

Whichever student who would cross my threshold today and shine would become my victim, er, draftee. Luckily, the first class of the day was a gold and orange combination. Beginners, yes, but a star at that level would have barely enough experience to take on the responsibility of student helper.

Her name was Katy, an eleven-year-old orange belt going on sixteen.

Fifteen minutes into class, I already had to call on her. The front door burst open, and I recognized the woman who breezed through the entrance to my studio. Buster's mom.

"You wanted to see me?" the woman said, pausing in the doorway as if she was modeling her leather jacket.

I rushed over to the edge of the workout floor, shook her hand, and welcomed her effusively. "Yes, I'd love a chance to sit down and conference with you."

"That's exactly why I'm here," she said. "Where can we talk in private?"

I hesitated, hoping that we could make an appointment for a more convenient time. However, I didn't want to send her away for fear of never seeing her again. "I'm in the middle of a class now."

Apparently, she didn't care. "This won't take long." She glanced at the clock on the wall. "I need to do this now. I am interviewing with the JC Corporation in less than an hour. You've probably heard of them? It's one of the top jobs in the Denver metro area, and it's headquartered right here in Boulder."

"JC? Nope, afraid not. Never heard of them."

"Jimmie Condo," she said with a sigh of exasperation.

That got my attention. And everyone else's. Students were staring. I could tell, because the room had fallen silent around us. "Shall we go into my office?" I didn't wait for her reply but turned to face my students. "Ten push-ups," I said, snapping my fingers at my gaping students who stood motionless in the middle of their combinations. "And then another set of twenty kicks, each leg, front kick and sidekick. Got it?"

"Yes ma'am." Voices called out in unison as the orange and gold belts dove to the floor.

But I needed to buy more time than that for my conference with Buster's mom. "After you're done you'll pair off, and Katy will lead everyone in white belt basics. Katy's in charge, and your moms and dads will be watching you."

I nodded at the parents in the bay window, cueing them for their temporary appointment of responsibility, and then I steered the talented eleven-year-old to my mirror position. An essential part of students' training was learning how to be in charge.

Katy beamed with pleasure and counted out the drills while I led Buster's mom along the taped-off path at the edge of the workout floor.

Her name on Buster's paperwork was Beverly, although I'd never had a two-way conversation with her to know if that's what she liked to be called. I saw her occasionally when she dropped off or picked up Buster, but I'd never seen her stay to watch one of his classes. She was an unemployed Ph.D. with a minimum of a dozen prospects always pending, which must beg her time and attention away from Buster's progress in karate. That she was physically here in the building was enough of a shock. That she'd showed up without Buster should upset the equilibrium of the universe.

"What line of work is this JC Corporation in?" I asked, keeping my voice pleasantly disinterested. Jimmie Condo was practically haunting me.

"The money-making line of work," Beverly said. "It's too complicated to go into detail. Can we move on to the topic of my son?"

So much for small talk. "It'd be great if Buster could join us for our chat," I said, sailing to the sink to fill a mug of water. Words tumbled out of me in my haste to get back out onto the floor. I knew my students would be okay for a little while, with their parents watching, but still. This was Katy's first time in charge. I couldn't let it last too long.

"That's not possible," Beverly said. "My son is too busy now, taking care of his dog-walking business in the neighborhood."

I put on my most positive tone of voice. "Buster is a great role model with all that initiative of his. Even though he's missed some classes, he's still going to do a super awesome job when he tests."

"*If* he tests," said Beverly from behind me.

I looked up from the sink. Water overflowed the mug. Her word choice, "if," gave me hope. Maybe she hadn't ruled out the possibility of Buster's staying on in this school. Maybe she hadn't switched him to Kim's school yet.

I spoke cautiously. "Do you have some concerns you'd like to discuss?"

"I most certainly do. He's far too upset to continue his ridiculous schedule at the moment. Something has to give, and I've decided it will be karate."

Whoa. I let out a long breath, not realizing I'd been holding it. "Is that what he wants to do? Maybe we should talk to him."

"He's too young to know what's best for him."

"He's put a lot of work into his martial arts. He's come such a long way. It'd be a shame to quit now." The hairs on my arms bristled.

"He's done enough," Beverly said. "He's at an impressionable age, and he's seen way too much trouble. And it's all your fault. Really. What on earth were you thinking? Exposing those poor, defenseless, helpless children to that horrible crime? It's simply the last straw. It has been giving my son nightmares, thank you very much."

As if I'd planted Francesca's body on the Flatiron. Just to torment Buster. Was this woman serious? I carried her mug over to the microwave and punched numbers. I'd like to punch something else.

"You're right," I said, gritting my teeth. "It was a difficult thing for any of us to see. Talking about it might help all of us, but especially Buster. I know he feels especially responsible because he chose that route."

"No he didn't. The little gal he wants to impress gave him the idea."

I spun around. "Rachel? Are you talking about Rachel?"

"I think that's her name. Does it matter? He's gone through enough. What else do we have to go through? You're not any better than that idiot you replaced. At least he didn't make the children take karate home with them, twenty-four seven. I am prepared to take the matter of your termination to Arlo's attention."

Now she was on a first-name basis with my boss. Oh boy.

She went on ranting. "I should have done so from the get-go, from that very first brawl of yours."

"If you're referring to the incidents a couple months ago —"

"That's one."

"That wasn't my fault." As soon as the words were out of my mouth, I realized they were the wrong response. I could almost hear my sensei, Master Hwang's voice chiding me in my head. *Nell, Nell! We never accept defeat. Turn weakness into strength.* I did some mental push-ups.

"No? There are some who might disagree. I suggest you be more careful. You're still on probation, you know."

I was? "Mr. Callahan didn't say anything about any probationary period."

Beverly waved an imaginary fly away from her face. "It's standard procedure. You should read the fine print of your contract."

I had. Beverly was just trying to intimidate me. It was one test after another, ever since I took on this job as head instructor a couple months ago. I was getting tired of it.

"Look, I appreciate your concern, but —" The microwave chose that moment to beep that the water had come to a boil. Sort of like me. "I didn't have anything to do with what happened to Francesca. Hers was an unfortunate accident."

"That's an understatement," Beverly said, "considering how fast the police came around to pay us a visit."

"Buster told me..." Luckily, I bit my words off in time before compromising Buster's trust in me. I handed her the mug of hot water and a basket of tea packages.

She ignored them. A vein throbbed at her temple. "What did my son tell you?"

"Um..." *Think fast.* I didn't want to give away the fact that Buster had been here when his mother had forbidden him to come. "He recognized the body," I said all in one breath. "He called her Fanny and said she'd done karate here at this school. Is that what the police wanted to talk to him about?"

Beverly huffed, apparently dissatisfied with my explanation, even though it was the truth. Maybe incomplete, but the truth.

"They wouldn't tell me beforehand," she said, "and so I wouldn't let them talk to my son. He's a minor. I have to protect my son's best interests."

"Of course. And I want to help. But since I wasn't employed here back when Francesca, or rather, Fanny, was a student here, there's not much I can do. Maybe you can fill me in. How well did Buster know Francesca?"

"And that's another thing." Beverly shook her index finger at me. "I try my best to shelter him from all the hanky-pank

186

that goes on, and this school seems to have more than its share. I shall mention that as well to Arlo."

"Hanky-pank?" It was so not fair of her to blame me for my predecessor's womanizing habits. My act was clean. Squeaky, shiny clean.

"If you ask me," Beverly went on, "that gal was just asking for trouble. And she got it. I'm not surprised."

"Francesca? What sort of trouble was she asking for?"

Beverly shrugged. "She spread hormone wars and cat fights everywhere she went. I should have pulled my son out long before now, but he insisted on continuing with all this. But enough is enough. I will not have my son infected by all that, not at his delicate coming-of-age stage."

I was trying to understand. "But if Francesca was at the heart of the problem, and now she's...gone..." Didn't that eliminate the problem?

How far would Beverly have gone, I wondered, to keep Buster from becoming "infected," as she claimed? I tossed out the suggestion that had popped into my mind. She was a squeaky wheel for sure, but she was also smart enough to realize that murder would not further her son's best interests. Maybe I was getting carried away with my sleuthing.

I tried again. "So you think it was one of Francesca's boyfriends who killed her?" Innis, I thought. Guinness Innis. And then there was the sender of flowers. Innis had implicated Jimmie Condo. I felt as if I'd come full circle. Everything came back to Jimmie Condo.

"Or maybe it was a woman," Beverly said. "There's nothing more dangerous than a jealous woman, do you not agree?" She didn't mean for me to answer her rhetorical question because she didn't give me a chance, as fast as she rattled on her accusations. "Perhaps someone who had been jilted by one of Fanny's many rejects took out her anger on Fanny."

That made my head hurt, untwisting her logic. Certainly, Lyle was rejected by Fanny, aka Francesca. Had he jilted someone else? Ham suspected there was a woman in Lyle's life, and I assumed he meant Francesca. But maybe there was someone else. Someone infatuated with Lyle? Someone who knew she'd never have Lyle as long as Fanny stood in the way?

But why would that same someone try to run Lyle down? Pure, nuclear-fueled anger? I knew something about that, thanks to Max.

I was still chewing on all this as Beverly rambled on. "Or it could have been anyone. Who knows what perverts lurk around this place considering how improperly lit the grounds are? We can't see them in all the shadows that surround this building, but I know they're watching our every move. I smell their bad breath every time I walk up the sidewalk. Who knows what goes on in the minds of such perverts?"

At least that was something I could do. "I'll speak to Mr. Callahan about installing new lights around the property. Would you let Buster come back to class if we had new lights?"

Beverly grimaced. "It's too late." She zipped up her leather jacket.

"But isn't there something we can do to convince you to let Buster stay on here?"

Beverly grinned, as if she sniffed the upper hand. "You could postpone the test."

That was the one thing I couldn't do. Other students had already prepared with that date in mind. Ten more days from now. I'd already cleared the date with my boss, and most important of all, he had it on his calendar. He was a busy man. It would upset his schedule if I tried to change the date now.

Calmly, I watched her stalk out of the kitchen. Then I picked up her mug and flung the cooled water across the room, following her wake.

FIFTEEN

My favorite time of the day was night, and my favorite time of the night was right after the last of my students had left. It was a down time when I was still buzzing from the adrenaline rush of working out. Night descended around me like black velvet, feeling both soft and staticky electric. I was alone, and I wanted to keep spinning.

Especially when someone provoked me, as Buster's mom had.

With Terra safe upstairs in the apartment, the front and back doors locked, and the workout floor empty, the floor felt mine. Finally, after a long day. And it called me. I inserted a CD of my favorite music, a mix of soundtrack overtures, not caring that I was a dinosaur behind the technology curve. I liked my old stereo and speakers. They comforted me. I turned up the volume, grabbed my bo staff, bowed onto the floor, and struck a pose.

When the drums rumbled, I twirled the bo, a six-foot piece of polished teak, first to my right, then curving around to the left. Bringing the bo out of its twirl, I slid it back through my fingers and then lunged forward, jabbing the bo into an imaginary foe. *Beverly and your attitude issues!* I pulled back, swung to the other side, tilted the bo up, over my head, and whipped it down atop my next evil shadow. *Aunt Cybil, take that, hi-yah!*

I released my energy as I went through the rest of the routine that I was working up. The *kata*, which we called a form in our nontraditional studio, was a dance of martial arts techniques against imaginary opponents. Much better than any video game. Choreographing a musical form with weapons was part of my personal progress towards earning my next degree under Master Hwang. He would check my form next month, and there were still a few moves I had to smooth out first.

The drums kept rumbling a beat too long, and I fell out of my flying side kick with a stumble. An extra sound had thrown me off track. Then I realized it wasn't a miscalculation of the music but another sound that I'd heard. Something *not* coming from the music.

Some noise — rattling trash cans? — came from the alley out back.

Instantly, my mind spun back to that time a couple months ago when I'd heard similar sounds in the alley, and that time hadn't turned out pretty. Lights from wall sconces dazzled the workout floor now as they had then, making me feel caught in the center of a blazing spotlight. I was on display to anyone outside who might be watching me through the windows from the dark hideout of the juniper bushes. Buster's mom was right about all the shadows surrounding the studio. How unsafe was that? I would have to ask Callahan for more than new exterior lights. We should replace those bushes with something less worthy of offering a hiding place for any peeping toms.

I rolled my bo staff across the floor to the wall and then executed a series of tornado kicks, twirling my body like a spinning tornado. In case any peeping tom out there was watching, he'd think these moves were part of my workout. Suddenly, I landed at the opposite wall, beside the light switch. With one flick of the switch, I doused the lights and sprinted toward the corner beside the window that looked out over the side yard filled with juniper bushes.

My eyesight didn't adjust to the sudden dark as fast as I'd moved, but even so, I thought I saw a branch move out there. Wind? I checked the maples and oaks that lined the street, but I didn't see any of those branches with their budding baby leaves moving against the street light. No wind.

Goosebumps tickled the back of my neck. Someone had been watching me through the window.

Part of me congratulated myself for giving the peeping tom a show of what I could do with a stick. Let that be a warning to him, should he try to mess with me.

Another part of me, the mom part, stiffened my muscles and spine and set my breathing to hyperventilating mode.

The rational side ruled out. It was probably a cat, leaping through the bushes, rattling trash cans. Or in this town, it was more likely to be a bear. Guardians usually brought their pets inside at night, on account of the bear population, not to mention mountain lions and coyotes. Bears came out of hibernation this time of year, and their favorite treat was someone's trash can that had been inadvertently left outside. Case solved. A bear had been searching for dinner.

For good measure, I hurried down the hall in the dark, groping along the walls to the kitchen office, where I flicked on the outside lights that Buster's mom claimed were insufficient. I peered through the window of the back door at the illuminated alley. Movement at the periphery of the lit area pulled my attention immediately to my Ghia, which was parked in one of the spaces next to the shed behind the studio. The shadowy outline of a solitary person passed beside my car and scurried toward the alley. Not a bear, unless the bear was wearing a human cloak.

My heart thudded. Had someone been tampering with my car? I unbolted the door, yanked it open, and yelled, "Hey!" through the screened-in porch.

The figure shot away into the shadows. Given the speed with which he suddenly moved, I was sure he'd heard me.

I unlatched the screen door and leapt out onto the stepping stones through the weeds of my backyard. I heard Master Hwang's voice in my head.

No be stupid, he said. *Stupid get you killed.*

My step slowed. In the distance, I heard a car door creak open and slam shut with a tinny click. Taillights glowed from the darkened end of the alley. The left one red, and the right a pinkish red, as if the light shone through tape that patched up a broken rear light.

The driver was probably the person I'd seen hurrying down the alley, the same person who hadn't stopped when I'd yelled. Why hadn't he stopped? Because he — or she — had been spying on me through my window. Why would he do that?

He was guilty of something, obviously. Guilty of spying, at least. Maybe more. Maybe guilty of pushing Francesca off the Flatiron.

But why would he spy on *me*? To gain information? I didn't know anything. Not *yet*.

My spy might not know that. Apparently, I was making him — or her — nervous. Because I was investigating the truth about Francesca's death. I was trying to clear my student Lyle from any suspicious involvement with her death.

Maybe my visitor had actually been the missing Lyle, coming to talk to me, but I'd scared him away.

I would have to investigate the area in the morning, in the light of day.

Wind stirred, and the screen door flapped behind me. The breeze cooled the droplets of sweat that lined my brow as a result of my workout. I hadn't imagined the peeping tom. That had been him running away just now. He'd driven away with a broken taillight to avoid getting caught.

For the first time I became aware that I was barefoot, standing outside in the dirt and gravel of the alley. Rocks pinched my feet, and I moved slowly back across the stepping stones to the porch, where I latched the door behind me. I crossed into the kitchen and closed and bolted the door locked.

A board creaked somewhere from within the studio.

"Mom?" Lights switched on in the hall, and Terra entered the kitchen, a shadow outlined against the light of the hall. "What's going down?"

"I'm just locking up. Let's go back upstairs." I hoped the board that I'd heard creaking was her footstep coming downstairs just now and not someone else's. An accomplice could've easily entered the studio during the diversion outside. An intruder could now be hiding somewhere inside. I pushed Terra up the stairs to our apartment, locked and bolted that door behind us, then scoured our three rooms, the bathroom, the closets, and under the beds. Sammy sat up, alert, in the middle of her nest-like bed and squeaked at me. If only she could talk.

"What are you looking for?" Terra asked.

"Nothing." I found nothing. No one. "I'm going to bed."

* * * * *

"So what was going on last night, Mom?" Terra asked me at breakfast the next morning.

"Nothing," I lied, figuring there was no point in alarming my daughter about a peeping tom. "The wind came up, so I went outside to batten down the hatches. You know how Mr. Callahan likes for me to keep things secure. Remember how the door came unlatched before? I'll have to ask Gramps to take a look."

"I didn't hear the wind," she said, slipping a blueberry to Sammy.

Sammy squeaked with each bounce as she wound around the kitchen table legs in her eternal quest for treasures.

That gave me an idea.

"Didn't you hear it? You must've been studying so hard that you didn't even notice how windy it was." I switched topics to keep her from probing too far into my fabrication. "Did you get all your assignments done?"

She grunted, which meant no.

"So we can order pizza for my sleepover this weekend?" she said. "And if my movies don't get here in time in the mail, you'll take us out to rent them?"

"Sure, honey, I think five girls can squeeze into my Ghia, don't you?"

"You don't have to be snarky about it." She fed Sammy her last berry, then stomped over to the sink with her empty cereal bowl. "I'm late."

"Not too late to brush your teeth," I said automatically, doing my parental duty.

"Watch the mail, okay?"

I nodded. As if our mailman would want to hijack teen angst movies.

I got her off to school — she could walk the short distance down the hill to the high school — and then picked up Sammy and ran down the stairs to the kitchen office. The back door stood open. My heart thudded in my chest. I'd locked it the night before. Hadn't I? I was sure I had. Terra had used the front door when she'd left for school a few minutes ago. I knew that for a fact, since I'd heard the rattle of the glass panes.

Had someone slipped in through the back door overnight? A chill shivered through me.

I set Sammy on my shoulder and closed and opened the door several times. I peered inside the cut-out in the side of the doorframe that housed the latch when the door shut. It didn't catch the way it should. I must've thought it was locked last night when really it wasn't. Anyone could've pushed the door open and entered in the middle of the night. Something else to fix.

Sammy jumped down from my shoulder and hopped outside. Her gait reminded me of a slinky, the way her long body scrunched up and then tumbled forward. She squeaked with each bounce.

"Hey, wait for me," I called after her. She wasn't an escape artist. I wasn't worried about her running away. She was just an obsessive explorer. Sometimes she forgot where she was in her eagerness to follow the trail of some shiny thing.

If there was anything to find in the alley that my peeping

tom had dropped the night before, Sammy would be sure to find it. So I let her go. She inspected the perimeter of each stepping stone and worked her way across the yard. She prowled beneath the Ghia, pausing to glance up at the pipework.

"Hey, Sammy, don't get any ideas. Don't climb up inside the engine, for heaven's sake." I dropped down onto my knees to drag her out from under the car.

She chittered in protest, and something dropped from her claws and rolled into a clump of dandelions. I pulled her leash out of my pocket and clamped it onto her, then fished around in the dandelions. It was a bead. Pink crystal and sparkly in the morning light.

Just then the door to the craft shop next door opened. The craft shop, I realized, would carry beads like this. I'd only met the owner a couple of times. Alice something?

From Alice's store stepped a man who looked vaguely familiar. It was too early for the store to be open for business. I wondered what other business he might've had at this hour of the early morning with the young, attractive Alice? Hmmmm? I stood there in the alley, clutching my crystal bead in one hand and Sammy in the other. Staring at the man, I wondered what planet he'd come off of. He wore a plaid jacket of intertwined spring colors of lemon yellow and grass green, white trousers, as if he was heading off for a golf tournament in a previous century, and a yellow and white polka-dot bow tie. I hadn't seen a bow tie since my dad had worn one to Max's and my wedding sometime in the middle ages. I felt my jaw drop.

His gaze met mine. How could it not? With all the vibes of shock and wonder that I must've been sending. He waved and smiled. I smiled back and pretended to be looking for the newspaper that the errant paper carrier wouldn't have delivered. Mr. Fashion Statement wouldn't know that, of course.

"Top of the morning to you," he said with a Brooklyn nasal twang as he sauntered over toward me. "Are you one of Alice's neighbors?"

"Yup, next door." I nodded at the karate studio. "Are you one of Alice's customers?" So to speak.

He tipped his head back and laughed from his gut. "You could say that. Jimmie Condo's the name." He held out his hand, noticed Sammy tucked into the crook of my arm, withdrew his hand and flinched. "Who's your friend?"

Time froze for me. He was the man on the telephone at the Denton mansion. That's where I'd seen him.

Then I remembered to respond. "This is Samurai Q. Ferret." I held her up, a fur wrap around my arm, but Sammy chittered, squirmed, and clawed her way around to my backside. I agreed with her reaction, but this was Jimmie Condo, for goodness sake. Here was my golden opportunity to finally quiz the man. And oh, I had soooo many questions. Where to start?

"I've heard of you," I said lamely.

He laughed another belly laugh, and that turned me grumpy. I wasn't that funny.

"So," I said, almost hearing the gears crank and turn in my head, "what brings you to our neighborhood on this fine day?" I squinted at the sky to double check. Sure enough, cerulean blue. I sniffed the air. Sure enough, mountain spring crisp. I took a deep breath, filling my lungs with its purity.

"On my way in to the office," he said, "I thought I'd stop off and check out a couple of pieces of property."

"I understand you want to buy my dad's farm."

199

He cocked his head at me and frowned. "And you are...?"

Oh yeah.

"Nell Letterly," I said, a couple beats late.

"Ah! The dumpy little Letterly place. It will be much finer once the golf club comes in."

My veins tightened. "Golf club? They're threatening eminent domain against my dad's farm for a *golf* club?" I didn't think it was amusing, but he gave me another belly laugh anyway.

"Where'd you hear that?" he said, once he recovered from his mirth.

"That's what your assistant told me. Phyllis Eberhardt."

"Ah, yes." He wiped moisture from the corner of his eye.

"It's true?"

"Indeed. But it won't come to that."

"You don't know my dad."

"True enough."

"But you knew Francesca Denton, didn't you?"

He massaged his chin and stared upward, lost in the Colorado blue. "Now there's a name for you. Denton. A local institution, wouldn't you say?"

"Maybe you knew her as Fanny Dent."

Recognition flamed in his freshly scrubbed face, reeking of English Leather. He lowered his lids and cleared his throat, but it was too late. I'd already seen it. He knew Fanny. "You sent her flowers," I went on.

"My, my, you are the inquisitive one, aren't you?" He adjusted his bow tie and tugged his collar away from his neck.

"I would encourage you to share what you know with the police, who are investigating her death. You must know about that, right?"

"My dear lady." He cleared his throat. "I will admit to a weakness for the fairer sex, but surely you can understand, a person of my position, and my, er, maturity. What would I have to do with a co-ed? A-hem. What would the press make of that?"

"I can only imagine." I met his gaze, noticing that he hadn't denied a relationship with Francesca. He just hadn't elaborated on what kind of relationship it had been.

"Well, I mustn't be late," he said, breaking my gaze. He made a move toward the back door of the karate studio. "There's no time to spare. Chop, chop. Do you mind?"

"We're not open yet," I called after him, running to catch up.

"That's okay," he said, "I don't mind."

"Maybe I do," I told his back.

That stopped him. He wheeled around and arched his eyebrows at me. "We have an appointment."

"What appointment?"

"Didn't anyone tell you? My assistant set it up. I believe you spoke to her."

I felt slightly dizzy, slightly winded, as if I'd just finished a series of tornado kicks. Phyllis must've spoken to Poppy. I should learn to check my text messages.

He turned around and marched on, toward my back door.

I ran to catch up again, only this time I inserted myself between him and my open back door. I held out my hand like a traffic cop. "Just a minute. If you thought you had an appointment, then I didn't get the message. Just tell me what this is all about, and I'll see what I can do for you." I wasn't going to let some strange man enter my private premises, no matter what line he served me. And this man was strange in countless ways.

The smile and sunshine lighting up his face slid off his face in a heartbeat, snuffed out by a dark cloud. But there wasn't a single cloud in the sky, let alone a dark one. He glowered at me. Apparently he was unaccustomed to not getting his way. He reached into an inside pocket of his blindingly spring jacket, pulled out a smartphone, and thumbed it to life. "You are the owner of this property?" he said, staring at the information flow on his phone rather than looking at me. I didn't see how a phone could own anything, other than its so-called owner, so I presumed he was speaking to me.

"That would be Mr. Callahan," I said from the top step leading up to the porch. From this vantage point, I could look down on him and the balding spot of his crown that gleamed through sandy brown wisps of surviving hair. "Arlo Callahan. He is the owner. I am the caretaker. If you wish to come back during business hours, that's up to you. Today we're open from three until eight. No, wait, today's our Bolder Boulder training run day. We open late today, at five."

He tapped his phone one last time, slid it back into his pocket, folded his arms across his chest, and grinned up at me. It wasn't a sunny grin, though, like it had been when he'd emerged from Alice's next door. Now his grin looked pasted-on, in what must be a painfully wide split. He looked as if he was trying to impersonate a used car salesman. Heck, maybe he was, for all I knew.

"Those hours aren't convenient for me," he said. "I can see that I'll have to take this matter up with the people who matter. Good day." He tipped his hand to his unruly wisps of hair in some sort of salute, or doffing an invisible hat, and charged into the narrow space between my junipers and Alice's lilacs that were about to pop into bloom.

I started to call after him and give him an idea of just how much I mattered. Didn't he know he was trespassing? Sure, he did. He just didn't care. He owned whatever space where he trod. But by the time I could've caught up to him, he was already halfway through the bushes to the street out front, climbing into a red Lexus. After all, the point was to get rid of him, right?

Somehow, I suspected that I hadn't seen the last of Jimmie Condo.

SIXTEEN

Thanks to the parental network I had taken great pains to establish with the parents of my daughter's friends, I had Bri's mom, Dagmar — the one who volunteers with the Pioneering Society — in my cell's contact list. I arranged to meet Dagmar for an emergency latte later that morning. She was a professor at the university and stopped off for her morning latte at one of the coffee shops along the university's perimeter. Lucky for me, that was only a couple of blocks away from the studio. A short, warm-up jog.

The air smelled thick with coffee beans. The whoosh of steaming milk blared into the heavy aura of lethargy of not fully awake clientele. We jostled into several loose lines, and by the time it was my turn to order, Dagmar showed up, looking harried. We exchanged the usual pleasantries and carried our scalding hot paper cups to a table that overlooked the bustle of Broadway.

"Bri's looking forward to Terra's sleepover this weekend," Dagmar said with a smile. "And so am I. I can really use a night off, not having to worry about where she is and who she's hanging out with."

I smiled back. "I'm glad we parents can stay in touch with each other." Too bad Max didn't agree. About staying in touch, that is. And Francesca's parents, hoo boy. That family made my family feel positively functional. I wondered if their angst had pushed Francesca away from them, into relationships with abusive boyfriends.

We exchanged a little back and forth about our girls' classes and end-of-year projects and compared notes concerning gossip and then I got down to business. "Terra told me that you volunteer with the Pioneering Society. That sounds interesting. What do you do?"

Her face relaxed, and she stopped glancing at her watch as she told me about leading walking tours and acting as hostess to some of our historical homes during open houses. "Are you interested in helping out, too?"

"Maybe. I've always thought it's such a fascinating story, the way miners came and staked claims. I wish I knew more about our history."

"That doesn't matter. Anyone can volunteer."

"Anyone?" I said. "Do you get many university students as volunteers?"

Dagmar sighed and glanced at her watch. "Sometimes. Mostly, if they have a term paper to write. Or if they need extra credit. Why? You thinking of going back to school?"

"Ha!" Max had derailed that dream. If I'd listened to my dad I would've ended up with a degree instead of two years at a college smaller than my high school.

"You could, you know," Dagmar said softly. "I'd help you get started."

"Thanks, I'll keep that in mind. For now, I'm happy doing what I'm doing."

But, was I?

Sure, I was.

Dagmar stared thoughtfully at me, waiting for me to go on.

"I get to help my students," I said, trying to convince her of my satisfaction. "That's an honor. To make a difference in their lives."

"So, who are you helping now?" Dagmar said.

I filled her in on the case building against my student Lyle and his connection to Francesca, the dead co-ed in the news. I told her about Lyle's accident and how he'd gone missing from the hospital. I had to find him before something worse happened to him. "Apparently, Lyle was volunteering with you guys, because Francesca was, also, and I wondered if you remember either of them. Or if you've seen Lyle."

Dagmar frowned for a while, peering into her nearly empty cup, as if her answer might lie in the residue of foam. Finally, she shook her head. "Not me. I can't recall them. But we volunteers don't always get to interact with everyone. Sometimes a volunteer is just focused on one particular project, and then moves on."

I described Francesca's red hair and her alleged fondness for pink. "Maybe she called herself Fanny?"

"Fanny?" Dagmar lifted from her cup study. "Sure, I know Fanny. But surely you don't mean..." Her face paled. "That young woman who died on the Flatiron was our *Fanny*?"

I sighed. "It looks that way."

"Oh my gosh."

"I'm so sorry," I said, giving her some minutes of sympathetic silence to process the bad news. Then I went on. "What do you know about her? And about her friends?" *Lyle, in particular.*

"I don't think she had many friends. Not like our girls, Bri

207

and Terra, have. I always felt kind of sorry for her in that respect. She seemed so aloof, as if she was above everyone else."

"Sounds like she didn't win any popularity contests. But what about boyfriends?"

"I wouldn't know about that." Dagmar mopped up a dribble with a napkin and muttered under her breath. She glanced at her watch again, then at her satchel resting against the wooden leg of her chair.

"The gossip among my students," I said, "is that Lyle was crazy about her. Her death seems to have made him freak out. I understand he was hanging out with some of your volunteers."

"Now that you mention it, there was one young man who seemed to admire her in spite of her lack of reciprocation. I'm certain he wasn't a martial artist, though. He's too quiet and awkward."

"Short and skinny?" I said. "Thick glasses and spiky black hair?"

Dagmar nodded. "That sounds like him."

"That's Lyle."

"Oh." Dagmar fell silent, as if thinking about it. Then she shrugged and went on. "Anyway, Fanny couldn't allow herself to just let go. I remember one time at an open house not long ago, they put her on clean-up duty, and she suddenly remembered that she had to be somewhere else. She walked out, leaving the other volunteers to rearrange their schedules to take up the slack. Your Lyle is the one who filled in for her."

"Did Fanny ever find out what Lyle had done for her to help her out?"

"I have no idea. Besides, she probably couldn't have cared less." Dagmar reached down and grasped her satchel. "I'm late.

I've got to go. Like I said, they're not *my* volunteers. We don't always intersect. Every once in a while there's an occasion. For instance, last week. Some bigwig catered a picnic party for a select group of volunteers. I couldn't go, not that I wanted to. But I was kind of curious about his house. It's one of those McMansions next to greenbelt, y'know? That's not where the party actually was, but that's where they started from. The volunteers got to help lug stuff up to the shelter house nearby on one of the trails. That's where the party was supposed to be."

"Do you think Francesca — I mean, Fanny — went to the party?"

"Who knows?" Dagmar shrugged.

"Who *would* know? Who could I ask?"

"Why don't you ask the guy who threw the party?"

"Good idea. Where can I find him?"

She described where his palatial house was located, and I realized that it was on the fancy side of the street just up the hill and around the corner from Hamilton Yeager's, where Lyle rented a room.

Which made his party site very accessible to the trail above the Flatiron. Where Francesca had died.

"And the name of the guy?" I said.

"Jimmie Condo."

I sputtered, choking on my coffee, as she swung away through the crowd of coffee drinkers.

* * * * *

I limped back to the studio, thinking all the way about this Condo character. He wasn't just satisfied with buying my dad's farm. Now he wanted to acquire Callahan's property. Which would put me out of a job. Did he carry a personal vendetta against me? He seemed to lurk behind every bush I passed. I somewhat believed in six degrees of separation, but really. This guy hung out at each degree. He was probably a witness to Francesca's fall.

If Francesca had been at Condo's party, then I bet Lyle had, also. I wondered if the party had been Monday night, and if it had been the cause of the reported ruckus the night before my students and I found Francesca's body. The night of the illegal campers.

Maybe that's where Lyle was hiding now. Up in the mountains.

I only had a couple hours or so free until drop-dead time, when I had to go back on duty, accompanying a group of my students on their training run. Not enough time for a mountain trip, but enough time to track down Lyle at the university, as long as I had some inside help.

Gillian.

My soon-to-be ex-sister-in-law was officially in some sort of business degree program, drawn to this particular university by Max's pull, so that she could follow in her half-brother's footsteps. I didn't know much more about it than that, because whenever I probed for specific information, she became evasive, so I dropped it. What I *did* know and respect was Gillian's ability to pull strings, call in chits, or what have you. When I needed to know something or get somewhere, I always called Gillian first.

She agreed to meet me on campus in thirty minutes.

Assuming Lyle hadn't skipped town, then the place that funded his rent money would surely have an idea of his whereabouts. I had to find him before the hit-and-run driver found him first, which might turn out to be the last time.

My quest for Lyle had become more than just a matter of clearing his name from the Dentons' scorecard. The future of the karate studio was at stake if I couldn't mollify the Dentons. And somehow, their determination to blame him seemed fueled by Jimmie Condo's desire to acquire my dad's farm. And now the karate studio itself. It had become personal for me. How Abby the roommate fit into all this, I didn't know, but I felt as if we'd known each other her entire life. We were two peas of a pod.

Five minutes early, I found the sandstone building where I was to meet Gillian. I marched up the steps, through the double doors, and wandered down the hall until I saw bulletin boards flanking an open door. People milled inside with coffee cups and computers, giving it a more administrative look than whatever they do in science labs to solve the mysteries of the universe. Me, I just wanted to solve the mystery of the dead coed in my corner of my little world.

No one paid attention to me. They kept on sipping their coffee and yakking about their exploits of the weekend. But then, I was only standing in the doorway, looking in, hesitant to cross the wrong threshold.

Footsteps clattered up behind me from the hall.

"Nell! Here you are," said Jill in her breathless, chastising voice that echoed, booming down the hall.

I grabbed her by the arm and pulled her to a stop next to the drinking fountain. "Thanks for coming," I said in a steady, soothing voice, willing my calming powers into her so that she would lower her voice. I was working on my Master Hwang impersonation, and I had a long way to go. But it almost worked.

Gillian lowered her voice. "You know *I* always answer a request for help."

Meaning that I hadn't. "Look, I already said I was sorry about last weekend, but something really important came up."

Her wide lips settled into a pink pout. "Well, in that case, we'll go this coming weekend. Now, what's this new emergency all about?"

"One of my karate students is also a grad student here at the university, and I need to find out where his lab is located on campus."

She tilted her head sideways, an indication of her interest, while I gave her Lyle's name and a hunked-up description of him. She was always interested in a male subject. I could save her the trouble if I told her that Lyle was definitely not her hunkish type, but I would withhold that information until after she delivered.

"Let's go find out," she said, swinging away from my grip and into the office. I followed in her wake. Her entrance instantly charged the room with her energy, and the coffee drinkers' chatter cut off in mid-sentence. They looked up at us, or rather, at Gillian, who mesmerized them. I didn't know how she did that.

"Good morning, ladies," she sang to them.

They hung on her words as she identified herself from a lesser performing department than theirs and congratulated them on their fine achievements, setting them up for a plea for a tiny favor, the whereabouts of Lyle Sawhill.

One of the office women sat down at a computer and frowned at the monitor while typing furiously. This eventually led to an address that Gillian seemed to recognize. She flashed them her broad smile, and we were off on the next stage of my hunt.

The lab, when we found it, smelled of chemicals and hummed like my mother's kitchen wall clock, an antique she'd acquired from the '50's. Apparently, some experiment was percolating. The back sides of three white-coated people presented themselves to Gillian and me at the open door.

"Excuse me?" I said, calling from the doorway.

Gillian strode inside, as if she had every reason to be here. Maybe they expected her, their new lunch date for the day. They didn't know? Too bad, their loss.

A young woman wearing safety glasses stood up from her stance, bent over her work at a long table holding equipment I had no idea what the pieces were. Her two colleagues ignored us. They even ignored Jill. "Wassup?" the young woman asked.

"We're looking for Lyle," I said. "Have you seen him? I understand he works here."

"Yeah, when he feels like it," the woman said, and she returned to her work at the table.

"Haven't you seen him recently?" I waited for one of the white coats to tell me about Lyle's hit-and-run accident, but they didn't seem to know about it.

"Not in something like a week," the woman said.

"A week? Don't you wonder why he's away that long?"

"Naw."

"Don't you need him for the work you do here?"

"He just gets in the way."

I tried again. "Isn't it unusual for him to stay away that long?"

She shrugged. "Depends."

"On what?"

"If he's off his meds or not." All three white coats chuckled.

"Really?" Gillian said. "Look, Nell, you didn't say anything about that. You dragged me over here for someone on medication?"

"Because it's not true, Jill."

"Oh, it's true enough," said the young woman. "What do you want him for? Did he violate his probation?"

"He's not on probation, either," I said, sounding more convinced than I felt.

"Too bad," said the woman with a frown. "The cops were here looking for him, too."

I shouldn't have felt surprised, but I did feel a bit dismayed. I always seemed to stay a step or two behind the police. Because the police were looking for him was probably the reason he was in hiding. How on earth was I going to find him now? What did I really know about Lyle?

"Hey, lighten up," said the woman. "It was just a joke. He's a nerd, but I don't think it's as bad as that."

That was a relief. Or was it?

I tried to get the conversation back on track. "Seriously, though, do you know where he went or why he's been away this long?"

"He said something about going camping," said one of the bent-over workers, a young man. "Remember?"

"Why would I remember that?" said the woman. "Who do you think I am? His personal assistant? Give me a break."

"So he's gone camping?" I said. "Isn't this a bit early in the season?" They were predicting a spring storm coming in, and the way temperatures had been falling, it could be snow, especially up in the high country. Where else did one camp? I hoped that wherever he went camping, if indeed that's where he was, it was in a legal campsite, and not, say, in Boulder's open space.

"Not if you're stupid."

"Lyle seems pretty smart."

"He's no rocket scientist," said one of the white coats, and the other two chortled.

"Aside from all that," I said, trying to recover control of the conversation, "how can he leave school now? Aren't finals coming up? Shouldn't he be doing something, like studying? Or at least grading papers for the professor he works for?"

"Naw. The professor he works with lost his grant this semester, so Lyle doesn't have any recitations or labs to lead at the moment. He's just doing an independent study this semester, and it's left him pretty much at loose ends. You ask me, he's gone off the deep end as a result of the grant going down."

"Did he say where he was going camping?"

"He never talks to us. You ought to ask that gal he hangs with over in Doctor Simon's lab. She probably knows."

"Unless she's gone with him."

"In his dreams."

"Yeah, that's about as far as it gets for him. Brilliant dude, with the social skills of a middle schooler."

"Doctor Simon?" I said, jumping into their back-and-forth. "Is that his thesis advisor?"

The white coats chuckled again. "Hell no, it's the snake lab."

I felt my blood pressure sky rocket. "What's he doing in a

snake lab? Isn't he an astronomy student?"

"Astrogeophysics," said one of the men.

"Simon's lab is where *she* works," the woman said.

My heart beat sped up, as my old aversion to snakes returned, along with the memory of Lyle's gun. I couldn't help it, not even with Master Hwang's mental calming exercises.

SEVENTEEN

The snakes would have to wait. My free time was running out fast. I made it back to the studio a few minutes before my student helper of the day, Jason, showed up. He was taking Buster's place this week as organizer of the group training run, and I had to approve his planned route. Hopefully, it would be less eventful than last week's.

While I looked it over, I gave him the task of assembling a make-shift tracking system now that the cops had confiscated my files. Losing those file boxes, even if temporary, added a new kink to the paper mess my crooked predecessor had left me with. I was becoming quite the expert at cleaning up other people's messes.

Not so good at my own. I needed something temporary fast, and Jason probably knew his classmates better than I did.

"What about Fanny?" said Jason, standing at the counter where he'd spread out the remains of what the cops had left us from my predecessor's paper mess. He waved a mangled green card at me.

"What about her?" I took the card from him and untwisted it. "Where'd you find this?"

"At the back of the knife drawer. That's why your drawer wouldn't close all the way. Look at this. Here's your proof that she was here."

I smoothed the card against the chrome rim of the kitchen table. It was a five by seven attendance card. "Dent, Fanny" – Francesca's public name — was written across the top in big black letters, thick from a marker, and slanted in a handwriting that I'd come to recognize as my predecessor's. The color of the card indicated that she was a green belt student here at Callahan's Karate. In our ranking system, green meant she was an advanced beginner, transitioning to intermediate.

I wondered if this card was what the cops had been looking for when they carried away my file boxes. I studied the haphazard pattern of only a handful of checkmarks and then turned it over to see if there was a secret message written on the back. There wasn't. For the life of me, I couldn't figure out why this card would've mattered enough to require a search warrant.

We used a system of attendance cards that some would call antiquated. We were low-end techie, which suited me just fine. Maybe that's another reason why Callahan chose me to replace mess-boy. Who knows? That's another story.

The system was simple, really. Each card represented a student. Each time a student arrived for class, he or she would take his or her attendance card from the box and then hand it to the instructor when bowing in for class. After class, I or my assistant of the day would record the student's attendance with a checkmark on the card and replace it in the box for the next time that student returned. We recommended three classes per week. With this system, I could see at a glance of the card how many classes each student had attended. When the card filled up with checkmarks, it was time for that student's next belt test.

Francesca's pitiful attendance record showed that she was

dedication-challenged. Not good considering her rank.

A sophisticated system such as ours required a separate box of registration cards for each student. Students never saw that box. Inside that one, the registration cards should be alphabetized, and the entire box kept in the office. Registration cards kept information about the students other than belt rank, things like their age, address, and contact information. That's what I'd assumed the cops wanted to see. But they'd taken the attendance cards, too.

Except for this mangled one of Francesca's that had been lost at the back of the drawer.

Deliberately placed there? Or just another result of mess-boy, my predecessor?

When I'd taken over this job, both sets of cards were misplaced, mis-filed, and didn't match up. I'd taken the office apart, all the way down to its old-house kitchen original purpose, but I had never turned up a registration card for Francesca. There was no record of who she was, how to contact her, or if she'd ever existed.

But I could guess. I had a pretty good idea that she was another of my womanizing predecessor's harem. Once he'd left, she would've had no more reason to keep coming to class. Was that really why she'd switched to Kim's Karate? Not because of her fight with frat-boy Innis at all. Without a registration card, she'd probably never paid a dime into the school, regardless of the check Aunt Cybil claimed to have written. Lack of payment was the official reason why my boss wanted to kick out my predecessor and replace him with me. My job was to stop losing money for him.

"From this," I said, adding Francesca's card to my

replacement stack of five by sevens, "it looks like the last time Fanny came to class was in February." When mess-boy was still the instructor here. "You were here then. Did you know her?"

"I wish." Jason muttered under his breath, and his neck flamed red. He looked away, flipping his golden boy bangs. "I mean, she was in college. She wouldn't have anything to do with us high school kids. I can't wait till I can graduate and get out of here."

"Did you ever take a mixed level class with Francesca?" I asked. "I mean, Fanny. What was she like?"

"Hot."

"You mean, she was good at karate?"

He laughed. "No, I mean 'hot', as in hot chick."

"O-oh. I get it." I could imagine Terra rolling her eyes at me. "So you had a crush on her?" As Terra had a crush on Jason. But Jason mooned over Francesca, and maybe that's why he never reciprocated Terra's attention. Funny, how these little romances settled into unrequited triangles.

He snorted and bent down to peer farther into a cabinet. "Of course not. Why waste my time?"

"Right." Gently, I steered him to one side. "I'll take over here. Why don't you check off the new cards and figure out who we're missing?" I turned my back on him, giving him space from his obvious discomfort. I could only pry so far.

I would have to add this to Dad's repair list. Maybe he could make adjustments so that these cabinet doors would close better. I probed around inside one of the cabinets. My fingers nudged something along the base that felt like a loose tile. A bell rattled as I moved the tile, and I jerked my hand back. I should know better than to reach into dark spaces.

I unsnapped a flashlight from its charging station on the wall and shone its light into the cabinet. Sparkles reflected off a jingle bell inside a caged ball. I laughed and reached in to grab a handful of Sammy's loot. "That ferret," I said. "She's always stealing shiny stuff and hiding it somewhere. Apparently I've found one of the places she likes to stash her treasure."

I opened my palm and examined the loot. Besides her ball, there were two paperclips, the pink crystal bead she'd found outside under my car, and a shiny, silver button. Like the buttons I'd seen on Phyllis Eberhardt's jacket.

Just then, the front door opened and then banged shut. Glass rattled. It was too soon for students to arrive for our training run. There was always the off-chance that it was a robber with an eye on my stereo out front, not so high-tech, but valued for its increasing rareness. Even Boulder had occasional crime. Although, if the door slammer was a thief, then he was the world's stupidest by announcing himself. Still, you can never be too prepared. I laid Sammy's treasures on the counter and positioned myself on the balls of my feet where I could see part-way down the hall that led into the workout space.

"Yoo-hoo?" called a woman's voice with a lilt that I recognized.

I tiptoed farther down the hall until I saw her. Jasmine. The lady who'd lost her snake. I recognized her sassy black curls and pert smile. Her emerald eyes gleamed, lighting up the place. She stood in front of the empty folding chairs lined up in the bay window and reserved for the parent observers.

"Welcome," I said to her. "May I help you?"

"Where is everyone?" she said, wiggling her derriere as she switched her weight from one foot to another.

"Our first class of the day won't start for a couple more hours, but a few students should be arriving soon for an extracurricular exercise."

"Oh, honey, I just come for that free class you said I could have." She flicked her pink fingernails at me. A bracelet of matching pink crystals jangled from her wrist. "I hope it ain't gonna ruin my manicure."

"No worries." My gaze fixed on the color of her beads. "We start you off slow in your first complimentary class. But before that, we need to make an appointment for your one-on-one introduction."

Her face fell. "Oh. Well, see, I'd sorta' hoped I could do it now. I just don't know when I could ever come back. I got to pick up my honey in a few minutes."

"Maybe I could squeeze you in," I said with a laugh. I was afraid that if I let her go now, I'd never see her again. We never turned away potential students. The key was to hook them on the free lesson, to make it tailor-suited for each individual in such a way to convince them how much fun karate could be.

"That'd be super," she said, jingling.

"Let me get you a sheet of information to fill out before we get started. Please have a seat." I waved at the folding chairs behind her and grabbed a clipboard with enrollment information that I kept handy in a box beside the shoe rack.

I couldn't take my eyes off her bracelet while Jasmine filled out the basic information. I wasn't sure how anyone could write with those cut pieces of glass or maybe rocks hanging off her wrist. They looked like the same crystals on Francesca's necklace. Rose quartz, Abby had called them. Samurai Q. Ferret had found one just like Jasmine's, glittering outside the studio, where the peeping tom had passed through.

I watched Jasmine pause over the blank spaces and then scribble in her information. Maybe I couldn't read it right upside down, but it looked like she had an address where she was living and even a job. She moved fast for just having arrived in town little more than a week ago. Maybe I'd misunderstood when I spoke to her on the trail above the Flatiron. Hadn't she said her boyfriend was finding them a place to live? The backpack she'd tried to hide under a bush suggested she didn't have a place to stay yet.

When she was done writing, I took the clipboard and glanced at it briefly while she removed her shoes and stowed them in the shoe rack. She'd listed her place of employment as the university. Her address was a Boulder street I didn't know offhand.

The trick to these introductory sessions was to make them as fun as possible, along with a useful tip to show the potential student how beneficial enrollment in this studio could be. Most important, we had to accomplish all of that fast, before the prospect's attention had a chance to waver. I went through the front punch demo, straight in and straight out, and then let her try it a few times. Her bracelet jingled, and she giggled.

Jason emerged from the kitchen office holding a stack of attendance cards for today's classes. He glanced over at us several times as he went about his business, filing the cards into the appropriate slots.

I showed Jasmine the front kick, snap it out and back, and then let her try. Not bad. She moved as if she knew what she was doing. As if she'd had some experience kicking. Kicking people?

Jason finished filing, and then he bowed onto the floor and sat down on the carpet to stretch out. Bending over his quads, he kept peeking up at Jasmine. She glowed, as if she could sense the attention. And thrived under it.

I finished up the quick intro with her and handed her a schedule to show her which classes she could attend for free. The point being, to commit the potential student to a convenient time to return.

She was getting impatient. "Oh, dear, I'm late," she said, noticing the wall clock. "Sorry, I got to run." She grabbed her shoes, snatched the schedule out of my hands, and darted out the door.

"No problem," I said to the rattling glass in the front door. I scooted around to the bay window and watched her run down the street to a blue car splattered with mud. As she maneuvered it out into the street, I noticed the Colorado license plates along with red tape covering up a broken taillight.

If that was Jasmine's car, then she must've been in town longer than a week, as she claimed. It wasn't likely she'd have our plates this fast. And I wondered, when I saw that red tape, if she'd lost a crystal from her bracelet on the night of the peeping tom.

Jason came to stand beside me and watch her drive away. "So he finally talked her into signing up for karate?"

"Who?"

"Lyle. She's been hanging around him for a while."

"You must be thinking of someone else. Jasmine only moved to town a week or so ago."

"Nope. Who can forget someone like her? She was around here back when Mr. Valencia was still the instructor."

Crawlies tickled my spine. Okay, Jasmine had lied. I'd already known that, hadn't I? I wondered what else she had lied about to me. If she was indeed the other woman in Lyle's life, I wondered if he'd jilted Jasmine for Francesca. How angry would that make her? Angry enough to kill Francesca, and then to frame Lyle for it?

EIGHTEEN

Next morning, I found Doctor Simon's lab. That is, I found the building on campus where the snake lab was housed, down in the bowels of the basement. Except, when I got to the door off the stairwell that would've led to that subzero level, a big sign was taped to the door saying "Danger! No Admittance." I tested the latch. It wasn't locked, so I pushed the door open and poked my head in.

The smell hit me first, a cloud of foul air barreling past my head. Sheesh. Didn't anyone clean around here? The hall looked sterile with highly buffed floors that reflected anything that walked. Looks were deceiving, because the place reeked like Sammy's ferret condo during finals week, when Terra didn't get around to cleaning it.

No one awaited me on the other side of the door, banning me from the floor, so I pinched my nose and stepped inside, onto the slicked, shiny surface. I caught whiffs of chemicals, combined with the odor of ungroomed animals and their fecal matter. Snake shit, in other words. With my eye on the floor, I tiptoed along the hallway, looking for the number above the door that would indicate Simon's lab, from what I'd been told.

I found it.

Two white-coated people knelt on the floor in the zoo smells, looking inside cupboards. Not a good sign.

"Hello?" I said.

They tumbled backwards in unison, landing on their glutes. The woman frowned up at me, revealing the stains that dotted the front of her rumpled lab coat. Her dishwater blonde hair hung askew from one giant clamp on the top of her head. "Holy crap!" she said. "Who are you? And how did you get in?"

"I walked in," I said.

"You're not supposed to be here. This place is off limits. Didn't you see the sign?"

"Sure, I saw it. You should've thought of locking the door if you really didn't want anyone to enter."

"Fire hazard. Besides, we thought the sign would be good enough to keep people out. What the hell do you want?" She dusted off her hands and stood up, then offered a helping hand to her chubby partner.

"I'm looking for Lyle Sawhill. Have you seen him? I hear he spends some time down here."

"Yeah, he's my roommate," the woman said, "and he's in big trouble when I get my hands on him."

Roommate? Or housemate, as Ham was clear to point out. There was a third housemate, too, Ham had said. He'd called her Chandra. This woman must be her.

"Why is Lyle in trouble?" I asked. "What's he done?" Besides getting accused of the death of the woman he admired, and then running away after nearly getting himself killed? What else could go wrong for him?

"He broke in here and let the snakes loose. That's why they don't want the public wandering around down here. It's for your own safety."

Oh good. I had a knack for ending up places I wasn't supposed to be.

Just then someone's cell phone rang. The woman roommate fished into one of her deep pockets and pulled out a phone. "Hang on," she said with a frown. "It's Lyle."

She held it up to her ear and said, "Hey." If looks could kill. She stared up at the ceiling, where pipes zigzagged across, and wandered out into the hall.

"Let me talk to him when you're done, please," I said as she walked away. But either she didn't hear me or she ignored me. Every once in a while I heard punctuations of her anger exploding out in the hall.

"You WHAT?" she said, and then moved farther away, apparently looking for a sweet spot of reception.

Meanwhile, it was me and the other white coat, staring at each other in a smelly room with snakes on the loose. He gave me a suspicious, wary, half-lidded look, as if he thought I was somehow to blame for setting the snakes loose.

"Soooo..." I said, letting out a big breath of frustration, "when did this happen? The break-in, I mean?"

"Last week. But don't worry. We've rounded up all of the snakes so far, except for one. He's probably hiding out somewhere on the floor, scared to death. Feasting on the mice from one of the other labs, I'll bet. We'll find him sooner or later."

I glanced up at the pipes above my head. Could he — I mean "it" — be hiding up there, waiting to drop onto my head? A chill rippled down my spine. Vertigo, from looking up.

"Why do you think it was Lyle who broke in and set the snakes loose?" I remembered how he'd aimed with his gun at the snake on the trail and figured he didn't love snakes anymore than I did. Breaking into a snake lab and setting the snakes loose just didn't sound like something he'd do.

"That's what Chandra says." He shrugged. "Me, I wouldn't know. Ask her." He nodded at the hall, where bits and pieces of her voice mumbled through the door, and then he eased himself back down onto his hands and knees. His moved in slow motion, as if his mobility was limited by his plumpness and his patent leather shoes. He reached into a cupboard and slid containers around.

Great. I heard buzzing all around me. Either it was my inner ear, my imagination, or the loose snake. I really wanted out of there.

Chandra finally breezed back into the lab. Her scowl was gone, but she didn't look happy. She wore a satisfied look on her face, as if she'd successfully terminated a pest. "I just know he's in here," she said to her partner, waltzing past me as if I didn't exist. I'd gotten a lot of that here on this campus.

"Lyle?" I said.

She shot me a look that read, "Who are you again?"

I introduced myself. "Did Lyle tell you where he is? Is he okay? I understand he was in an accident, but he left the hospital before I could get a chance to visit him there."

"Yeah, that drunk messed him up bad. He had to get out of the hospital so he could get over to his Chinese doctor and get stuck by a bunch of needles. He's being a porcupine today."

"Acupuncture?" I said. "But he has a bullet wound."

Chandra brushed off my concern. "The bullet just grazed him a bit. Besides, I doubt they'll poke him there."

It didn't add up. "Isn't acupuncture kind of expensive? They told me over in his lab that he'd been laid off this semester." I wondered how he had extra funds for a procedure like that.

Chandra shrugged. "I don't think money is a problem for him."

Ah. Another Boulderite living off his trust fund. I'd had no idea. He'd never dressed in designer jeans or anything fancier than holy jeans and a tee shirt. "Did he say how he's doing? Did the acupuncture help him?"

Chandra snorted and fell down on her hands and knees beside her partner. "Not great enough that he feels like he can haul his telescope out tonight for stargazing. I have to do it for him. And he only ever wants to go out at two a.m."

"No wonder he keeps off hours," I said, watching the two of them poke around inside cupboards. "Why are you so sure it was Lyle who broke in here last week?"

"Because I saw him," Chandra said, leaning back to peer up at me.

"But why would he do such mischief? It just doesn't sound like him."

"You're right. It doesn't. He must've been high on something. Or hypnotized, maybe. Anyway, I was alone in the lab. Darren was supposed to be here." She nodded her head at her partner. "So was Simon. Actually, I thought he was somewhere around. I had to go to the bathroom, and it wouldn't wait. Something I ate the night before, I guess. It was no big deal to leave the lab unattended for a few minutes. So I came out of the bathroom and caught sight of Lyle's back side as he was heading out. I yelled at him that I was here, in case he'd been looking for me, but he didn't stop, just kept running up the stairs. He wouldn't turn around or say anything, and I thought that was odd of him.

Oh well. He can be strange sometimes. I went back into the lab, and all the cages were empty. Then I saw a few of the snakes, slithering away on the floor, hurrying to hiding places. Who else could've done it but Lyle?"

Who else, indeed. But it didn't make sense. He'd stolen a snake, even though he hated snakes, to plant on the trail where he could shoot at it. But what on earth did he hope to accomplish by that? Had he just wanted to frighten us? *Why?*

* * * * *

I was jogging back to the studio when my cell phone beeped. I broke stride long enough to slip the phone out of my pocket, and then I stopped dead in my tracks when it identified the caller.

Dad. Dad never called this number. If I was a Luddite, he was a dinosaur.

"Hi Dad, what's up?" I said into the phone.

"Nellie? You okay? You're breathing heavy. What's wrong?"

"Nothing wrong with me, Dad. I've been running, that's all."

"Sure you have, but the question is why have you been running?" He was shouting at me, telling me that he couldn't hear well. Voices in his background were shouting, too, so maybe he was trying to raise his voice to be heard over theirs.

"What's going on?" I shouted back. My heart pounded with alarm. "Who are those people you're with?"

"Some volunteer firefighters is all. You know, there's some of 'em who live down the road from me. They saw the blaze first."

"What blaze, Dad?" My heart skipped a beat, and I held my breath.

"It's okay, calm down. They've got it under control. I just thought you'd want to know."

I *do* want to know, I thought, gritting my teeth. "I'm on my way," I said instead and sprinted the last few blocks.

The only thing that kept me from driving like a crazy person across town and out to the periphery, where the town was spreading east into what used to be open countryside, was the knowledge that Dad had had enough of his wits about him to make the call. When I hadn't answered my house phone, he must've thought to phone The Other Number. Terra had trained me to always make myself available by keeping the cell on me, and I figured "why not?" No one else but family had my cell number, so who else would call? Then Terra had worked on Gramps to convince him that my cell number was one that would always reach me, so why bother to call the landline? In fact, why bother to have a landline? Because she was dealing with dinosaurs, that's why.

I tried not to hyperventilate as I fought with all the suburban drivers that the sprawl into the countryside had spawned. How much of the farm where I'd grown up had been consumed by fire?

It turned out to be the tool shed that was hardly ever used anymore. Mother had used it for the orchard and her garden, mostly. Now, Dad hardly ever touched it. Still, the fire could've spread to other buildings, to the barn where Cinnamon our horse lived, and from there to the farmhouse. It was too close for comfort.

It was too early to determine the cause of the fire, but I could already leap to the conclusion that someone had set it. We'd had no nasty weather with lightning that would've touched it off. There were no chemicals or wiring anywhere near the tool shed that could've triggered an accidental spark. Nothing could've gone wrong, not on its own, not without someone's intervention. Someone had deliberately started the fire. But that someone hadn't wanted to hurt anyone. Maybe just scare us. Or warn us into cooperating.

Jimmie Condo?

Who else had any sort of agenda with my dad?

I stayed with Dad as long as I could, until my drop-dead time to return to the studio and earn my salary. Dad seemed all right, but I didn't like his being out there by himself overnight. I tried to talk him into coming back into town with me, spending the night at my place. I'd feel better that way. He just hooted at me, said he wasn't alone at the farm. Cinnamon was there with him. But, he said, that old nag was far too old to watch over things. That's why *he* needed to stay. No one else could do a better job there than Dad.

Reluctantly, I left him. But I made him promise that he would check in with me personally before he went to bed for the night.

NINETEEN

Storm clouds loomed all the way back into town. They were promising us a late spring snow. Just what I wanted to do in the morning: shovel more snow. At least the storm would squelch any lingering hot embers in the remains of Dad's shed.

All through classes, I kept thinking and worrying about Dad. I couldn't leave him out there alone. What if the person who'd set the fire came back later tonight? I wasn't satisfied with his promise of a phone call, but I didn't realize what I had to do until my last class bowed out for the night.

Terra came with me this time as we headed out to Dad's place. Hopefully, we'd catch him before his bedtime. He was already dressed in his terrycloth bathrobe. I tried again to persuade him, face to face, but I still couldn't talk him into moving in with me while his shed was repaired. He'd had a good life, he informed me, as if he expected not to wake up in the morning. He wouldn't even agree to stay overnight at my place. Stubborn old man. I suspected that he was eagerly awaiting the opportunity to confront his adversary in the middle of the night.

Well, fine.

I roared out of his driveway one more time.

Spring snow was falling with a fury by the time we finally left the farmhouse, later than wisdom dictated for my teenager.

The roads were sloppy from the wet snow, not yet icy.

Funny, how you could get used to aggressive drivers. I hadn't noticed them so much before starting to teach my fifteen-year-old how to drive. After that, I noticed them everywhere. It seemed that everyone I met on the highway was someone whose business was far more urgent than mine. They got right up on my bumper, roared around me, always in a no-passing zone, and often times, they even shot me the bird as they went.

Anything less than road hostility was becoming the exception.

So I couldn't help but notice the pair of headlights we picked up just down the road from Dad's. What made the driver so noticeable was that this guy wasn't roaring up to my bumper like the rest of the world. He hung back at a respectful distance and remained there as we put miles between us and Dad's. I kept looking in the mirror, but he didn't close the gap. What was his problem? Driving carefully on account of the snow?

I turned west onto Valmont, the main highway into town, and so did he. Then the road curved, and momentarily he disappeared from my mirror. But farther on, I watched him speed up coming out of the bend, as if he was trying not to lose sight of me. Mind made up, I suddenly wheeled into one of the subdivisions near the jail.

"Mom, where're we going?"

Instead of answering Terra, I frowned at the rear-view mirror and watched the headlights turn, too.

My daughter twisted around in the passenger seat to stare out the back window. "Is that car following us?"

"Let's find out."

The Ghia fish-tailed into the quiet neighborhood as I

236

tried to remember its boomerang-shaped layout. Terra had some friends who lived here. Many of the streets were dead ends. I didn't want to get stuck in one of those with a stranger shadowing us.

"The school teacher," I snapped. "Where does she live?"

"Huh?"

"You know. Your friend whose mother is a school teacher."

"Well, there's Bri, Hilary, Marissa —"

"The one who had the Halloween party."

"Oh, you mean Kelsey!"

"Where do I turn to get to her house?"

Terra leaned forward and scrutinized the dark street dotted with pools of light. Silent dollops of snow streamed past street lamps. "You missed it," she said. "Why do you want to go there? Oh, I get it." She glanced over her shoulder at the headlights following us. "You're going to call the police, 'cause you forgot to bring your cell phone, right?"

I thumped my frustration on the steering wheel as we sloshed past the indicated street.

"There's another way to Kelsey's house," Terra said. "You can turn somewhere up ahead."

I brightened as I approached the next corner. "Here?"

"Yes. No. I don't know."

I'd already turned.

"I don't think this is it, Mom."

If I hadn't been certain before about being followed, I was now. Sure enough, those headlights had turned onto the street that wasn't Kelsey's. While maintaining a discreet distance, he'd matched each variation in speed, each random turn I'd made. Now I took advantage of the distance he allowed me, and I sped up. The street curved ahead. My tail disappeared behind me while I rounded the bend, then I spied a van sitting in someone's driveway. I spun the wheel hard and slid the Ghia into a space I created in the protective cover of the van. I turned off the engine, doused the lights, and took my foot off the brakes.

"Mom, this isn't Kelsey's house."

"Shhh." Did I expect our pursuer to be able to hear us? Vinyl squeaked as I turned in my seat to watch out the back window. Lightbeams bounced off the house across the street.

Terra squirmed for a better look. "Looks like one of those small wagons."

Her interest perked as my dread grew. All I saw was the broken taillight. I bit my lip and held my breath.

No sooner had the broken taillight vanished at the end of the street than I breathed again. I started up the Ghia, and keeping the lights off, I backed the car out of our hiding place. I scooted back the way we'd come. It wouldn't do to make a wrong turn now and come face to face with our shadow.

"Who would be following us, Mom?"

"I dunno." Too busy to pay attention to conversation, I monitored both the rear-view mirror and the pools of light ahead. Only street lamps illuminated the way for us.

"Have you been holding out on me? Are you in some kind of trouble again?"

"For God's sake, Terra, would you help me find my way out of this maze?"

"Turn there," she said, pointing.

"Are you sure?"

"Sure. Well, sorta."

It looked as good a place as any to turn, and since I didn't see anyone else around, I turned.

"Look!" Terra shouted, pointing straight ahead where Kelsey's neighborhood fronted the main highway. "There it is! That wagon!"

I slid to a stop behind the nearest parked car. Fortunately, I hadn't yet turned on the headlights. We sat there in dark silence watching as the low boxy shape of the vehicle materialized in front of us from a side street. Splashing through slushy snow, it headed for the corner, signaled, then turned onto Valmont. As it cruised under a street light its broken taillight winked at me. Apparently he'd given up on us, for he'd left the subdivision and was speeding away toward the highway to Denver. Suddenly, I pulled the Ghia away from the curb and stepped on the gas. "Let's see where he goes."

"What? Are you crazy?"

"Probably, but don't worry. He wasn't exactly keeping himself out of sight from us." My attention riveted on the set of lights ahead of us that belonged to our pursuer. Turning the tables on him, I navigated through the slop, matching his speed.

We followed the taillights all the way south, through town. But instead of turning onto the highway to Denver, he turned west. Toward the mountains. I dropped farther behind as the streets became more residential, where traffic was more sparse.

We made several more turns, and eventually I realized where we were. Lyle's neighborhood.

"There it is, Mom! The wagon! It's stopped, dead ahead!"

Across the street from Jimmie Condo's mansion. Where the red Lexus sat in the driveway.

I wheeled into the closest space curbside, under a pine tree, behind another parked car. Now what? Part of me wanted to march over there and confront the driver of the car with the broken taillight, the same car whose driver had spied on me at Callahan's, creeping me out.

But the mother in me remembered my daughter sitting beside me.

Now, I wasn't sure I wanted to know who my pursuer was, considering the recent turn of events in my life. Was he involved in Francesca's murder?

Was I sure I wanted to face him alone, in an empty, nighttime street, where I should be protecting my daughter instead of dropping her into the middle of a bad situation?

"Stay here!" I whispered. "And lock the doors behind me."

"Mom, you're not going out there!"

The rise in pitch in her voice almost made me change my mind. "If I'm not back in five minutes, go drive for help."

"Me?" she shrilled. "I don't have my license!"

"Don't worry, I'll bail you out." Before either of us could say another word, I slipped out of the car and into the shadows.

Shoot. Who did I think I was? Nancy Drew?

I slipped behind the trunk of the pine tree and pressed my nose against its scaly bark, catching a whiff of vanilla. I ducked behind parked cars and darted to a row of shrubs. Wet branches slapped ice particles in my face as I pushed through the shrubs, keeping well away from the street lights. I ran closer, until I could make out the figure of the driver, climbing out of the front seat and thumbing through her key ring. Jasmine.

Well. This put a new light on things. Jasmine marched up the sidewalk to Jimmie Condo's front door as if she owned the place. So much for her lies. She held out her key ring and inserted a key into the lock of the front door. It opened, and she disappeared inside, shutting the door behind her.

The image of Francesca's secret key flashed through my mind. Did it unlock this house? Jimmie Condo would have given it to Francesca, along with the roses. He might've given one to Jasmine as well, but I thought it more likely that Jasmine — my peeping tom — had broken into the studio to steal Francesca's key from my jeans pocket.

TWENTY

Saturday morning, the cloudless sky screamed blue, a shade so intense that it almost looked fake. By the time classes let out, the couple inches of snow we'd had overnight had evaporated like the magic show of springtime in the Rockies. I headed over to Dad's, just to make sure he was safe and the fire hadn't flared up in the night. Terra stayed behind in town, running some errands for her sleepover party, which would be that night, starting with pizza for dinner.

Nearing his place, I saw right away that Dad had a visitor. A white pick-up truck splattered with mud parked in front of the farmhouse and blocked the middle of the circular driveway. I pulled up next to it. The driver's side displayed the green shield logo of Boulder's Open Space. I climbed out of the Ghia and sucked in my customary lungful of country air. And inhaled the ashy smell of stale smoke.

The sound of voices led me around to the back of the farmhouse to the charred remains where the shed had stood up until yesterday. Dad was talking to a short and solid man dressed in the uniform of a ranger, and I startled, as if from a feint. I recognized him. Rock.

I crunched to a stop on the gravel. "What are you doing here?"

"Ah, here she is now," Dad said with a scowl, a signal to remind me of my absent manners. But he couldn't blame me after all we'd been through.

"Sorry, Dad. Were you looking for me? Is everything all right?"

"This fine young man will tell us, I'm sure."

Rock scuffed the toe of his boot along the edge of ash. "They were talking about your fire at headquarters. With the wind, and all, we wanted to make sure no stray ember spreads. Since I'm on my way out to one of the nearby trailheads, I thought I'd stop and check on things."

It sounded fishy to me. I wondered how much beer he'd consumed the night before. "Wasn't a crew of firefighters going to stay overnight and monitor things?" I asked.

"You just missed 'em, Nellie," Dad said. "But they'll be back. They drove off to patrol other perimeters as long as the ranger was going to be here. He's a volunteer firefighter, too."

"Is that a fact?" I said, giving him a cool assessment. "Have you seen Gillian recently?"

"Last night, in fact. She's the one who thought you'd be here just now. She also thought you'd want to know what I learned from my bud the cop."

"Detective Hennessey?"

"Right, Sean. He has a room at my house."

I nodded. "Go on. What'd he tell you?"

"Don't go spreading this around, you understand. I wouldn't want him to get in trouble. I wouldn't tell you except Jilly insisted."

If Gillian knew, it could be no secret.

"Okay. You can trust me."

"So the coroner's report finally came in on that Francesca Dent. Guess what she died of?"

"A broken neck?"

"Wrong."

"Internal injuries from her fall?"

"Wrong again." He folded his arms across his chest and grinned. "Snake venom."

* * * * *

I played it cool, refusing to give Rock any idea that his bombshell had blown me away.

I kept remembering the snake we'd seen on the trail, the one that Lyle had shot at. He hadn't stolen it from Simon's lab to plant on the trail to frighten us. Regardless of how the snake had come to be there, it was probably the same one that had killed Francesca. And all along, I thought we had a killer on the loose, a killer terrorizing my students.

It was a snake. There was no killer.

I got Dad settled, watched Rock drive away, and then climbed back into my car to return home for chaperone duty. I burst out laughing in the car, and I hooted all the way home.

The killer was a snake. Sure.

It wasn't funny, but I couldn't help myself. M*A*S*H humor. All along, I'd thought the killer was stalking Lyle and almost got him in that hit and run. And stalking me, too, in the form of a peeping tom.

I wiped my eyes as I pulled into my parking space off the alley. Still... Even if she'd died of venom — and that, truly, wasn't funny — something, or someone had made Francesca fall from the top of the cliff above the Flatiron. I didn't think a snake could do that. A snake might startle her into falling, but then, would it slither down the side of the Flatiron to catch up to where she'd hooked herself into the crevice and bite her fatally, that is, if she hadn't already died from her injuries?

No.

If the snake had bitten her *before* she fell, then she would've hiked out for medical help. Snake bites didn't have to be fatal. But even if she didn't head out for medical treatment, for whoever knew what reason, someone nudged her over the edge. Maybe that someone had been there while she was being bitten.

Jasmine, the woman who'd lost her snake? How deadly convenient.

But I was rushing to assumptions with only minimal information. I wasn't likely to get anymore than that. If I phoned the cops to pester them for more information, then Hennessey would get into trouble for having told Rock that much. Maybe it was better in the long run to keep that flow of information open.

I checked the ground beneath the car before I climbed out, just in case there were any errant snakes patrolling the studio. There weren't. But I remembered the pink crystal bead that Sammy had pulled out of the grass and stashed along with her other treasures in her hiding hole behind the kitchen cabinets.

Francesca's favorite necklace consisted of pink beads of rose quartz, according to her portrait and her roommate, Abby. It had gone missing. Was Sammy's bead from Francesca's missing necklace? Then, only a couple days ago, Jasmine showed up here for her free lesson, wearing a bracelet of pink crystal beads. A coincidence, probably, since Sammy had already stashed her single bead before Jasmine showed up with hers. But was it a coincidence that Jasmine's pet rattlesnake was also missing? Hmmm. Obviously, there was a connection. If only I knew what that connection was. Especially, considering that Jasmine's and Francesca's paths never intersected.

Or had they?

I didn't know, so I let myself into the studio and climbed the stairs to the apartment to set to work, baking a chocolate cake for the midnight snack for Terra and her friends. You could never go wrong with chocolate.

* * * * *

The girls started showing up. When Bri's mom, Dagmar, the history professor, dropped Bri off, she walked inside with Bri.

"I brought you something," she said, handing me a slip of paper. "It's a list of websites you can check out."

I studied the list of multiple w's and gave her a quizzical frown.

She explained. "You said that you were interested in our mining history, right? And that you'd like to learn more about it."

"Oh, right." In all my copious spare time, I would do that. Then there was the issue of actually using a computer. Technology was always a battle for me. My time would be better spent working out with my bo staff.

"Well, here's a starter for you," Dagmar said, stabbing the paper in my hands. "You'll probably have a late night, so here's something you can do while the girls are watching their movies."

"Okay, thanks." I smiled at her, and she scurried away.

The girls spread out their sleeping bags upstairs in our living room, arranged for best viewing of the television. The ferret sat in the center of her fan club, chittering with delight that so many of Terra's friends had come to dote on her.

I escaped downstairs to the empty workout floor and did a few turns with my bo staff, working out details to my form. Each time I executed a jab or an overhead strike, or a spinning chop, I couldn't help but think of imaginary opponents standing there, waiting to take the end of my stick. My techniques worked better, drove harder, if my imaginary targets were people with excessive doses of attitude who rubbed me the wrong way. Not that I would ever carry out my fantasies in real life. I used their images in my head as props and imagined them circling around me, attacking me. My fantasy opponents took on the shapes of people connected to Francesca. Some of them were even suspects in her death. I'd already knocked down most of them, back when Gillian helped me organize my theories.

But a few different possibilities lingered, and some of the ones I'd knocked down already, came back to haunt me.

I whirled around and faced an imaginary Phyllis, who had somehow managed to scramble back up to her feet, in spite of her pencil skirt and three-inch heels. All because I'd found the button from her jacket, hidden among Sammy's treasures. That meant she had been *here*, on these premises, where she'd lost her button for Sammy to collect. Why here? To spy on me? To take Francesca's secret key out of the pocket of my jeans that I'd left in my duffle bag that night someone had forced the studio door open? I jabbed with my bo, but imaginary Phyllis resisted with a side-step.

Shifting to the other side, I faced Jasmine, laughing and

bobbing her curls. She'd proven herself a liar, so maybe she did have a connection to Francesca that I knew nothing about. Or maybe I did know it but didn't know I knew it. Jasmine could be the jilted girlfriend of Francesca's rejected boyfriend — Lyle. Jason, my student helper, had seen Jasmine and Lyle together. Jasmine knew how to handle snakes, too, and not only had Francesca died of snake venom but also a deadly snake had gone missing from Lyle's roommate's snake lab. Had Jasmine stolen the snake to help her eliminate her obstacle to a relationship with boyfriend Lyle? Jasmine drove the car with the broken taillight. Jasmine had been here the night of the peeping tom, and again on the highways from Dad's farm. I swung my bo up and over my head to crash down on an imaginary Jasmine, but her ghostly image evaded my strike.

Standing in the shadows between the imaginary Phyllis and the imaginary Jasmine was an image of Jimmie Condo with a wide grin splitting his face and tilting his bow tie. I turned the opposite direction, and he stood there, too. An image of him stood in each corner of the room, laughing at me. I jabbed and jabbed, but I couldn't strike his image away. He'd sent flowers to Francesca, who'd thrown them away. He probably wasn't accustomed to rejection. He'd practically confessed outside my door that he'd been in a secret relationship with her, or else he'd pursued her but couldn't capture her heart. He was old enough to be her father. She wanted a father figure, but that's not what he wanted to be. If word got out about a relationship between them, his professional image would be tarnished, maybe ruined forever. Condo had given the party the night Francesca died. Innis had stolen her away from the party, but Abby the roommate said that Francesca didn't return her text messages for two days before that. Had Condo kept her locked away in his McMansion? Was that why Francesca allowed Innis to steal her from the party, so that she could finally escape?

Innis's tousled and bloodshot image staggered in and out of shadows, under the influence. If he couldn't have her, no one could. Was that enough reason to kill Francesca? He'd complained about Lyle. Was he the drunken driver who ran Lyle down that night? I jabbed, but he bounced away.

And then the shadows lifted, and all of my imaginary foes vanished. I stood in the center of the workout floor, panting, just me and my bo staff. I stretched my tired muscles and strained to hear sounds from upstairs. A murmur of television voices floated down the stairs along with footsteps.

Terra rounded the corner. "Mom, what are you doing?"

"Just working out a bit. And thinking about whose paths crossed with other paths."

"Huh?"

"If I find a connection, then I might figure out who's doing all the stuff that's going on."

"Like the fire at Gramps's?"

"That's one. What are you doing down here? Why aren't you upstairs with your friends?"

"I've already seen that movie a hundred times, and they're just like watching it. So I got bored and thought I'd...do something else." Her gaze flickered towards the kitchen office, although I could tell from the way she ducked her chin that she was trying to hide her wandering attention. The only thing of interest in the office was the computer.

"Terra! Don't tell me you use the computer without asking permission first."

"Okay."

"That's the office computer," I went on. "So, do you?"

Her chin shot up and her lower lip thrust out with defiance. "I wouldn't have to sneak around if I had my own computer. Aunt Jill says I should have one."

"Does she, now? How are you going to pay for one?"

"I have my own money."

"Which you use for your music lessons."

"Yeah, well, Aunt Jill says she could help me out, since you won't ever."

"Honey, I *am* helping you." Except, she didn't realize it yet. "You need to go back to your guests, whether or not you want to watch the movie. Go on, now, scoot."

Terra rolled her eyeballs at me and tromped back up the stairs.

I headed down the hall into the kitchen, flipped on the lights, and powered up Mr. Callahan's computer. I found the list that Dagmar, Bri's mom, had given me, and got to work. Long after I'd scrolled through pages and pages of information, I found it. A story about the origins of the Denton family's ancestor, the one who'd built the family's fortune from a silver mine. It seemed that there was a controversy about his claim. He'd claim-jumped the mine from another miner by the name of Eberhardt.

Eberhardt — any relation to Phyllis? — had died on site, trying to guard the claim that he ended up losing to Denton. He'd died after a rattlesnake bit him.

TWENTY-ONE

The coincidence of it all nagged me throughout the night.

When I finally slept, I dreamed of snakes. I was not sorry to awaken early the next morning as Terra's friends gathered up their sleeping bags and went home.

I was gulping my third cup of coffee when Gillian arrived to drag me away in her sporty Audi TT. Terra was off the hook, since she had to stay home and clean up from the party, but not me. I couldn't avoid my duty any longer. I had to accompany Jill on a family mission. She was the only one left in the family who was entrusted with such business, now that Max had gone missing. Since I was technically not out of the family yet, I got the honor of holding her hand. Never mind that it was my day off.

I decided to enjoy the scenery whizzing past. We headed west through neighborhoods of gingerbread houses, towards the mountains — where all the silver and gold mining had taken place in our state's history. Where Phyllis's possible ancestor had died of snake bite.

Soon Gillian and I left the city limits behind. Mountains soared up around us. Her Audi shifted into low gear to climb the forested slope.

"Why do you want to buy mountain property?" I asked, my head throbbing with images of miners, mines, and rattlesnakes.

"For the investment, silly. The family has investments all over the world, not just here. But we especially like to buy property in places where family members live. It's easier to keep an eye on things that way."

"And deal with troublesome renters?"

Gillian turned to look at me instead of the road. She lifted one eyebrow and said, "we don't always rent out our properties. We like to use the places ourselves and then flip them for a profit. I thought it'd be fun to have a getaway cabin. You and Terra could use it, too."

Now she was talking.

"So what are we seeing today?"

"There's a previewing of a house on Pine Nugget Lane. I managed to worm the information out of Van. I guess there are other nibbles on the property, so he wasn't going to bother telling me about this place. If he wasn't such a hunk, I'd find another realtor. No way am I going to miss out on a hot deal just because someone else gets there first."

The name of the place sounded familiar to me. Where had I heard that before? "And you wanted me to go along with you to beat up the other buyer? Or to be your muscle so that you don't have to be alone in the mountains with a stranger realtor?"

She took her eyes off the road again and shot me a scathing look. "Van is meeting us up there. And anyway, if I'd wanted a bodyguard, I would've found someone a little bigger than you. I know a few hunks, you know. Not only at the B school."

Meaning, she wasn't desperate.

And also meaning that her love life had branched out.

Again. "Tell me about him," I said.

"Who?"

She was a pro at playing innocent. "The new boyfriend."

Gillian swerved too close to the bend in the road, and we nearly plummeted over the edge, down into the tailings of one of the many old gold mines that pocked these hillsides as reminders of dreams that had gone bust. Here in the west, we'd been dealing with eastern prospectors, investors, and fortune hunters for most of our recorded history. The Gannons were no different. They were just the modern equivalent of a gold mining company.

"Hey, look out," I said. "Want me to drive?"

"Don't you wish. Daddy would kill me if I let just anyone touch this car."

Her knuckles gripped the leather-wrapped steering wheel, and now she steered the car too far left. Not that this dirt and gravel road had actual lanes. It was barely wide enough for one and a half car widths. Still, I kept my eyes on the dust cloud forming ahead, telling me that around the next bend a car was coming.

"Hey, Jill, relax. I'm just looking out for you. I want to make sure this guy measures up." Actually, I wanted to make sure that Rock wasn't the guy.

"Believe me, honey, *you're* the one who needs looking out for. That's why I thought you needed to get out of that little hovel where you've moved my niece to."

"Our apartment is not so little, and it's definitely not hovel-like. You yourself thought it was charming. That's what you said the first time you saw it. And cute, too."

"What I said was 'quaint.' That's different."

"Quaint is good. Quaint is character."

"Honey, when are you going to learn that not all character is adequate for my niece?"

It was clever of Gillian, the way she'd managed to distract me from the topic of *her* new boyfriend by bringing up Terra. Lord help the boy who ever tried to become Terra's boyfriend. Terra couldn't help being fifteen. We all had to go through it at one time in our lives. Bringing up my daughter would always distract me from whatever other subject was supposed to be under discussion.

"But back to my question, Jill, about your new boyfriend. Is it Rock?"

Woops, the car swerved again. That was too close. Okay, I was getting it. There must be something wrong with the new boyfriend.

"Okay, never mind. Tell me later." I decided to take my mind off my inquisitiveness by watching where we were going, since Gillian wasn't doing such a spectacular job of that. What was her mind on? No, never mind, I didn't want to go there, either.

The dust cloud was upon us. A dark blue car barreled around the bend ahead, and for the instant that it poised on the curve, it looked aimed for us, as if it intended to plow into us. It looked as if it had hit a few other cars in its history. Gillian swerved the TT far enough to the edge of the cliff that I only saw air beneath my door. We sat there, balancing, waiting to be hit broadside.

Sitting ducks, that's what we were.

"Damn!" Gillian said, and she swore a few other words, too, words that I'd wiped from my vocabulary back when I became a mother of a language-absorbing toddler.

Then the blue car, a Subaru wagon, slid past us with a hair to spare. I twisted around in my seat to watch it plummet on down the slope of the road that we'd just climbed. It braked before the next curve, and its right taillight shone through red tape.

"Jasmine!" I said. "She drives a car like that. What's she doing up here?"

Gillian shrilled. "Hit us! That's what she meant to do!"

"But why on earth would she be willing to sacrifice her own car just to hit ours?"

"Because it's a beater. She has nothing to lose."

"Only her life," I said. "The force of the collision could've pushed all of us over the cliff. We would've ended up down there." I pointed at the greater than forty-five degree slope that spilled away to at least three humps of yellow dirt, indicating tailings. Far away below was a creek. Not that I could see it. I knew it was there, hidden beneath the line of pines at the bottom of the canyon. The main road was down there, too.

There was no guard rail to keep a car from rolling over the embankment and plunging into the canyon far below. We would've rolled, end over end. The car would've been crushed like a can of pop. It would've been certain death for its occupants. Death for *us*.

Jasmine meant to kill us.

And I had begun to think the killer might be Phyllis.

I was doing it again, leaping to conclusions, just because Phyllis had anger management issues. And a possible ancestor who possibly gave her a motive for revenge against the Dentons. Silly me. It was Jasmine all along. Of course. Jasmine and her snake.

Gillian started up the car and pulled slowly, cautiously out into the road, away from the edge of the cliff. She checked the rear-view mirror at least a half dozen times as we continued ten miles out of town, almost straight up, around one switchback after another. She was either checking her lipstick or looking for the blue Subaru. Had it turned around and was now following us?

Gillian slowed the car when the road snaked around to the north side of the mountain. There were still unmelted snow drifts along the side of the road with occasional patches of ice in the shadiest dips in the road. Carefully, she maneuvered around the snow and ice. That's what I thought she was slowing for, when in reality, she came to a stop outside a driveway of two rutted lanes through a patch of snowy woods that led off the main road up another hill. A barbed wire fence lined the roadside, and where the rutted lanes intersected, there was a gate, hanging loosely open and decorated with a couple of deflated, orange balloons.

"Ten miles might be just a bit too far for a daily commute to town," Gillian said. "Know what I mean? I can't waste all that time on the road, and I can't afford to get snowed in. You can see how likely is that. This is May, for goodness sake, and we could seriously still get stuck here!"

"I noticed. You're not going up there, are you? Jill, you'll get stuck. I don't know about you, but I don't have all day to wait around in the middle of nowhere for a tow trip. I have laundry to do."

"No problem," she said. "There are fresh tire tracks, so other cars have made it. So can I." She turned the car into the two ruts and gunned it. We bounced uphill, splashing through puddles of melted snow, sliding a little to one side with each spurt of the car's power. Somehow, we crested the top of the hill, where it flattened into a meadow. The grasses were greening up with little spots of color where the first wildflowers burst through as snow retreated. At the end of a long driveway stood a rustic cabin. Not run down, but made of logs. The real thing when it came to rustic.

Except for the red sedan parked in front. That shining piece of modern machinery took away from the cabin's rustic image. It was a Lexus, and fire-engine red. Like the car Jimmie Condo had parked in my space in the alley behind the studio.

Gillian slowed the TT to a stop next to Condo's car and turned off the engine. "It's so peaceful here," she said, climbing out.

My hand hesitated on the door handle. Peaceful, my eye. This place looked like a trap. The front door stood open, and a squeegee propped up beside it. The freshly mopped porch seemed to be saying "Come in! Come in to my parlor!"

And what was Condo doing here? That man turned up everywhere. Now that we thought we'd safely escaped getting side-swiped by Jasmine, here we'd arrived in Condo's territory. How safe were we from that character? Last night I had fought imaginary images of them all as possible opponents, along with Phyllis...

Then I remembered why Pine Nugget Lane sounded familiar. It was the address of the listing I'd seen lying on Phyllis's desk. Marked "Denton." This cabin was either property the Dentons were selling or interested in buying.

Reluctantly, I climbed out to follow Gillian before she could blindly walk into a trap against one, or possibly all three, of my opponents. I wasn't so sure just how imaginary they actually were.

The sun felt good on my head, luring me onward. There was nothing like spring sunshine in your face, warming the last of the lizard-cold blood that turned my veins to ice during the winter months. If I were a cat, I'd stretch. Oblivious to the trap awaiting us ahead that the open door and the red car flagged.

Maybe this red car wasn't Condo's. A long, thin scratch marred the side of the driver's car door. I didn't remember a scratch there before, but then... I wondered if a hit-and-run accident with a bicycle would've put such a mark there. Had Condo been so impaired that he hadn't even noticed he'd run over Lyle? I couldn't imagine it being deliberate.

"That's odd," Gillian said, glancing first at the car and then at her wristwatch. "Why is Jimmie here?"

I echoed her. "*Jimmie*? You're on a first-name basis with Jimmie Condo?"

"I was going to tell you," she said, "but you never gave me a chance."

"Jimmie Condo is your new boyfriend?"

"Not yet. We've only had one date so far. But where's Van? Why isn't he here yet?"

"Let's wait for him outside in this delicious sunshine," I said. *Purrr-r-r-r.*

Gillian strode up to the porch. "The front door is open. Jimmie must be inside, filling in for the seller's realtor. He surely heard us drive up."

"Wait, Jill! You brought me up here to keep you safe, and you're right. Something feels odd. We'll wait for Van outside."

"What's wrong with you? I've never known you to be afraid."

260

"It has nothing to do with fear. It's stupidity, that's all. You're asking for trouble to walk into a situation that's off, the way this is. You don't know who could be hiding behind that door, waiting for us, luring us in there with an open door."

"Now who's the paranoid one?"

"It's not paranoia, it's just common sense. The best self-defense is not to have to defend yourself. Someone could be hiding in there, waiting to ambush us."

"Oh, Nell, you're so negative all of a sudden."

"Me? You're the one who planted the seeds of doubt. Don't go in there, Jill. I'm telling you."

She plowed forward.

Just then, a car's engine rattled, straining up the incline of the driveway. A dented blue wagon crested the hill and rolled across the meadow towards us.

TWENTY-TWO

The blue car raced closer. Sprays of melted snow heaved in waves to either side of its bumpers as it bounced over ruts, aiming at us. I yelped at Jill. "Let's get out of here!"

But it was too late. Gillian froze in place at the foot of the porch, her eyes wide. I crouched, ready to sprint out of the blue car's path. My fingers hovered within touch of the Audi's door handle, while I waited to see which way to jump. Hesitating, I was unwilling to abandon either Gillian or her Audi, our escape mechanism. The dented Subaru careened to a stop only inches behind the Audi's bumper, blocking us in. We weren't going anywhere until the blue car moved, not unless we wanted to get stuck in a snow bank or mud puddle.

I retreated sideways, towards Gillian, angling myself so that I could see both her and the driver of the blue Subaru, using my peripheral vision.

Jasmine sprang out of the driver's seat, her frizzy curls bouncing. "Thank goodness I caught you in time. Don't go in there, y'all."

"Why on earth not?" Gillian asked, sounding like a defiant child who'd been told not to touch the pretty vase. I thought Jasmine's words sounded more like a command than friendly advice.

Gillian turned on her heels and marched on, through the open door. No one was going to stop my sister-in-law when she wanted something. In this case, this cabin. She disappeared from view inside the cabin, and then she screamed.

"I tried to warn her," Jasmine said, but her sly smile suggested she hadn't tried very hard.

I leaped up the steps to the porch. "Jill, what's wrong?"

"You'd better not go after her," Jasmine said behind me. "I'm warning ya."

My skin prickled. I'd been right. It *was* a trap. If I was going to help Gillian, then I couldn't entrap myself, too. I backpedaled off the porch, out into the open, and then turned to face Jasmine. "What's in there?"

Jasmine turned her head, aiming one ear at the open door. "I hear him now. I thought he'd be happy up here in this high country with his own kind, rather than down there in that awful city laboratory. But he sounds scared."

This crazy woman who talked to animals wasn't talking about any human, I realized. I took another step backwards, farther away from the cabin.

Gillian screeched from inside. "S-s-s-snake!"

"He ain't no Clara," Jasmine said. "No one can take Clara's place, even though I thought Willie would be grateful to be liberated..."

"Willie?" I asked, my voice cracking.

"He used to live down in the city. In a filthy cage, waiting to be experimented on."

"A snake went missing from Dr. Simon's laboratory at the university."

"That's him. That's Willie."

"Are you the one who took him — I mean, it?"

"I didn't *take* him," she said. "Willie wanted to go home with me and my honey. Besides, I didn't think anyone would miss him much. My honey said they had too many snakes in that place, anyhow."

"Your honey said that?"

"Sure, and he ought to know, since he's been rooming with that woman who works there."

"Lyle."

"That's right. I believe you know my Lyle."

My Lyle, she'd said, as if she owned him. Jasmine was the woman in Lyle's life, the woman who had been upsetting him. Maybe stalking him. Maybe she was the reason he carried a gun and got jumpy when he saw snakes in the path.

"You killed her," I said, stepping farther away from Jasmine. My moves put me closer to the cabin. And closer to the snake that held Gillian captive. "You killed Francesca."

"No! Not me!" Jasmine started to cry.

"You used your snake. Clara. Or maybe Willie. Because Lyle started paying attention to Francesca, and you couldn't have that."

"He-yell no! You got it all wrong. It wasn't me. All I done was borrow her necklace so I could use them crystals to calm down Clara."

Gillian started to screech.

I tiptoed onto the porch and poked my head through the open doorway, cautiously scoping out the snake's den. Then I saw it. A long, skinny body slid across pine floorboards, hugging the baseboard.

Gillian stood in the center of the room, screaming and doing a tap dance number on the balls of her feet, as if she'd suddenly stepped onto a bed of hot coals. As long as she kept moving, they couldn't burn her. As long as she kept moving, the snake couldn't get her.

She screamed and screamed, and the snake kept slithering along the length of the room. Slowly coming around to the open door. To me.

"Come to Mama," said Jasmine, brushing past me, jangling the crystals around her wrist. Francesca's missing necklace, reconfigured.

"No!" I yelled. Was she crazy? Maybe I was the crazy one for hanging there in the doorway, when I could've run away. But I wouldn't abandon Gillian. "It's a rattlesnake. Stay away from it."

"I can't. Don't you see how scared Willie is? I shouldn't have left him here before he had a chance to adjust to his new surroundings. Don't worry, he'll calm down once I show him the crystals."

Another shadow moved on the opposite side of the room. I switched to defensive mode, having to use my peripheral vision to track that movement while still maintaining watch on the snake. And on Gillian. And on Jasmine. I definitely didn't like these numbers. In such a case, a fighter didn't look at any single opponent but at a spot in the middle where all opponents could be kept more or less in sight. I was never very good at this drill, but then, I never had the motivation of a poisonous snake thrown into the mix.

Where the shadow moved, a doorway led from a back room. That shadow sprinted toward the center of the room, where Gillian did her tap dance. The snake had slithered halfway around its circuit of the room, inching its way closer to my position in the open front doorway. Jasmine crossed the room, cutting off the snake, at a V-angle to the shadow. I kept my focus fixed on the center of the room, and then the shadow emerged into my vision's range, materializing into the shape of Phyllis.

Jasmine expertly scooped up the snake, holding it by its jaw.

Phyllis held a gun in her hand, aimed at the snake. "Stand back," she said, pushing past Gillian.

"Oh god oh god oh god," Gillian said, whispering her mantra.

"That looks like Lyle's gun," I said.

"Don't shoot him!" Jasmine cried. "It wasn't his fault. He didn't mean no harm."

The snake's body whipped, shaking its rattles like the sound of sliding grains inside a maraca. Jasmine twisted with the motion and never lost her grip on Willie's jaws.

"What are you doing with Lyle's gun?" I said.

"Oh god oh god oh god."

Phyllis swiveled the gun around to aim at me. "Better to shut you up with."

Gillian let out a mewling sound as her attention focused on the end of the gun in Phyllis's hands.

My mind raced. Ham had told me that Lyle's gun was too small to do any real damage. "It was you all along," I said, challenging her in the hopes of confusing her. Distraction was a valid technique, even in the ring. But we weren't in the ring now. Here, anything would go. I just wished we could do this without a snake in the equation. I stayed where I was, standing rooted to the threshold. "You took the gun from Lyle, didn't you?"

"Of course I did," Phyllis said. "Why would I create a record by buying my own gun?"

"You're the one who hit Lyle with Condo's car. Condo lets you drive his car, doesn't he?"

"Shut up about Jimmie," Phyllis said, her eyeballs rolling back and forth in her head with a look of feverish frenzy.

"You hit Lyle deliberately," I said. "So you could take his gun away from him."

"I tried to tell y'all not to come in here, didn't I?" said Jasmine, panting as she wrestled to keep her grip on the snake. "Now look what you gone and done."

Gillian's tap dance drummed to a stop. "Hello?" she said, her voice wavering. "You better stop this now, because Van will be here any minute. Tell them, Nell."

Phyllis spit out a laugh. "That's what you think. I already told him we were going to split the fee. No point in his being here, too."

"He has to be, if he wants his percentage," Gillian said, taking a tiny step backwards, towards me. "Otherwise, the deal's not legal."

Phyllis waved her gun. "Hold it right there. The law won't help you now."

"You don't think much of the law, do you?" I said. Keep her talking. Small talk. Distractions.

"Honey," Phyllis said, aiming the gun at me again, "what's the law ever done to help you?"

"Not much, I guess. Just like you." The cavalry wouldn't rescue us, but maybe I could distract her until she made a mistake. Then rush her. Take the gun away. The best defense against a gun was to be a moving target. Moving targets were harder to shoot.

But then, there was the snake.

Phyllis snorted. "Yeah, you and me, we're both natives. We have to carry on the legacy. Sometimes we have to take the law into our own hands, like they did in the olden days."

"I can understand why you resent the Dentons so much," I said, my mind spinning, searching for a weapon. I remembered the squeegee propped beside the door on the porch. "On account of your ancestor."

Phyllis tilted her head to one side. Her gun-aiming arm dropped half an inch. "If you're referring to that silver mine, it was rightfully my great-grandfather's. Denton stole it."

Wow. "And you still carry a grudge, after more than a hundred years?"

"I'll make them pay, one way or another."

"By murdering Francesca Denton?" Murder by snake venom. How fitting.

Her arm quivered and dropped another half inch. "That wasn't part of the plan. I didn't mean for her to die. I only ever wanted the money. And to scare her. But just enough to settle what she owed me."

"I figgered it was you all along," Jasmine said, relaxing her grip. The snake pointed at me. "See, she's Jimmie's secretary, and so I figgered she killed that girl you was telling me about. I know, 'cause she didn't like it none when I got hired on to cater one of Jimmie's parties, and I said all my problems would be solved if only I could make Jimmie Condo my sugar daddy."

"Shut up!" Phyllis waved the gun up and down.

Jasmine clamped her fingers tighter around the snake and went on. "It was just a joke! Anyhow, we was in his kitchen, gathering up things for the picnic he was giving for those pioneering volunteers. Her and me was talking." She nodded at Phyllis. "Well, she saw one of the vials I used to keep Clara's venom in, after I milked it. The next day when I went to look for it, it was gone. I thought at first I might'a misplaced it, but then a couple days later, that same day you come up there on top of the rock?" She turned to me. "I was looking for my missing vial. I figgered she'd used it, maybe to splash into that gal's face, and so her and me needed to talk again, and —"

"That's not how it happened, you idiot!" Phyllis screamed.

"Why don't you tell us how it really happened?" I said softly, buying time. I shifted my body weight a fraction of a degree, in the general direction of the squeegee.

Phyllis panted. Her cheeks flushed. Her gun arm swung from me to the snake to Gillian to me again.

"Oh god oh god oh god."

"That's all the talking you're going to do!" Phyllis shouted. "You got nothing on me!" Then she leveled the gun at Gillian, who was gurgling on her screams. "I said, shut the f*** up! You think you can waltz in and take Jimmie out from under my nose?"

"No!" Gillian's mascara ran down her cheeks. "I don't think that! Tell her, Nell. Tell her I don't think that."

I was watching the snake, whose body tightened in Jasmine's arms. "That's right. Gillian changes boyfriends as often as the rest of us change our socks."

"You calling Jimmie a used sock?" Phyllis waved her gun again. "You think he's no one? You don't know. No one appreciates Jimmie. No one knows the things I do for him. I made him who he is. And what thanks do I get for all my trouble? He's mine, I tell you. Not yours. Not hers."

"We understand," I said soothingly. Keep her talking. "We can help you."

"It's too late. Nobody can help now."

"Tell us. We're listening." I summoned the *chi*, the invisible force that pumped through my body, and flung it her way. It was a trick I'd seen Master Hwang do, but could I?

My *chi* must've smacked her broadside, because she flinched and gasped on a deep breath. Words tumbled from her. "She found out." Her voice took on a pleading tone. "I had to stop her."

"Stop Francesca? Stop her from doing what?"

"Sticking her nose in our books."

"Was there something wrong with your books?"

"Not after I fixed them."

"But how did Francesca do that? How could she take a look at your books?"

Phyllis breathed deep and choked. "By pretending to be a student. Wanting to intern with us. That's what she said."

"But she *was* a student."

"No, that was just an excuse to live next door to the office. I didn't know she was living there, not until Jimmie recognized the Denton aunt one day when she dropped by. By then it was too late. Teasing Jimmie was bad enough. But no. She wanted to spy on me, too. So she was going to have to pay."

"How were you going to make her pay?" I asked, focusing on my *chi* to pin her in place.

"It should've been easy. A hypodermic needle of snake venom in her buttocks. Just a warning. Let people think a snake bit her. Jasmine's snake. All I wanted was for both of them to leave Jimmie alone. All she had to do was give me the money she owed me, and I would've helped her. It *could've* been easy, but she fought me. And she fell. Her fault, not mine."

"And you thought you were going to get away with that?" Jasmine said, tsking.

Jasmine's voice broke the force of my *chi*.

Phyllis sucked in air. Her eyes widened and her nostrils flared. Her gun arm trembled, lifting up to aim at Jasmine. "Just like each of you is going to pay."

A bullet zinged through the air.

The snake's body whipped, jerking itself loose from Jasmine's arms. It fell with a thud to the floor. Jasmine fell next to it, crying, clutching her stomach. Blood trickled from between her fingers.

Gillian screamed bloody murder, and Phyllis turned the gun on her.

I lunged backwards for the squeegee, not taking my eyes off the mound of snake. Its body wound around and around, mesmerizing me as it coiled into a thick lump beside Jasmine's bleeding huddle.

Time froze as Gillian screamed.

"Run, Jill!" I yelled, swinging the handle of the squeegee as if it were my polished teak bo staff. I slammed it down onto Phyllis's arm that held the gun.

The gun fired, clattering to the floor. The snake rattled, shot out of its coil, and struck with the speed of a dart.

Phyllis screamed, dropping to the floor, shaking with violent sobs. "It... b-bit me!"

I grabbed Gillian, and we ran outside to call 9-1-1.

TWENTY-THREE

It was a dark and stormy night. I swear to God. But I wasn't going to let a little weather stand in the way of our big night, the first belt test I would conduct as head instructor. Besides, these spring storms usually blew through the Front Range quickly. I only hoped the rapidly dropping temperatures didn't change the soggy day into a winter wonderland overnight. Springtime in the Rockies. Heck, someone had to live here.

Dad was the first to arrive. He wanted to get his pick of the parking spaces, or so he claimed. He had agreed to act as my administrative assistant tonight, setting out extra folding chairs, checking in students, telling them where to wait, where to stretch out, and where their parents could sit. One by one the students dripped inside, bringing the smell of wet air indoors with them. Each time the front door opened, the howling wind whistled inside too.

The door opened again, and Gillian walked in. "What's going on? There's not a place to park within five blocks. I parked next door at Alice's, since her car is gone."

"You'd better move your car before she gets back," I said, striding along the taped-off walkway with a box of my improvised cards. I set them down in front of Dad at the folding table he'd set up.

"Where's Terra?" Gillian asked. "Is she ready to go? She

didn't forget, did she? We're taking her to dinner."

"We? Jill, I'm conducting a test tonight —"

"Not *you*. Tucker. He's waiting in the car. Terra won't mind, will she? I thought since she loved that Thai before, we could introduce her to Ethiopian tonight. Someone has to broaden her horizons."

Terra marched down the stairs. "Sorry, Aunt Jill, I'm staying in tonight. I wouldn't miss this test for anything."

"Just because Jason is testing?" I said, teasing.

Terra rolled her eyes at me. "He's like so yesterday."

The door opened again, letting in more rain and wind. "Hi," Buster said. "Since I can't test this time, I thought maybe you'd like some help."

"Hallelujah," Dad said. "Sit yourself down over here, young man, and show me how these cards work."

I smiled and patted him on the shoulder. "You're just in time. We need someone to check to make sure every tester's belt is tied correctly and his or her uniform is spotlessly clean."

"Yes ma'am," he said and pulled up a chair next to Dad.

"But what about your mom?" I asked. "Does she know you're here?"

"She knows. She's cool. You caught the killer."

"Well, it wasn't exactly *me*," I said. "Willie stopped her from doing anymore harm."

"Whatever. As long as I get to come back. Rachel's coming, too. Not just to pick up her stuff, either. She says she misses all of us. She wants to come back." He turned to Terra. "How about you? Did you make up your mind yet?"

I looked back and forth between Buster and my daughter. I remembered now that they had been brewing up some sort of plan when I caught them conspiring together in the foyer. "What's going on?" I said.

"Nothing, Mom." Terra turned back to Buster. "But I'll keep it in mind. That's why I want to watch tonight."

"Keep what in mind?" I asked.

Buster turned to me. "She's thinking of taking karate! I told her she'd like it. I'll help her, too, so she doesn't have to —"

"Shut up," Terra said.

Was this true? I tried not to show my glee. I had to turn away from them to keep from bursting with smiles.

Gillian apparently thought I was happy for her, probably on account of her new date. She hugged me and ran out into the rain, nearly knocking over Mr. Callahan, who was climbing the porch steps. Once inside, he hung his raincoat over the railing and pulled out a handkerchief to mop the beads of rainwater streaming from his face.

"Why'd you come in the front door?" I said, swiping a towel from the bag shelf and mopping him. "You're soaking wet."

"Some red Lexus is in my parking spot out back," he said. "I had to park five blocks away and walk."

"Oh no," I said. "Jimmie Condo shows up again."

"Condo is here?" Callahan said.

"No, I don't think so. I haven't seen him. Why would he be here?"

"Because he wants to buy us out."

"Oh no!" I'd forgotten about that, in all the excitement.

"Don't worry. I turned him down. Lazar sent me a bonus, a token of the Dentons' appreciation for your job well done. They're not interested in forcing me out anymore, now that you found out who really did it. They'll leave us alone from now on.

Why would I accept Condo's offer? No way. Let's get this show on the road. We're still in business."

I checked the wall clock. It was almost time. I glanced at the list of testers that Dad had checked in. There were still a few missing names. I would give them five more minutes.

The door opened again, letting in another burst of wet wind. Lyle limped inside, patting a slick wave of hair hanging in his face.

"What, no star-gazing tonight?" I said with a grin. "How are you? I haven't seen you in ages."

"I'll live. And so will Jasmine and Phyllis. I just came from the hospital, and I thought you'd want to know about them. Phyllis had it kind of rough, but she's going to pull through, her hospital guard says. Then she moves over to the jail. For murder."

I shook my head, amazed by how I'd deceived myself, thinking Phyllis wasn't capable of the crime just because of the way she dressed. I should've known that appearances are deceiving.

"I hope they put her away for a long time," Lyle said. "Long enough for me and Jazzy to get back together. Did you hear about Jimmie Condo's offer?"

"I sure did," I said, "but don't worry, it's not going to happen."

"It's not?" Lyle frowned. "But he offered Jazzy the job that Phyllis was supposed to be doing. You know? The one where she was supposed to keep the books and manage property and all that? The one she messed up."

"Oh. That one."

"Yeah. And now Jazzy is going to be doing it. That means

we can finally buy a place together. Small, but it's a start."

"It sure is. There's only one thing I don't understand. Why did Jasmine follow me that night I drove home from my dad's farm, after the fire at his place?"

"That was Phyllis."

"It was Jasmine's car. And I saw Jasmine get out of it."

"Yeah, but Phyllis is the one who hired Jazzy. She didn't care if you spotted her or anything. Phyllis just wanted to keep you busy while she broke in to your place. Phyllis confessed to setting the fire, too, just to pull you away from here."

"She must've been here more than once," I said. "What on earth did she want?"

Lyle's face flushed. "It was that key Jimmie Condo gave to Fanny. Any time Condo paid any attention to another woman, it made Phyllis go crazy."

I had seen that crazy streak, oh yeah. "But the key was already missing."

"This key, Mom?" Terra pried a key away from Sammy's claws.

"That's the one. Sammy! Have you been hiding more treasures?" I scolded the ferret, took the key, and pocketed it.

Lyle's voice caught as he sniffed back tears. "Jazzy's real sorry she ever got involved with Phyllis. She didn't mean any harm. She was just trying to earn a few bucks here and there."

"It's okay, Lyle. Life's lessons don't come easy. But how about you? Are you going to come back to Callahan's Karate once things settle down for you? I could use some adult help."

"I'm here, aren't I? I guess I can't test, but I can watch, so I'll know how to do it next time."

"As long as you don't have a gun on you, you can come on

in and have a seat."

"Don't worry. Jazzy's giving up her snakes for me, so I don't have to carry a gun around anymore."

The door blew open again, and Detective Rosenquist stood in the doorway. Past his shoulder, I saw flashing lights, where he'd stopped his car in the middle of the road. "Where do you want this?" he said, heaving my box of files in his arms.

"Just put them down here," I said, pointing to a corner of the foyer, "and I'll put them away later. So, you're done with them?"

"Nothing in them that we needed. It was a false lead. Next time it won't be. Next time you won't get off the hook so easy. You better watch your step."

I sighed and pulled Francesca's secret key from my pocket. "Then I'd better turn this over to you now."

There would be a next time. I could hardly wait.

* * * * *

NELL LETTERLY'S SELF DEFENSE TIPS

Sometimes amateur sleuthing will land you in trouble. If, like Nell, you are a magnet for trouble, then here's a review of five basic safety tips from *Murder with Altitude*:

1. Avoid trouble. The best defense in martial arts is not to have to use any defense techniques at all. Sometimes this means hanging back when a situation doesn't feel right. You won't go there. You won't let anyone egg you on. You just won't.

2. Don't look like a victim. Stay positive and remember not to go to dark or remote places by yourself. Remember, there's safety in numbers. Thugs don't want to make it harder for themselves.

If this doesn't work, and you find yourself cornered:
3. Distraction is actually a valid technique. For example, look up to telegraph a high punch, and then kick low. Sometimes switching tactics startles your opponent just enough that you can escape.

If you find yourself outnumbered:
4. Use peripheral vision. A fighter doesn't look at any single opponent when surrounded but at a spot in the middle where all opponents can be kept more or less in sight, using peripheral vision.

If, heaven forbid, someone is taking potshots at you:
5. Run! Moving targets are harder to shoot.

Good luck, have fun, and remember to stay safe!

ABOUT THE AUTHOR

Sue Star writes mysteries about families in chaos. She is the author of *Murder in the Dojo*, the first of the Nell Letterly mystery series. Like her character, Sue has also trained and taught the martial arts, but unlike her character, Sue believes her life is more stable. She enjoys hiking, traveling, and just hanging out with her family.

Sue has also collected several stand-alone short mystery stories in *Trophy Hunting* and *Organized Death*. She is currently hard at work on the third novel in the series, tentatively called *Murder for a Cash Crop*.

Find out more about her writing at

http://www.dmkregpublishing.com

http://rebeccawriter.blogspot.com

http://mysteristas.wordpress.com

https://www.facebook.com/pages/Sue-Star/546146592165545

Contact Sue at suestarauthor@gmail.com

LIKE TO READ ANOTHER NELL LETTERLY ADVENTURE?

Murder in the Dojo (#1 in the series): The book that started it all. Read an excerpt on the following pages.

Available **now** from your favorite bookstore in trade paper or e-book format:

Coming in 2015:

Murder for a Cash Crop (#3) When growing pot in beautiful Colorado begins to involve real money, things turn deadly.

Sue's short story collections featuring other strong women:

Available **now** in e-book format on all the e-reader platforms:

Organized Death: Even the most organized women stumble when a crime occurs.

Trophy Hunting: Trophies come in all forms.

Read selections at: www.dmkregpublishing.com

Murder in the Dojo

Chapter One

Suburban moms like me don't usually go to Boulder's Hill after dark. The Hill is university terrain, having evolved over the years from a shopping mecca of the 1950's for the well-dressed college student to a hippie center of drugs and riots of the 'sixties. Ever since, the place has battled between gentrification and decay. Decay keeps winning.

And yet, here I was, wandering up the long, sloping streets, searching for the address on Callahan's business card. I wasn't looking for any more confrontations — I'd had enough of that today. Lucky me, tonight the Hill appeared dead. Odd, for a party land of off-campus housing. Odd, for a Saturday night, three weeks before spring break.

Then a clang and a yowl erupted out of the distant shadows. I gripped my duffel bag tighter and hurried up the middle of the cracked sidewalk, staying as far away as possible from bushes or parked cars, where thugs could hide. *Relax, Nell*, I told myself. *It's just a cat.*

In Boulder, Colorado we didn't have a serious crime problem. A few mountain lions, maybe. And sometimes cast-off couches got torched, but still... In this neighborhood, I was clearly outside of my suburban comfort zone.

Comfortable? Who was I kidding? Practically ancient at forty-five, I had a failed marriage, a husband who'd bailed, and a half-page resume. I had to make a living somehow — that's why I'd ended up here, with nerves on edge. And I had a teenage daughter to raise, even though she thought the raising was all done.

My friends took my problems in stride because, after all, Boulder is a city of support groups. What they'd never been able to handle, however, was two years ago when I got my black belt in American Freestyle, a non-traditional version of Tae Kwon Do. There's no support group for the mad housewife turned karate kid.

I found the address. From the outside, Callahan's Karate looked like somebody's family home, a bungalow built of sandstone from the era of the 1920's. With all of its original mortar and shingles. No benefits of yuppie restoration practices here, I thought, clambering onto the wooden porch.

Light shone through the beveled glass panels of the front door. I knocked, then waited a few minutes, studying the way the door stood slightly ajar. No one came, so I pushed it open and stepped into a foyer. A locker-room smell of moldy socks hit me in the face.

The foyer opened onto an empty studio, a long and narrow floor space interrupted in the middle by an archway. A thin, faded carpet of sea green and dust drew the hollowed-out rooms together. The floor rippled from the buckles of nearly a century of settling. This place was the opposite end of the scale from Master Hwang's state-of-the-art studio where I'd trained — until the money ran out.

I called into the empty space. "Mr. Callahan?" My new boss. I still felt dazed by today's turn of events that brought me here. It didn't make sense that he'd chosen *me* for the job. Not that I was complaining.

A thud sounded from the back of the house, then floorboards creaked. From the shadows of a curving passageway, a low, male voice asked, "Rick?" Then his hulk filled the hall's opening, and I relaxed.

He was dressed in a white uniform, rumpled as if it had been wadded at the bottom of Terra's laundry basket for a month. A crisp brown belt, tied incorrectly, hung around thick hips. He looked dumb-founded, his innocence all the more pronounced with a baby-face. His top gaped open in a "V," exposing a sparse crop of chest hairs among a field of inflamed pimples.

"You're not Rick," he proclaimed, reaching into a bag of potato chips.

"No, I'm not," I agreed.

"Look, lady, we're closed tonight."

I watched, too shocked for words, as crumbs sprinkled onto the carpet. How could anyone show this much disrespect to his uniform and the workout floor and still earn such an advanced rank as his? It would be quite a leap for him to achieve the next promotion.

I cleared my throat. "Is Mr. Callahan here?"

He snorted. "Naw."

"I have an appointment with him," I said.

"I ain't seen him."

I glanced around myself at the scuffed interior of the studio. "Then, I'll look around a little while I wait."

"Does Rick know about this?" the over-grown kid asked.

"I really have no idea." I removed my shoes and placed them along with my bag into one of the empty racks beneath the stairs. In case Callahan wanted me to demonstrate my abilities, I would be prepared. Then with a bow of courtesy, I stepped onto the workout floor.

"I don't think it's such a good idea," the kid said. "Rick won't like it."

Sighing, I gave up. "All right, who's Rick?"

His eyebrows shot up like two spastic, wooly worms. "You don't know?"

I shook my head.

His potato chip bag rattled, falling to the floor. "Hey. I know who you are. I heard about you." His eyes narrowed, maybe with understanding, maybe something more. He studied the length and breadth of my body with the assessment of a man far more mature than himself.

The force of his examination made me take a step backwards, toward the front door. Something about his manner told me that I was an uninvited guest at his private party.

"*Rick* is the instructor here," he said.

I stopped, stiff with surprise. "Mr. Callahan will be here any minute, and he'll clear up everything."

The illusion of the boy's maturity vanished as he chortled. "You don't know much, do you?"

Mothers of teenagers never knew anything, I started to point out, but something clanked and hissed about that time. I glanced up.

"It's just the furnace," the kid said with a grin.

I summoned a stony look to turn on him.

"I was supposed to lock up," he said, smirking, "but I guess Mr. Callahan can do that, if he's coming here like you say. I've got to split, and anyhow, the two of you probably don't want me around." He winked. "If Rick shows up, tell him Eugene — that's me — couldn't wait. I'll see him over at Kim's." He snatched his potato chip bag from the floor. "By the way, don't tell Callahan that's where we're going."

Kim's Karate? I felt my veins tighten at the memory of Mr. Kim, the man who'd organized the demo earlier today — along with my humiliation. But so what? I'd ended up the winner in the long-run, getting this job, never mind that the circumstances puzzled me.

Before I could refuse to commit to any promise to Eugene,

he disappeared back down the hallway from which he'd emerged. He was a confused student, the first of many challenges I would probably face. Apparently, I'd just replaced "Rick" as head instructor here.

Liking the sound of my new title, and liking it better with the kid gone, I closed the front door and glanced at my watch. The air smelled dusty, and I was glad I'd kept on my socks as I returned to the carpet. I turned in a slow, wide circle, taking mental notes of the tasks ahead of me. Fresh paint. New mirrors to hang on the barren walls. The Korean and U.S. flags. Displays to cheer up the place — framed certificates, different colored belts, and the glass case Dad had built for my kamas.

The case would fit perfectly on that strip of wall between the mullioned windows.

I'd been carrying my kamas with me today in their velvet-lined travel case as a sort of talisman. They must've worked, because here I was. I hurried back to my duffel bag and carefully lifted a kama in each hand. One of the martial arts weapons that originated from farmer's tools, they looked like a pair of stubby sickles. Macho-men would die for this set that I owned. They had blades so sharp they could shave my legs just by looking at them.

The steel blades made them top heavy, and I gripped the leather-wrapped handles tightly, for I had no desire to lose any bodily appendages. These weapons were just for show — they were far too deadly for a non-showy martial artist like me to actually perform with them. Just holding them gave me an extra boost of power. I struck a stance, and their power flowed into me. Then I carried them over to the wall space between the windows and held them up for size. Here, they'd make a great focal point. A power point. For me.

A distant clang sounded outside, breaking the spell. Through the window beside me, I saw something move in my peripheral vision. Callahan? Branches scritched against the panes of glass. The wind was picking up. Probably had blown over someone's trash can in the alley out back.

Then a floorboard creaked overhead. Maybe my new boss had been upstairs all along. But I couldn't imagine why he hadn't responded to my calls. More than likely, the house was still settling after a century of use.

I put my kamas away, then padded up the wooden stairs in my stockinged feet to check out the creaks. On the landing at the top of the stairs, I paused before a closed door, scuffed and scratched. This was apparently the apartment that would become Terra's and my new home.

I tried the knob. Unlocked. "Mr. Callahan?" I said, pushing open the door. Inside, blank, canary-yellow walls faced me. A smell of stale beer permeated the air, and pizza boxes from Tío Tito's littered the hardwood floor. No furniture. Good. I had plenty to bring over from the suburbs.

Dust bunnies rolled across the floor toward another door, as if someone's recent passage through here had stirred them up. Chasing the bunnies, I explored a bedroom facing the street and another one overlooking the alley. I found a pile of women's lacey underwear, monogrammed with a curly "M," but no Callahan. Where in hell was he?

A new sound, one that didn't come from creaking floorboards, or the furnace, or upset trash cans, suddenly broke into my daze. Something mewled outside, like the unearthly hisses of cats poised to fight. I expected another eruption of yowls and clawing sounds, but the silence that followed was even more ominous.

Then something squeaked — not the sound of a house settling

— and thumped — nor branches scraping against the exterior.

Maybe a mountain lion had come down from the foothills and cornered its prey. There were always several encounters per year with the cats around here. After all, this town jammed up against the base of the Rocky Mountains.

Maybe its prey was Callahan.

I bounded downstairs and hurried across the workout floor. Down the narrow hall where Eugene had disappeared, I followed the curving passageway to where it ended in an old kitchen. A sleeping computer resided there now, covered with sticky notes and surrounded by a mess of paper. A linoleum floor, looking like a checkerboard, led me out to a screened-in porch.

The mewling sounds had stopped by now. My nose pressed into the musty wires of the screen door. Bushes rustled from somewhere out there in the dark, beyond the house.

Groping along the plaster dust of the wall, I felt a light switch and flipped it on. An outdoor floodlight illuminated a small patch of yard with overgrown and dried-out grasses surrounding the house. At the edge of its ring of light, a small shed sagged by the alley. No mountain lion. No Callahan.

Across the alley rose the jagged outline of a student apartment building, haphazardly ablaze with a few squares of light. Someone, I thought, must've had too much to drink at a college party and was being sick in the bushes of the alley.

I could almost hear Terra's protest, "Mo-o-om," in my head.

So I waited for the noise to come again. It didn't, but the door of the shed in the back yard heaved. A gust of wind slammed it shut, as if the shed were something alive, breathing.

Okay, maybe I was wrong about the drunken college student. Could my new boss be out there, in trouble? He'd said he needed a caretaker for the place, which hinted at possible problems. What had I gotten myself into? Whatever it was, I'd agreed. I'd shook on it. My word was as good as a contract. I hadn't signed one yet, but now I had to see this through.

I pushed against the screen, swinging it open, and tip-toed onto the back porch step. Another blast of wind found its way under the loose tail of my oversized work shirt.

I was accustomed to going without shoes, but not outside in the dark in unfamiliar territory. Goosebumps tickled the back of my neck. If Callahan was out there, needing help, I couldn't afford the delay of going back for shoes.

My socks gave me enough protection from loose pebbles on the flagstone path that led from the porch to the shed, but I wished I had something more. A flashlight would've been good. Maybe a weapon, too. I scrabbled around on the ground for a handful of gravel that I could fling into a surprise attacker's face if necessary, then slipped into the shadows beyond the reach of the floodlight.

Callahan wasn't being mugged, I told myself. This was Boulder, after all. Safe and snug. Not the big city. As caretaker, I would have to secure the door. That was my job. That's all it was. Doing my job.

Still, I paused to let my eyes adjust to the dark. Master Hwang had trained me to observe my surroundings. Not to march blindly up to any banging door without knowing what might await me from within.

Then I spied a small window and inched toward it. Dirt and grime coated the glass pane. Something *inside* the shed glowed. This wasn't a shed, I realized, but a garage that faced onto the alley. A car sat inside, nearly filling the interior. Not just any car, but a sporty little model, something my errant husband would've lusted after. The driver's door stood open, giving off the glow of the car's interior light. Something dangled out of the open side of the car and touched the dirt floor of the garage. It was an arm. An arm in a purple sleeve. It wasn't moving.

www.ingramcontent.com/pod-product-compliance
Lightning Source LLC
Chambersburg PA
CBHW021340250626
47155CB00002B/716